Falling Light

THE SHADOWS OF FATE
BOOK ONE

by

Crystal L. Kirkham

FALLING LIGHT

editor@darkbrewpress.com

ISBN
Paperback: 978-1-7774408-6-2
eBook: 978-1-7774408-7-9

Cover design by Crystal L. Kirkham
Interior design by B.K. Bass & Crystal L. Kirkham
Editing by Sam Hendricks

www.darkbrewpress.com

BOOKS BY CRYSTAL L. KIRKHAM

<u>Saints and Sinners Series</u>

Road to Redemption

Depths of Darkness

Little Stories in a Big Universe

Gateway

Alert

<u>The Shadows of Fate Series</u>

Falling Light

Rising Darkness
(Coming Soon)

Penumbra

ACKNOWLEDGEMENTS

There are so many people to thank for making this entire series a reality that I almost do not know where to begin. I ended up writing two pages worth of dedications and acknowledgements to some of the most influential people in my writing life.

Being a writer isn't always easy between my job and other commitments, but I've been very lucky. I have so many people who have been wonderful and unwavering in their love and support of me on this journey. Most of you know who you are, and I thank you from the bottom of my heart—you know, the one that may or may not be in a jar on my desk. That one. I thank you from the bottom of it.

I have specific people I want to mention but I'll spread that out through the next two books in this series.

CHAPTER ONE

Anela stood in the middle of the farmer's market and luxuriated in the feeling of the ebb and flow of the humanity that pressed in around her. There was an energy here that fed a need within her, a need for something more than this corporeal existence provided. Though there were moments when that void was filled, when she could entangle her essence in that of someone else. A fleeting emotional bond that kept a different, darker hunger at bay.

She closed her eyes and reached out with every sense she had. There was no shortage of human emotion for her to touch, to feed into that great void. It was beautiful in a way that nothing else was, but she still yearned to be closer to what she craved. Unfortunately, that required an intense openness that she would not find among the strangers that surrounded her.

Most of the time, Anela enjoyed being human. There were benefits to this life that she had learned to embrace. Benefits that had never existed in what she could remember of the place that she'd come from. A richness of senses beyond any her kind had. Raw and jarring once, she enjoyed it now. Touch, sight, smell—the sweet things had made the most recent half of her six thousand years in this place bearable.

With a sigh, she relaxed until there was nothing beyond her own emotions and thoughts. She had come here, not just to be around people, but for the more mundane task of shopping. Though there were dozens of each kind of stall; she had long ago found those that were the most honest and trustworthy—and the ones where the vendors flirted always made her smile a bit brighter.

With her first destination decided, Anela stopped midstride as a prickle at the back of her mind caught her attention. It was a strange sensation; one she'd never felt before, but familiar at the same time. Occasionally, strong emotions would break through to her even when she wasn't open to them… except there was no emotion here. This was something else, and it wasn't human. She ran through the possibilities as her eyes scanned the crowd for the source of the phenomenon.

Anela touched the cell phone in the pocket of her jeans. She considered calling Samir—he would want to know about this—but she hesitated. She didn't know anything yet, not even if it meant danger. It didn't feel dangerous, but things were deceiving. No one would think by looking at her that she had almost destroyed the entire world.

Once again, that strange sensation broke into her thoughts and demanded her attention. This time, she didn't allow it to fade, but focused on it and tried to pinpoint the source. It didn't take her long; he was staring at her with the intensity of a thousand suns. The flicker of his eyes as he studied her was the only movement, otherwise he stood like a deer caught in the headlights of an oncoming truck.

She wasn't ashamed of the fact that she was doing the same. Everything else faded into the background: the people swarming about, the noise of children playing and screaming, the enticingly sweet smell of mini donuts. There was only her and the stranger standing across the plaza.

Asian, well-dressed, long dark hair tied back in an elaborate bun, and amber eyes that seemed to shine even in the bright morning light. Surface observations, though, did her no good. She needed a closer look, a deeper look. She took a few steps towards the man—if she could call him that, for he was obviously only as human as herself—and stopped. This was not a place to ask the questions that needed to be asked.

His head cocked to one side as she met his gaze and nodded slightly. He returned the gesture, his understanding and curiosity filling her mind. There was no doubt that he too had the sensation, an odd feeling that was welcome and familial. There were no words to describe it in any human language she knew.

Anela walked away from the crowd, and the streets the market had overtaken for the day. There was no need to check and see if the stranger was following her, she could feel his presence as distinctly as her own body. It was a tangible, undeniable thing. When they were finally alone in an empty alley, she stopped and faced him. He stood a mere few yards away but edged back as she turned, maintaining his distance.

Though not much taller than herself, he had an intimidating presence and wore his face like a mask—expressionless, unmoving. She wasn't scared of him, but her tongue still twisted itself in knots as she struggled to find the words she needed.

"Who are you?" she asked when no better question could be found. She kept her voice low, not wanting to be overheard even though she could sense no humans nearby. It was why she had stopped here. She did her best to project a quiet curiosity and assurance. It wasn't something she had done often—most humans weren't sensitive to such things, not unless you tried to force the emotion onto them.

He stared at her as if he didn't understand the question. None of the multitudes of emotions she could sense churning just below the surface broke through that calm demeanor. Picking them apart was second nature to her: curiosity, suspicion, wariness, anger, and hunger. It was the last one that concerned her the most; that same hungry void, the emptiness that she did her best to fill—he hadn't. He was starving.

His blinding fury seemed directed at the fleshy prison that contained him. It reminded her of the person—no, monster— that she once had been before she'd learned to accept confinement for the gift that it was. It wasn't perfect, but it was better than being feared or revered. He hadn't learned to tolerate this limited life or to enjoy the pleasures of being human, to allow in those small pieces of emotional connection that their kind craved.

Anela smiled and waited for an answer as she tried to decipher more of what lay behind those bright amber eyes. Uncertainty and hesitation, a hint of excitement, and fear that wasn't directed at her. She wanted to repeat her question but held off. He would answer when he was ready.

His eyes narrowed as he took another step towards her. "I would ask the same of you."

She was surprised at his total lack of accent, as if he had been in North America his entire life. Anela had always enjoyed the lilt of her voice, the rounded sound of her words compared to how others in this country spoke. She was usually okay with being thought an outsider, but here she was, self-conscious of her accent for the first time since she'd left the Institute. "You can call me Anela. Anela Masterson is the name I use."

He didn't respond immediately, and they both stood staring awkwardly at each other for several seconds. He walked the last few steps to stand within touching distance of her. "Keeler, Keeler Lim is my chosen name."

"Nice to meet you, Keeler," Anela responded automatically before blurting out the question that she was longing to ask the most. "How long have you been here?"

"Longer than you, judging by that accent," Keeler responded sharply. She could feel the apology in his emotions if not his countenance or words. "Although, I suppose you did not mean in this country."

"Not entirely, no." Anela smiled as sweetly as she could. She knew the effect her practiced smile had on most men, but there was no reaction from Keeler. She wasn't surprised by that. She was all too aware of the necessities of the superficial in this world, but she was seldom swayed by it herself, and she had no doubt he'd come to the same conclusion. Deciding to do away with human protocol, she dispensed with her questions and stated what she knew. "You're not human."

"Neither are you," Keeler said. "I so rarely meet anyone like me. I was unsure if I should even approach you. Not all I've met have been friendly or familiar, but there was something different…"

He let the sentence hang in the air, but she knew exactly what he meant. There was something here that she had never sensed before. Being in the Institute for so long, she had met many others that weren't human. Some trapped in a shell, some that could take the form of a human on their own, but she had never felt this kind of connection with any of them.

"Yes, I feel it too." She wanted more than anything for Samir to be here. He would know, but she doubted that this newcomer would welcome any member of the Nergal with grace. If he had been around even half as long as she had, then he would know of the Nergal and what that organization typically did to beings like them. No doubt the topic would come up if they talked.

"Now what?" Keeler asked.

"Do you want to grab some coffee and talk? Perhaps we can figure this out. It is always nice to have a friend," Anela proposed. She needed to know more about him. Though time was one of the things she had far too much of, she wasn't willing to let this moment of connection slip by.

A single terse nod was accompanied by acceptance flooding over her. Grinning, Anela motioned for Keeler to follow as she headed towards one of her favorite places.

CHAPTER TWO

Samir watched the two men across the street carefully. There was nothing odd about them on the surface, just two average blokes having a quick lunch—but it wasn't their appearance that held his attention. He'd been in town for a few days tracking down the source of some unusual readings. Nothing extreme, no new intrusions into the world, which is why he had decided to take care of this one on his own. Even Liana hadn't been able to protest against him doing a bit of field work.

Plus, it gave him a chance to see Anela. It had been too long since he'd stopped by. Technically, he was supposed to be checking in on her no less than once a month, but he'd let that slip. Not that anyone would complain so long as nothing went wrong. He trusted Anela, and she was too fond of her freedom—and humanity—to allow for any mistakes that could put that at risk.

So far, these two weren't registering high on the radar. Samir was curious to find out exactly why they had set off even the slightest of pings. From his observations of the last few days, they were doing nothing more than sightseeing. But there was no way of knowing without a full interrogation, and he didn't want to bring in a team if they were harmless.

His phone buzzed for attention and he spared it a quick glance, grinning at the name on the call display. Anela.

"I miss you, Sami. When you gonna visit me? Xoxoxox."

He hadn't told her that he was near because, had she known, she'd insist he stay with her. Though the accommodations would have been better and the company far more enjoyable, she had a habit of being distracting, and he was here to work this time.

He texted back a single word knowing it would send her into a tizzy.

"Tomorrow."

It looked as though he was nearly done here, judging by the luggage these two had hauled out of their cheap motel. Tags on the suitcase indicated that they had flown here, so, once he made a note of where they were heading, he'd have the rest of the day to write up a report and send it in for Liana to double-check. It didn't matter if he outranked her, recon was her domain and he would follow protocol in that respect. His phone buzzed again, and he was surprised there wasn't a wall of text and questions.

"Lunch?"

It was strangely short for Anela, but he was grateful that he wasn't going to have to listen to his phone buzz for the next five minutes. Movement caught his eyes and he glanced up to see the men were paying their bill and preparing to leave. He slipped some money under his unfinished coffee and walked to his car to wait for them to get in their own rented vehicle.

They seemed to be taking their time. Not wanting to leave Anela waiting, he sent a quick message, *"Sure, where?"* before tossing his phone onto the passenger seat. As he had predicted, the two men went straight to the airport. With skill born of practice, he followed them unobtrusively towards the ticket counter once inside. He noted the destination on their screen. Between that and their names, someone else could figure out if the flight to Houston was a final destination or a layover on the way to somewhere else.

Samir sauntered out of the airport and back to the car. He checked his phone and, as expected, there was a novel to read. Anela had given him two different times, a list of possible places to eat, and buried in the middle of it all was a phrase that made him groan. *"There's someone I need you to meet."* She was always trying to set him up with someone, convinced he wasn't going to be happy without another person to share his life with.

He humored her, but dating wasn't the highest priority on his list. She meant well, and might even be right, but his job was where all his time and energy went—and she knew that. It had often been a source of mild disagreement between them, though his goals would benefit her the most in the long run. After three failed attempts to try to text her back something that didn't sound mean, he gave up and called her.

"Sami!" Anela's warm voice washed over him before he even had a chance to say anything. "I'm so excited for lunch tomorrow. I just can't wait. Did you get the list of restaurants? Do you know what time will work best for you? Oh, I've missed you."

Samir laughed at the barrage of questions. "Yes, I got your message. Noon will be fine, but why don't you choose the restaurant? Send me the name and address of where to meet you, and I will be there on time."

"I can do that. Are you coming into town for work or for pleasure?" Subtlety was not a game Anela played well, but he cherished that about her.

"I have a few days off and I figured I'd visit my favorite person," Samir said. "However, I was calling because of that one little phrase you tried to hide in the middle of the last text. I told you last time, no more setups. No more blind dates. They never work out."

"Well, they would if you would just give someone a chance. They were all nice people, moderately successful—"

"And how do you expect me to explain the work I do? Besides, they're always here. I know you only want me to settle somewhere close by."

Anela laughed, a rich and velvety sound. "If that were the case, then I never would have set you up with Mandy. She was certainly not marriage material, but she would have shown you a great time or two. Maybe helped you relax a bit."

Samir groaned and shook his head at the memory of that disastrous date. They'd had nothing in common, and as pretty as she was, he wanted more than just a fun night with a random person. He'd sown his wild seeds in youth, that wasn't who he was anymore. "I don't need to relax, Anela. Things are fine, and you can save all those lovely dates for yourself. I'm sure Mandy was quite happy you rescued her from that disaster as well."

"I still say that you really missed out. The things that woman could do with her tongue—"

"I really don't need to hear the details. Not again." Samir was glad Anela couldn't see him right now. He could tell from the warmth in his cheeks that he had gone as red as a tomato.

It was one of the reasons he kept a bit of a beard. It helped to hide the fact that his face flushed at the slightest provocation. He didn't even need to be embarrassed; her teasing him would just make it worse.

"Fine, but what about the one before that? He wasn't so bad," Anela pushed.

Samir sighed. He was sure that she would never give up on her goal to see him happily married—maybe because it was something that she couldn't have.

"No, he wasn't, but that is not the point. I told you last time that I don't want to be set up anymore. Not by you or anyone else."

"Who else in your life cares enough to try and set you up?"

He wasn't going to argue that. Most of his friends were colleagues or subordinates, and none of them would even consider trying to arrange a blind date for him.

"Not the point. Please, Anela, can we just have lunch and catch up? No dates."

"I promise," Anela agreed. "No blind date."

"Thank you." Samir sighed in relief. "I will see you tomorrow. Text me the details, not options."

"See you tomorrow, Sami."

Samir drove back to his hotel and typed up the report. A part of him wondered, with the amount of time left in the day, if he should surprise Anela by dropping by early and making her dinner. He decided against it. He had never enjoyed surprises and, though Anela wouldn't mind, he was going to enjoy a quiet night by himself for a change.

No work, no interruptions. The moment he had filed that report, his vacation had begun. If he did agree with Anela on one thing, it was that he worked too much—but he was doing it for a reason. He'd long ago made the decision to set out on this difficult path, and that wasn't something he was willing to give up on easily. Even if he never managed to achieve change within the Nergal, at least he'd rest knowing he had given it everything.

CHAPTER THREE

Samir smiled the moment he caught sight of Anela waiting for him outside the restaurant. She stood out against the drab business crowd in a bright rainbow dress that complimented her dark skin. She'd even clipped colored extensions into her hair to match what she was wearing. Her flamboyant nature was something that Samir had always loved about her.

She wrapped her arms around him the moment he was in range and squeezed—thankfully not as tightly as she was capable of. Laughing, he returned the embrace and kissed her on the cheek. "I've missed you."

Anela grinned and ruffled his hair. "You grew it out some. I like it. Very handsome, goes well with a beard. I approve."

Samir smoothed his hair back into place. "Thanks. So, lunch?"

"Yes, I like this place and it's convenient." She linked her arm in his and walked through the glass doors of the restaurant. She nodded at the hostess as they marched right past her. He glanced down to see that her casual smile had become a mischievous grin. It was a look that he knew all too well and, the fact that she had gone right by the hostess, meant they were expected.

He put on the brakes before she could drag him any farther in. "Anela, I don't know what you have planned, but you promised no setups."

"What makes you think I have anything planned?" She batted her eyelashes at him, trying to look innocent, but Samir knew her too well to be fooled.

"I don't want to hear it," Samir said, glaring at her. "Tell me this isn't a blind date."

"This is not a blind date," Anela assured him, unfazed by the withering gaze. With another tug on his arm, she got him moving reluctantly towards the back of the restaurant.

"But?" he prompted. Even if this wasn't a date, something was going on and he would be damned if he walked into any sort of ambush—no matter how benign.

Anela didn't respond, and as she slowed to a halt, her eyes scanned the partially empty seating area, looking for someone or something. "Ah, he's here."

"He, who?" Samir asked trying to follow where she was looking but seeing only a wall in the way.

"Well, there is someone I want you to meet, but it is not a blind date. I did promise, and I meant it," she assured him even as she led him around a wall that created a semi-private alcove at the back of the restaurant. Only one person occupied the space and he didn't look up to acknowledge their arrival.

"Then what is this and who is he?" Samir demanded. If it was a blind date, for once, she had chosen someone he considered rather attractive. Not that it mattered if she were telling the truth. And, if it turned out that she was lying, then he would have to stand by his principles and leave anyway.

"Well…" Anela dragged the word out. It wasn't like her to beat around the bush on things. That left two possibilities, this was a date or there was something far more serious going on. He gave the man another good look and wondered if perhaps Anela was looking to settle down, but that would never be allowed. Not with a human and, if he wasn't human that was an entirely different matter.

"Anela, what's going on? Tell me now," Samir demanded, though his tone was gentle with her. He was rarely one to raise his voice, but he wasn't going to let her avoid giving him a straight answer.

"Please don't be mad about this, but there was no other way," Anela blurted out. She held up a hand to Samir and he waited as she took a deep breath and recomposed herself. "I think the explanation might work better if I do the introductions first. Come."

Samir allowed her to drag him the rest of the way to the table. He was willing to give her the benefit of doubt rather than jump to conclusions. She was often impulsive, but she rarely lost control of her emotions. This was important to her.

Now that they stood beside the table, their presence prompted the man to finally look up at them and Samir caught a flash of anger in those unexpectedly bright amber eyes. As soon as he noticed the emotion, it was gone. Replaced by an excessively neutral expression as he pushed out of his chair. Anela didn't even say hello, she crossed her arms and glared at him—her annoyance evident as she pressed her lips together. If this was a blind date, and Samir doubted that now, then this man hadn't been aware of it either.

Not a word passed between them, but there was a sense of communication that Samir couldn't shake. Whatever it was, Anela seemed to have won the silent argument as the man lowered himself back into the chair. Smiling, Anela proceeded with the introductions she had been so keen on before. "Samir, this is Keeler Lim and I think he's from the same place I'm from. Keeler, this is Samir Amin and, yes, he is a member of the Nergal, but you can trust him because he will keep your existence a secret if I ask nicely."

She turned her gaze to Samir with those last few words, her tone of voice becoming more forceful, but he was too shocked by her introduction to respond. This wasn't what he had been expecting and most people didn't know who the Nergal were. Those few that did, had cause to be aware of them. There was a reason they were considered one of the last real secret organizations.

"Won't you, Samir?" Anela pressed for a firm answer in a tone that he remembered well from his youth.

"Um, yes? What's going on here?" He hadn't intended to agree so readily. It had slipped through his lips without a second thought. He was still in shock over the introduction. He would have preferred a blind date over being blindsided like this.

"I met Keeler a few months ago. Like me, he's imprisoned in a human shell, trapped and mostly powerless. From what we've been able to discover, we've been on this world for approximately the same amount of time," Anela explained more gently as she pressed Samir into the chair across from Keeler. "He refused to meet with you and, since he was unwilling to do so with knowledge, I figured I would just make it happen because he needs to meet you. I need him to meet you."

"Um, okay. Hi?" Samir stammered as he struggled to wrap his head around what was going on. Keeler leaned back and crossed his arms. It was clear that he probably felt ambushed as well. Normally, when it came to his job, he was prepared and confident in what he was doing, but his brain still hadn't managed to catch up to that point.

"Now, talk. Figure things out." Anela gave them both a stern look. "When I come back, I expect you both to still be here and have actually conversed beyond the ordering of food."

"Excuse me?" Keeler spoke up for the first time since they had arrived at the table. Anela glowered at him until he huffed and looked away. Samir coughed to cover up his amusement. She was a force to reckon with when she was determined. It's one of the reasons she'd managed to gain her freedom.

"Now, be nice, talk, I will be back," she ordered, before marching out of the restaurant and leaving them alone in awkward silence.

Samir looked across the table at Keeler who still kept his gaze fixed on the spot in front of him and seemed intent on not speaking. It would be up to Samir to break the silence, but he had no clue what to say to this stranger. It wasn't often that he sat down to lunch with unknown beings from another dimension. A part of him wanted to go right into work mode but, if what Anela had told him was right, it was the last thing he should do.

Nergal protocol dictated that he should treat this intrusion as potentially dangerous—subdue, detain, interrogate. It was no wonder Keeler didn't want to meet him. If he'd had interactions with the organization in the past, it would have cemented a less than favorable opinion of any who worked for it. Samir had different opinions on that matter. First things first, he had to get Keeler to talk to him and, if he had been stuck as a human—trapped and powerless—for as long as Anela, then it would only be fair to treat him as a person.

"So, Keeler, right?" There was no response to his question, not even a nod of acknowledgement. Samir cleared his throat. "It's, uh, nice to meet you. So, um, well…"

Samir had no idea what to say. This was the same issue with every date that Anela had set him up on. He was never good at casual conversations. Except, this wasn't a date or small talk at a party. This was work, even if he couldn't treat it as such, and that was something he was good at. All he had to do was make Keeler see that he meant him no harm; convince him to open up and start talking a little.

"Anela certainly can be forceful when she wants her way, can't she?" Samir smiled, trying to focus on one of the few non-work things he could talk to Keeler about with ease. "I've known her for a bit over thirty years, since I was just a little thing. She's always had an impressive presence about her. Hard to say no to sometimes, but she's a good person, never maliciously dishonest. It's one of the reasons why I consider her my closest friend. To be honest, she's really more like family."

Keeler still hadn't looked up and was seemingly ignoring him. Samir took it as a good sign that he hadn't left yet though he had hoped Keeler would respond to the gentle banter. He tried not to let it get to him. If casual banter couldn't break the ice then he would try something else instead. "Anela says you have determined you both have been around for about the same amount of time?"

Keeler cocked his head slightly and looked up at Samir. He took it as encouragement to continue. "Must have been hard for you. I've read the records of when Anela first arrived here, at least what few records there are, and what she remembers of those times. It sounds like a confusing thing, to find yourself not only in a new world but to then be trapped and cut off from everything you are. Trapped in a shell that is unlike anything you've ever known. I cannot imagine how difficult it must have been for you, trying to understand what was happening back then.

"I know, for Anela, it took time for her to adjust to this new life and, for the most part, she had people around her that knew what she was and that the adjustment would not be easy for her. I mean…" Samir let his voice trail off as he thought of how some of the Nergal had treated their prisoner before more recent times. It was not something she talked about, but he had access to those files and what he had read had nearly moved him to tears. It was one of the many reasons why he had dedicated himself to his job as he had. Things had changed over the passing centuries, but they needed to change more.

Samir refocused his thoughts on the present and continued talking. "I won't lie to you. Not everyone was sympathetic to the struggle she went through, but to deal with such a transition without anyone around who could understand or help. It could not have been easy."

"Can I get you drinks or are you ready to order?" Samir startled slightly at the waitress that had approached from behind. He had been so focused on Keeler that he hadn't been paying attention to his surroundings which was unlike him. Normally, he was aware of what was going on around him. A habit from so many years working in the field.

"Um, yes, I would like a, uh, water for now. Thank you." Samir cursed at himself for stammering on such a simple order. He hated that he was this off-balance today. He needed to get himself together and act like the professional he was.

"And you?" She turned to Keeler, her professional smiled fixed on her lips as she waited for him to say something. He remained stubbornly silent, responding with a shake of his head and dismissive wave of his hand. He watched the waitress leave before fixing that silent stare back on Samir.

"Uh, well, as I was saying, it could not have been easy for you and…" Samir sighed and leaned back in his chair. This seemed like a useless task. He was getting no response from Keeler to anything he said. He had no idea how to get through to him. He'd needed to try something else.

"Look, I know she sprung this on you. She surprised me as well," Samir admitted in hopes that blunt honesty might get him further than sympathy had. "Normally, I would be all prepared with the right things to say and this would go far more smoothly. I am sure, if you've been around for as long as Anela said, then you have formed your own opinions of what I might be like. A member of the Nergal, someone whose job it is to stop intrusions from causing accidental or intentional damage to this world, but I am sure she told you that I am not going to do anything other than talk to you. I've been working for change in the organization, a more rational and modern approach. All I want to do is talk. I promise, that's all."

Still, no response. Samir tried not to get frustrated with him. Instead, he did his best to try and see it from his point of view. He understood the reluctance, but it seemed that Keeler was as taciturn as Anela was garrulous. Such opposite ends of the spectrum. It was a thought that struck a chord in his mind, one he hoped would help.

"Okay, you don't need to talk to me, but I had a thought and it would be easier to make sense of this thought if you could just answer a few small questions." Samir leaned forward intently. "Whether I intended to or not, I did give Anela my word. I won't tell the Nergal or the Institute about you. I cherish my friendship with her, and I won't go against my word. So, for this moment, can you please trust me enough to answer a few small questions or at least tell me if you're not comfortable answering any particular question?"

"Okay," Keeler agreed. Samir tried not to be too elated that he'd finally gotten a response. Still, he would have to tread carefully.

"You both already determined that you'd been around for about the same amount of time, right?" Samir asked.

"Yes." Monosyllabic answers were a start, but Samir hoped for more. It would take time to gain Keeler's trust, and he was willing to try. He'd already promised Anela he wouldn't tell the Nergal, but that didn't mean he wasn't going to do his job even under that restriction.

"And you're tra…" Samir let the word drift off unfinished as the waitress returned with two glasses of water.

"I brought two just in case, have you had a chance to figure out what you would like to order?" she asked as she set the glasses in front of them.

"Not yet, thank you, we'll flag you down when we're ready." Samir smiled warmly at her and waited until she was far enough away before continuing. "As I was about to say, you're trapped in a body, like her, correct?"

"Yes." Another one of those head tilts that had Samir wondering what Keeler was thinking.

"And do you know how that happened?" Samir leaned forward over the table again. Intent on the answer.

"No." Another single word answer. Samir had hoped for a little bit more this time, but he still had a theory to work with.

"It's not often that we find intru…" Samir didn't want to upset Keeler by using the language the Nergal would use. He needed to be careful there. "Your kind are very rarely trapped in a body without the Nergal being the ones to do it and, even then, those ones aren't entirely powerless. It's a temporary binding and there is no way that it could be an accident. I mean, there are so few ways for something like that to happen that I doubt it could be a coincidence."

Samir grinned at Keeler who said nothing in response. He wondered if he had said something wrong. It was hard to tell since he barely showed the slightest hint of emotion. Although something seemed different, but he wasn't sure what it was.

"Are you—" Samir stopped mid-sentence as Keeler looked past him and waved to someone. He glanced behind to see the waitress sauntering over in their direction.

"Yes, are you ready to order?" she asked with a smile.

"Chocolate, please. Your richest, most decadent chocolate dessert. Thank you." Keeler ordered without having looked at a menu. He fixed her with a stare that made Samir uncomfortable.

She trembled slightly as she turned to Samir. "And you?"

"Oh, um…" Samir struggled to think of something to order. He hadn't eaten yet today, but the interaction had distracted him. Not knowing what else to do, he ordered the first thing that came to mind. "How about a burger and fries? Something with bacon and avocado on it would be wonderful. Can I do that, please and thank you?"

"Yes, of course." She scurried away with one last, quick glance back at Keeler.

Samir watched her go. He had an idea of what had happened, he'd seen Anela do it on more than one occasion. It wasn't something that he approved of, less so in this situation, but he wasn't in a place to question Keeler about it. He made note of the incident and tried not to read too much into the fact that it had been done while ordering chocolate. It was what Anela craved the most when she needed to suppress that hunger or the darkness inside of her.

"You were saying," Keeler prompted. Samir wanted to smile and took it as a good sign to continue, even if he couldn't shake that slight sense of unease.

"Um, right, so there is a concept we've come across a few times before. Not often, but enough that we have a record of it, and it reminded me of this situation. At least, it's the only correlation I can think of." Samir realized that he was babbling. He paused and took a deep breath. He was reading too much into everything and he needed to focus on what was real. "It's a concept we refer to as 'usesima'. When two of intru... uh... two beings such as you and Anela are vitally connected in a way."

"Vitally connected?" Keeler leaned back in his chair. "What do you mean by vitally connected?"

"Essentially you are kind of like one being split into two." Samir took a sip of his water to prevent himself from continuing. He had never considered that Anela could have that kind of connection. No one seemed to have thought of it before. He'd read everything they had on her dating back a few thousand years.

Usesima were some of the most powerful intrusions that the Nergal had on record. It must have been much harder than anyone thought for such a formidable creature to be reduced to living inside the limits of a human shell without going insane.

"That could explain the oddness of the connection I feel for her," Keeler mumbled.

"It would. It's not something we see too often," Samir said as his mind spun with the possibilities. It was an incredible opportunity to learn more about such a unique connection. Plus, showing that it was more than possible for beings such as this to live within society would help him prove that these intrusions were not the menace the Nergal and the Institute believed. "I would love to do a few tests to find the extent of the connection and how it works. We've categorized a few different types of usesima based on the energy of the connection and…"

Samir stopped as he saw a hint of the earlier anger flash in Keeler's eyes. He'd overstepped himself, talking about his work. He had let himself get carried away. "I'm sorry about that. I do stand by what I said earlier. As much as I would like to know more about the connection, I wouldn't do so without your permission. Honestly, if you've made it this long in life without triggering any events to get the attention of the Nergal, I see no reason why we should disrupt your life like that. We could do it off the record though if you're interested. It'll be difficult to arrange, but not impossible."

"Right, perhaps we should end this conversation. I should go." Keeler glanced down at his phone. It hadn't even been an hour, but enough time had passed for him to be able to make up a good excuse to return to the office.

"And what about your, uh, chocolate?" Samir asked, trying to keep his mind off the potential meaning of such an order. "We can talk about other things. For example, are you doing okay for yourself? Is there anything I could do for you to make things easier or better on you?"

"I'm doing fine for myself," Keeler stated stiffly.

"I see, that's good. I'm glad to hear that." Samir sipped at his water. He'd screwed up and he wasn't sure he would be able to recover the conversation. "If you want to leave, I am sure the waitress can make your order to go."

"Yes." Keeler pressed his lips together tightly for a second before adding, "Perhaps we can talk another time."

"I am sure Anela would appreciate that and… Oh, food's here," Samir said, surprised at how quickly their order had arrived. The waitress kept her eyes averted from Keeler as she fumbled to put the plates down without dumping them. Samir wanted to do something to put her back at ease, but there was little he could do besides give her what Anela referred to as his million-watt smile.

Samir nibbled on a fry until the waitress had left them alone again. "Or you could stay, talk, and eat?"

Keeler stared at him, and Samir tried to keep his emotions open and welcoming. As the silence stretched, he tried not to get his hopes up. Finally, Keeler dug into the chocolate torte that had arrived, taking an obscenely large bite of it. After he swallowed, he answered, "Fine, talk."

CHAPTER FOUR

Keeler stared blankly at the computer screen in front of him, unable to focus on the work that normally consumed his time. He was trying—and failing—at not thinking about what happened at lunch. He wanted the entire incident behind him, but it was proving to be hard to do. He'd always been good at pushing things out of his mind: the hunger, the past, the memories he wished he could forget.

He had been furious with Anela when she brought that Nergal agent to meet him against his wishes. Had it not been for the promise made, and the fact that Anela was the closest thing he'd had to a friend in hundreds of years, he never would have stayed. He'd have cut ties that day, changed his name, and moved on to a new life. It had been his habit for so long. Staying under the radar of the Nergal was something he had mastered. Reinventing his life, his identity, over and over again.

It was tiring and he had hoped to stay here for a while longer. This current life, everything he had built here, was only just beginning to come together. He had it all planned out and if that Nergal had been typical for his kind, it would have ruined everything. Except, he wasn't typical, he was… unexpected.

His gentle attitude and the obvious affection Samir had for Anela didn't add up. It wasn't possible. His few interactions with the Nergal during his long life had told him a different story about the kind of people they employed. To them, his kind were things, sub-human, barely worthy of a second thought. Yes, there were many non-corporeals that could be dangerous—he'd encountered one or two in his time here—but they were all painted with the same brushstroke by the Nergal.

He wanted to hate Samir for what he represented but that anger had faded when he had talked about his relationship with Anela. Friendship, family—even she had used those words. It wasn't something he expected to hear from a Nergal, and it picked at his peace of mind. It had been a mystery that he couldn't leave well enough alone.

With a sigh, he leaned back in the chair, his normal stiff composure gone though that neutral mask remained. A habit built from centuries of determined un-involvement. He shouldn't have pried, and he wondered if he was going to regret allowing himself to form a connection to Anela. Although, he wasn't sure if that were even a choice he could make. His draw to her was like the pull of the moon on the oceans—a force stronger than either of them.

It had been the genuine sympathy Samir had expressed towards him when talking about how hard it must have been—being alone and lost. That had been the last thing he expected from any Nergal. It had drawn him into the conversation in a way that nothing else could. Made him wonder what sort of man he was dealing with.

He had reached out, allowed Samir's emotions in. He searched for anything that would tell him that this was only an act, but none of what he associated with the Nergal was present in him. No animosity, no feeling of human superiority. There was only kindness, and an unexpected softness to him.

It was that softness that had most piqued Keeler's interest and made him want to solve the fascinating conundrum that had been presented. It would have been easier with touch, but he wasn't willing to take that chance. It had been risky to even attempt to reach out as he did, but he needed to understand the soul within no matter the energy it took. He had expected the usual muddy dichotomy most humans carried inside them, but instead he had found a sweetness, a purity that lived in the energy and essence that was Samir.

Though he could not taste—not without physical contact—there was no denying the sweetness he sensed there. Sweet, not like sugar, but like the gentle, life-affirming flavor of an untouched artesian spring. He had tasted the souls of many people in his long life, but not once had he ever sensed anything like this. He'd found himself so wrapped up in the beauty of it that he had forgotten to listen to what Samir was saying.

Even after he had pulled back, when all he could sense were Samir's emotions, he found himself unable to focus. Knowing the essence of that man had awoken in him a hunger he had suppressed for longer than he cared to think about, and he found himself craving more.

Anela had been pestering him about feeding the void, about getting in touch with humanity, but the man across the table should be the last person he wanted to get close to—

despite what his hunger demanded. He was starting to think she was right. Perhaps if he had not been starving himself, the urge would have been easier to control.

It was something he tried not to think about—that hunger that had once driven to seek connection. It had led to nothing more than pain and death. These were memories he would never be able to escape. Reminders and warnings of why he lived as he had for so long now. He would not be responsible for the death of one more person.

He had needed to curb his hunger quickly before he did something he might regret. But the strength of this attraction, the relentless screaming of a hunger that he could barely control was something he'd never felt before. He hadn't even been sure that chocolate would be quite enough. It was why he had pushed the waitress, demanded that urgency to deliver his order. It had been a mistake to do that.

Thankfully, Samir's excitement over his work had helped him to get his head somewhat in order, though it did little to dampen his hunger. It was a reminder that the man was not to be trusted. The essence that made Samir who he was and his hunger for it couldn't fully take away from the fact that they stood on the opposite sides of a divide. Human and not-human. Nergal and intrusion.

He should have left then, but the chocolate arrived. Samir had apologized with true sincerity and his own curiosity had gotten the better of him.

"Sir?"

Keeler sat up straight at the unexpected interruption and quickly composed himself. "Is there a reason you're disturbing me?"

"I've been trying to buzz you." Jenny never seemed to be intimidated by him, it was one of the reasons he'd hired her out of the hundreds who had applied for the job. She was driven, intelligent, and strong-willed. He was almost sad thinking that her five years with him would soon come to an end. He never kept any assistant longer than that in case they got suspicious about his lack of aging.

Although, he'd soon have to step away from the public eye and she was a good candidate to run things for a few years while he stayed in the background. It would help keep the rumors at bay. Keeler glanced at the time, even as his thoughts already began to wander away from why she'd come in. He didn't have any meetings this afternoon. There were few reasons for Jenny to need his attention. "And?"

"I wanted to let you know that the background research for the AFI acquisition came through and I don't think the client is going to be happy about it. I know it's not the top of your list, but I thought you might want to take a look."

Keeler switched screens and saw the email listed as high importance that had gone unnoticed. Had it been in his nature, he would have cursed. "Your attentiveness is appreciated in this matter."

She stayed there staring at him, her curiosity muted, but noticeable. Keeler fixed her with a cold look. "Is there something else?"

"Are you okay, Mr. Lim?"

It was not a question she'd ever asked him before. He wasn't. He was troubled, he was still craving to taste that sweetness—though the urge was muted with distance and chocolate. He didn't know how to answer, and it bothered him that he was in enough of a state from lunch to have prompted such an inquiry. "Please leave. I have work to do."

Without another word, she closed the door. Keeler took a deep breath, a habit born out of pretending to be human for so long. Though he could remember little of his origins now, he was determined not to let humanity claim him, but one thing was clear.

He was going to have to find a way to sort out this issue with Samir as soon as possible. It was a distraction he could ill afford.

CHAPTER FIVE

"I would love to say that I can't believe you'd do that to me except I know you better than that," Samir complained.

He was right. She did know him well enough to know that he was not a fan of surprises. Anela laughed. "Oh, Sami, darling, you can make all the play you want of being mad at me. It's the way it had to be. It would have been a disaster if I'd stayed. You know I dominate any conversation I'm a part of, and I wanted you to get to know him. Tell me what you think."

Samir chuckled and sipped at his wine. "Right. I already told you that I couldn't get much of a sense of him. It was an ambush for us both, and you really expected me to be prepared? It was almost worse than a blind date."

"Oh pish." Anela waved a hand at him. Despite his words, his true feelings were easy for her to read. He had enjoyed himself. "You did solve one thing. You think he's my usesima, which explains so much. I have never met another being with which I felt such a connection. It is as though I have discovered a missing part of me."

"And I'm glad for that, really, I am, but do you think I could have a conversation with Keeler when I'm a little more prepared?" Samir elbowed her lightly. "Although I am glad that work brought me to town. I did miss you and, despite the circumstances of it, I'm happy to have met him."

"What are you doing here anyway? You never did say." Anela curled up against him as she enjoyed her own evening glass of wine. She had been pleasantly surprised when he'd sent the message saying he would be in town. He rarely visited her without a good reason to do so, and as far as she knew, there was no good reason for him to be here.

"Ah, just some reports of suspicious energy levels in the area. Nothing to be concerned about which is why I came myself. We were concerned that something was going on but weren't sure what." Samir shrugged. "Not important."

"You always say it's not important." Anela grinned. "I would think the world would be ending and you would say it wasn't a big deal."

Samir laughed. "That isn't true, but I'd rather talk about Keeler than work. How did you meet him? When did you meet him?"

"In the spring at the farmer's market, so it's been a few months." Anela poured them both another glass as she recounted the tale of meeting him. She tried her best to describe it well, but she was sure she missed a lot of details.

"You've kept this from me for months?" Samir asked. "And here I thought we had few secrets between us."

"A girl must always maintain her mystery." Anela tried to hold a serious face as she said it, but she broke out laughing. In truth, there were secrets she kept from Samir. Only one of which was her own secret to keep, the rest were not hers to tell. Her own was kept to protect him. She was too fond of him to risk the career he worked so hard for because of a single mistake she once made twenty years ago.

"Sure, sure. Maintain your air of mystery." Samir snorted. "Keeler was interesting though. I feel a bit sad for him, alone for so long."

"Yes, I am amazed he has managed as well as he has," Anela agreed. Push as she might, he had been reluctant to talk about his past and much of it was a mystery to her. "I cannot even begin to imagine what it was like for him. My memories may not all be good from my time with the Nergal, but I had guidance and time to learn to be human. There was no way it was easy for him."

"Mmmm," Samir mumbled into his wine. "He seems to be doing fine now and I would hazard a guess that he is good at staying off the radar of the Nergal. I haven't done any searches yet to be sure. I don't want to trigger anything specific. When I have a chance, I'll do some roundabout backdoor searches to see what encounters we may have had with someone of his description."

"If he's good at avoiding the Nergal then you won't find much. There is one odd thing about him though. Something that I still don't understand." Anela shrugged. "It might be nothing."

"How often is it nothing?" Samir asked.

"Not often." Anela stared into her wine glass. As she thought of how to phrase it. He had always listened to her and trusted her instincts about people, even if technically Keeler wasn't human. Right now, he was giving her a lot of leeway in that regard, for which she was grateful. If anyone in the Nergal found out that he knew about an undocumented intrusion and never reported it, he'd be in a lot of trouble despite the position he held. "I know the Nergal have documented a lot of different types of intrusions. There have been few documented that were like me, but those that you have found have always been attracted to connecting with the emotions and energy of others. We feed off it in a way. Some of us more than others."

"And?" Samir prompted. This was all stuff that he knew, and it was something she had struggled with before finding a way to satisfy that hunger. She had found her solution long before he'd been in the world, and it was a source of a few jokes between them. People were at their most open to a connection during their intimate moments, and Anela's string of lovers was impressive.

"Well, he is starving for that connection and I've been trying to convince him to embrace the human experience and humans." Anela bit her lip and looked up at Samir. "I don't know if that was wise of me, but he is so unhappy here and part of it, I think, is because he is so hungry and unconnected."

"I think you did the right thing," Samir assured her. He took her empty glass, placed it on the table and held her hands. "You know more than I do about things like this and if you think it will make things better on him in the long run then I stand by that. Okay?"

"Thank you, Sami." Anela smiled. She couldn't thank her lucky stars enough that he was in her life and that the Nergal had allowed her to keep him as her watcher. She could not have made it through another few years with one of his ignorant colleagues. He was a good man, her Samir, too good sometimes. "He is resistant to the idea though but will not say why."

"I am sure you will manage to talk reason to him. You've always been good at that." Samir yawned and placed his now empty glass aside. "Anyway, early morning tomorrow. Once I have an idea of what is going on, maybe we can arrange another lunch with fewer surprises. M'kay?"

Anela chuckled. "Agreed, no more surprises."

CHAPTER SIX

Connor let his gaze drift over the small crowd before him. He had their full attention and they hung on every word he was saying. It wasn't the crowd he had hoped for, but any gathering that served the purpose was a good one. He lowered his voice and watched as they leaned forward, eager to catch every nuance of his sermon. He had them right where he wanted them. Soon he'd provide the miracle they had all gathered here to see and then he could be done with these people.

"My friends, some folks will say that they don't believe in miracles, and I would tell you that I used to be one of those people, but miracles are the reason we're here today. I have learned to place no limit on what God can do because if you begin to limit God, then there is no God. With no God to guide us then we will be lost completely. And so much of this world has already fallen into corruption. It is a nest of anarchy, an incubator of misery, squalor, dishonesty, and all that is vile.

"You can't argue against sin. It's here to stay because the oice of the devil is sweeter than honey. If sin weren't so deceitful it would not be so attractive. The devil doesn't let a man stop to think about what he is doing, that in every added indulgence he grows more unworthy of the light. More prone to turning to the devil for help. It is such a tragedy and it can happen to any one of you because his lies are so alluring. They draw you in and make you think that they're the truth, that they are the words of the Lord but, my friends, they are not. These gateways to sin can be such small, simple things."

Once again, Connor let silence fall over the small congregation that had gathered. Some were dedicated followers that he knew well, but there were some faces here that he didn't know. It was to them that he directed himself. To them that he tried to hammer the point home. It was these new people that provided the best options for funding his research and furthering his great purpose.

"Envy!" He let the word explode out of him, shocking the silence. He lowered his voice again, playing the crowd as he would a violin. "Like the envy many of you have felt towards those that can afford the best care and doctors while you and your loved ones cannot. It is not just the sinner who suffers. No, my friends, when one man sins, we all must suffer for it.

"So, do as you please. Lie, steal, drink, fight, or fornicate. God won't stop you. Go ahead and sin until the undertaker comes to put you six feet under but remember, it will not be long before you and I go to the beyond. Lives of pleasure shall have an end, the wicked and unworthy shall not live half their days, but all is not lost. No, my friends, there is always hope."

Connor smiled. It was a look that he had practiced a million times over in the mirror. It was meant to draw people into him and show an innocence of spirit that he did not feel.

He relaxed his posture slightly, enough to look approachable. To give the sensation that he was like them—another ordinary person living an ordinary life.

"It takes great faith to stop the devil in his tracks! Faith to know that those sweet words are not honey, but a bitter fruit. A terrible poison to the good people of this world. We must take care to not let the wicked and unworthy of this world bring us down to their level and that takes great faith indeed!

"It is faith in the Lord that allows me to reach out a helping hand to my fellow man. It is through this which I have been given the strength to heal. And you too must have faith in the Lord. Faith in his vision. Faith to fight off those evil words that his servants bring to you."

Two people that he knew well slipped silently through the door. Most didn't even notice them come in, but he did, and he tried not to let the annoyance of their intrusion color his words. "Those who listen to the deceitful words of the devil have been barking at my heels from one end of this land to the other. I have been lied about, vilified, insulted, defamed since this great gift was given to me, but let me tell you, any man can revile me and talk about me until he is blue in the face and I will not give up my fight against the devil until I breathe my last breath. And if you think that anybody is going to frighten me, you don't know me yet."

Another practiced smile as he stood there with arms wide to show that he was being open and honest with these people. He always made sure he put on a good show, but the best part was yet to come. "We are all one and the same. We are of a kind and, friends, today I have been told by the Lord that I may heal one of you. I have been given this blessing in his faith, but I cannot choose who it will be. You must decide who amongst you is most worthy of this gift."

Connor let them discuss his offer amongst themselves for a bit. Allowed them to argue. He never really cared who they would choose, but they had to choose someone. It wasn't until he heard a small voice amid the loud adults consoling her own father. A voice so small and weak that it called to him over the noise and chaos.

"No, Daddy, it's okay I'm fine."

Connor searched for the source of that tiny voice and found a little girl who sat on a plastic chair her fingers clutched around a tattered old teddy. Her skin was so pale it was nearly translucent, and her hair was long gone from radiation. An oxygen tank was perched on the chair beside her. Cancer, that much he knew. That much was obvious. His heart went out to her as he studied the man that hovered over her. The one, he assumed, that she had referred to as her father. His weathered skin, the bags under his eyes from late nights watching over his child. Connor was sure that normally he was a gentleman, but his grief had become anger as he fought for his daughter's life with every ounce of strength and will he had left to him. He wanted her to be the chosen one and for this nightmare to be over.

"That's enough!" Connor shouted out over the arguing crowd and there was immediate silence. "Look at yourselves. Listen to the words that are coming from your mouths. See how easily the devil can corrupt you? Where is your mercy? Where is your love for your neighbor? Because I'm not seeing it here today. I'm not hearing it in your words."

A few faces looked away from him in obvious embarrassment. He walked through the crowd of people to the little girl, the heel of his cowboy boots echoing on the linoleum of the rented hall. His 6' 5" frame made the girl look like little more than a porcelain doll. She had suffered long and hard, far too much for one so young. It wasn't often that Connor felt any sympathy for those who sought his healing touch. Normally it was just a part of the performance, but this girl made his heart ache.

"Except for this little angel right here. Her heart wasn't on herself. Her heart is good and pure," Connor said softly as he knelt beside her and smiled gently. "What is your name, my child?"

"Melissa," she whispered, her blue eyes wide and large as she looked up at Connor.

"Well, Melissa, the Lord has spoken to me and you deserve another chance. You are too precious for this world, but it needs you. It needs your kind heart." Connor took one of her hands and let it rest in his. "Just close your eyes little angel and let the Lord reach his hand down through me to help heal you of this terrible disease."

She closed her eyes and he placed his other hand against her cheek before closing his own. "Oh Lord, you have called on me to heal this child of yours. She is an angel, but she does not yet belong among the angels."

He paid little attention to the words that he uttered. It was a show and nothing more. What he did had nothing to do with the words he said. Instead, his focus was on the malignant cancer that had spread through her body. He could feel its poison inside of her, killing her slowly. Radiation and chemo had done little to slow the process. How long she had been plagued by illness, he had no idea. It didn't matter.

Every bit of energy he had, he focused on those diseased cells. They shone in his mind like beacons and he crushed each of them, turned the lights off one by one. This time he was reaching, extending himself more than he liked, but he couldn't say no to this child. He couldn't let the world lose something so precious. It took little time for the task to be done, but it felt like an eternity to him before he stumbled backwards away from her.

Melissa inhaled sharply, her eyes somehow wider than before as she stared at Connor. Had he the strength to smile, he would have. Sweat clung to his brow from the effort. One of his assistants pressed a piece of chocolate into his mouth. Sugar helped; it would take a lot to replace the energy he had spent here. Connor fixed his gaze on the little girl and smiled at her, his first honest smile of the evening. "How're you feelin', angel?"

Her tiny fingers clawed away the air tubes that clung to her face. She took another deep breath and looked to her dad who was watching with a precarious hope shining in his eyes. "I can breathe again, daddy."

Hope turned to tears of joy as the man wrapped his arms around his daughter and lifted her into the air in a tight embrace. His words were barely audible as he sobbed. "My baby. Oh, my baby."

Everyone else looked at him expectantly, but Connor didn't care about the rest of them. He had the energy to do one miracle like this every now and again. He was glad that this child had been here to receive that gift. So often he chose the person who would have the greatest impact with the least amount of energy expended, but it felt good to help someone who deserved it. He accepted the hands that assisted him to his feet, but he couldn't let the crowd go yet.

"Remember this, friends and witnesses. Remember this moment when a young girl, pure of heart and soul, showed compassion and caring. This is a girl who earned her heavenly gift. So, go forth with the knowledge that those who are pure of heart, those who truly show their caring and faith can receive the gifts of the Lord! Be kind, be humble and be generous. Do not let the wicked and unworthy take you from your path of righteousness. Remember this day, remember this earthbound angel as you go forth to spread the word!"

Connor leaned on the shoulders of one of his many true followers. Those who knew the truth of his powers and followed him anyway. They knew this was no miracle of the Lord, but a magic that had been learned through years of careful study. It was easier to make the masses believe that he was healing through divine intervention. It was their money he needed, not their faith. Money that served to further his plans.

He was glad that he had found the well-hidden secret of a healing touch. Doing it was draining and not something intended for most, but he was creative. He'd played with the rituals he'd discovered until he had created a way to boost his energy. It had been worth the time because nothing brought in money like faith healing.

He didn't let his guard down until he was away from the prying eyes of the crowd as Paul led him into the old Winnebago that he called home. He leaned back in a threadbare fabric seat as the two men that had come in during his sermon followed him inside. They said nothing as Paul fixed a cup of tea for Connor and added a generous helping of honey.

He'd drunk half the cup, feeling better as his energy returned to him. "I take it you found something, or you wouldn't have interrupted me like that. You know I need to be able to focus to do these things."

"Yes, sir," one of them said with a sideways glance at his partner. "We found the one you've been searching for. We did everything as you said, and we found the one."

Connor sat up straight, his tea and exhaustion entirely forgotten. "Are you sure? Absolutely sure?"

"Yes." The other man seemed reluctant to look at Connor as he spoke. Instead, he stared down at his hands that he held clasped together in front of him.

"Then I guess it's time we left the dust of this town behind us." Connor grinned and finished the last of his tea in a single gulp. He had wondered if this day would ever come when he first read about the being known as Zi Asbu in the old texts he read. A great and terrible darkness that was meant to consume the souls of those who were unworthy.

Soon, his plan would be set in motion, and the Earth would be cleansed.

CHAPTER SEVEN

Anela passed the mug across the table to Keeler. She had been barely able to hide her surprise at his unexpected visit to her. He'd never dropped by unannounced before, but he couldn't get the meeting with Samir out of his head. He needed to know more about this strange man, so—on a whim—he left work early to talk to her.

"What brings you by today?" Anela asked.

"I've had time to think." Keeler sipped at the tea she had made and placed the cup aside. "Perhaps I should have been more willing to talk to your Samir. I wasn't the most forthcoming with him."

"He's hardly 'my' Samir." She chuckled. "Maybe you should have been, but I think he enjoyed meeting with you."

"He was not what I expected," Keeler admitted and glanced around the house. He knew no one else was here because hers were the only emotions that he could sense. "Where is he anyway?"

"Shopping," Anela smirked and he tried not to bristle at her amusement. "He should be home soon."

"Ah." Keeler nodded, wondering how long he had. What he wanted to know the most was not a question he thought should be asked out of the blue. He needed to build up to that. "How did you become such close friends with him?"

"Friends, family. Same thing in this case." Anela waved a dismissive hand. "He's the closest thing I have ever had to family in this life. His parents were once my keepers. They were kind to me. A kindness that he shows to me as well. I watched him grow from a small boy to the man he is today."

"I can't imagine knowing any one person that long." Keeler stared at his mug. He'd spent his life hiding what he was, moving around and moving on. Even now, as settled as he was, he spent much of it alone. Those few people who had close contact with him never stayed long, he made sure of that.

"Now I have you. You are also my family and I would like you both to know each other." Anela grinned. "One little, happy family, yes?"

Keeler shook his head. "I'm not sure it works that way. It would be nice if it did, but that is not the reality I've experienced."

"A girl can dream." Anela let her smile fade away. "I know it may not be reality, but sometimes we all need to dream a little."

"I've done fine on my own so far." Keeler wasn't about to admit to her that for the first time in well over a thousand years, his own hunger for a deeper connection with another being had been awoken. He was barely able to admit it to himself, even if it was the reason for his visit here today.

"You've done okay, but you are living half a life," Anela chided him. "Start small. Stay for dinner."

It was a conversation they'd had several times over the last few months, and she wasn't going to let it go until he admitted that he deserved more than what he was letting himself have. He wasn't ready to do that. Not yet, perhaps not ever.

"I don't know if that's a good idea." Keeler reached for the teapot to pour himself another cup. As much as he wanted to give talking to Samir a chance, he didn't want to do it in such an informal setting. He was hoping for somewhere a bit more public. It was safer that way.

"Sami promised to cook me dinner tonight. He always makes too much and he's a good cook." Anela poured some more tea for herself. It was one of the few things that she could make well.

"Actually, before he gets here, I meant to ask you something." Keeler stared at the table, still unsure if he had any right to inquire about it, but he couldn't get it out of his head. No soul he had touched, not even those few that he had opened up to in the past, had ever felt like Samir. There had to be a reason for it. It couldn't be natural.

"Yes?" Anela prompted, but the opportunity passed as the front door opened.

Samir stopped short as he caught sight of Keeler and Anela sitting in the kitchen. "Oh, um, hello. How are you?"

"I should be going," Keeler said abruptly, sliding out of his seat.

"Oh, no. No, stay!" Anela pleaded. "Please stay for dinner."

Keeler hesitated, not sure that he wanted to leave. He couldn't deny how drawn he was to Samir and the sweetness of the soul that lay inside. Anela knew the draw to connect with another soul, the need to feed the void that formed without, and he longed to experience what he could sense.

There was only one way he knew to do that from the prison he was stuck in.

Samir placed the bags of groceries on the counter. A smirk echoed the amusement Keeler could feel from him. He could only assume it was directed at his indecision over everything. It was rare for him to be invited anywhere for a home-cooked meal, and he struggled for an excuse to leave before something happened that he might regret.

Samir smiled warmly at him. "Yes, stay. There is plenty here for an extra person. It would be nice to have someone else to cook for. I don't often get the chance."

Keeler slid back into the seat. It was the warmth in the smile that had convinced him to stay, a warmth that went deeper than the surface. "Okay."

"Fabulous!" Anela grinned and walked over to the counter to snoop through the groceries. "What is for dinner?"

"Nothing fancy. I was thinking pork chops, potatoes, and asparagus," Samir said, not looking at either Keeler or Anela as he pulled ingredients from the bags and placed them on the counter. "Although, since I am staying a few days, I did pick up some extras."

Anela laughed and shook her head. "Of course, you would. You always do. I will be left with a freezer full of healthy and delicious meals."

"You know me well." Samir grinned back at her and pulled a bottle of wine out of one of the bags. "I'm sure you have plenty, but I thought this might be nice for tonight."

"Delightful." Anela grabbed it from him and snagged three glasses from the cupboard. She filled them up and passed one to Keeler and one to Samir before she took a sip from her own. "Ah. Perfection."

Keeler sipped at his wine in silence as he watched Anela and Samir interact. He spent more time observing their playful banter than taking part in it. He couldn't hide the hint of jealousy that he felt at their closeness and familiarity with each other. Both did their best to engage him, but he only participated as much as was necessary. He was amazed that, as the dinner ended and the night wore on, he was enjoying himself.

Anela told anecdotes about Samir, and Keeler was amazed at how easily he blushed. Still, it wasn't enough to distract him from the unasked question that burned in his mind. They were several bottles into the night when Anela excused herself.

"I have work tomorrow," she said with a little wink as she got up to leave. "Finish the bottle off and don't worry about me. I sleep like a rock."

"Good night," Samir said firmly, a touch of redness coloring his cheeks. He poured the last of the bottle into his and Keeler's glasses and took a sip. "She's right though; might as well finish it off."

Keeler didn't pick it up. He stared at it instead, fighting the wisdom of leaving with his desire to stay. This evening had been a distraction that allowed him to forget about the hunger. Now that they were alone, it had come back stronger than ever.

"Are you glad you stayed?" Samir asked. That same warm smile that had convinced Keeler to remain here earlier played upon his lips.

"It's been an enjoyable night." He looked away, glad that Samir wasn't able to read his emotions, let alone the thoughts that ran through his head at that smile. He'd grown comfortable tonight, forgetting the promises he'd made to himself and who this man was. He was Nergal—an enemy—

and not to be trusted despite Anela's opinion of him. But even that reminder wasn't enough to subdue the rising hunger within. He wanted to taste that sweet soul now more than ever.

Keeler picked up the glass to distract himself, swirling the wine and watching how the deep red liquid reflected the soft light in the living room. He took a large sip; he'd had far too much to drink already. As quickly as he could recover from such things, it still had an effect on him, breaking down his normally firm resolve. He knew that he should've left when he had the chance. The words slipped from his lips before he could stop them. "I have a better question, though."

"A better question?" Samir smiled.

Throwing caution to the wind, Keeler placed his glass aside and turned to face Samir directly. His eyes narrowed, and he licked his lips as he tried to convince himself not to give in to that demanding hunger, but his hand reached out of its own accord. He took the wine glass from Samir and placed it on the table. Their fingers brushed lightly as he did so. Samir gasped; a spark of longing flared too brightly to be ignored. That one touch undid the last bit of fight Keeler had within himself. There was nothing now but the need to feed the void.

He leaned in closer until his face was only inches from Samir's. His eyes focused, studying the man before him and tracing every emotion to be found there. Desire, fear, confusion. He forced himself to hold back, take his time. He may never get another chance, and he didn't want to waste this one. "What I want to know is, what makes you so different from everyone else?"

"I, uh, what?" Samir's face flushed. There was still that hint of fear but no revulsion—that alone may have been enough to give him pause.

Keeler's lips curled into a small, genuine smile. It was a rare thing for him. Normally, his expressions were carefully crafted, planned for effect. As much as he was not human, his body still reacted as if it were, and his heart beat frantically as he reached out and placed a hand against Samir's cheek.

Accessing a small part of his power, Keeler submerged himself into the icy, pure sweetness that he had desired since they first met. It was like nothing he had felt before and it was better than he could have imagined. Samir pressed into his hand; his eyes closed in bliss.

Warm, affirming, welcoming—Keeler gave of himself, everything he could not express, and he received so much more in return. It reflected to him a version of what he was emanating. Six thousand years and he had never known what it was like to be the person whose soul he tasted. It wasn't exactly the same, but something more, something new as his own essence mixed with Samir's. His hunger, that dark void that was being fed for the first time in a long time, cried for more than this paltry touch—this shallow taste of what was craved.

He had the ability to make that happen and it took every bit of willpower to not give into the temptation to force those emotions onto Samir. It would only serve to drive him away if he did that, but there was no denying that he desired more.

Keeler bit the inside of his lip and wondered how far he could push his luck or if he had pushed it too far already. It didn't matter, he had to know if there was a chance for more than this fleeting taste. Without another thought, he leaned in and pressed his lips to Samir's; tracing them with his tongue, begging for entrance and savoring the moment as he silently screamed for more; hoping for acceptance and fearing rejection.

His risk was rewarded as Samir responded to the touch with an openness he had never expected, allowing him a deeper taste of the incredible sweetness that lay within.

He wanted more, but he dragged himself away before he could deepen the kiss itself, knowing that if he let this continue it would be harder for him to control himself, to stop his emotions, wants, and needs from affecting Samir. For now, that hunger was partially sated, and it was easier for him to not let it drive his actions. He picked up his glass and took a sip as he waited to see what sort of response it would bring beyond the confusing swirl of emotions he could sense.

It took another few seconds before Samir opened his eyes and looked at him. His mouth parted slightly, but no words came out. Instead, he reached for his own glass with a trembling hand and took a careful sip. Keeler continued to watch him intently as he sorted through the many emotions that clouded Samir's mind, trying to read into the longing and desire that he sensed there.

Silence built between them before Samir licked his lips and spoke. "Maybe we should, um, call it a night?"

"Maybe we should," Keeler agreed, letting his free hand come to a rest on Samir's knee. One last touch, one last light taste—something to take with him into the night. He found courage from the fact that Samir didn't move away and allowed his hand to drift a little higher. He nearly smiled as Samir's face turned a deeper shade of red.

"Yes, well, uh..." Samir stammered.

Keeler removed his hand and finished his glass of wine in a single gulp. "I'll call a ride."

"Okay." Samir's voice was shaky, the emotions behind it swirling once again. "Good night."

Keeler nodded in response before stepping out into the cool evening air. Though it had gone well, he couldn't help but feel as though he had made a grave error in judgement. Away from Samir and with his hunger subdued, he cursed himself. He'd spent so long trying not to entangle himself with humans, to put someone in harm's way again simply by association and here he was, not only doing that, but putting himself at risk as well.

Clearly, coming here had been a mistake and he would do better to stay away. As the car drove off, he chanced a glance back at the quaint little house and longed to return. To find something more than the emptiness that he had chosen so long ago.

He groaned and leaned back against the seat still unable to turn his thoughts away no matter what logic told him to do.

CHAPTER EIGHT

Samir pressed his hands to his temples as he stumbled into the kitchen. Water. Coffee. He needed something to help his dry mouth and aching head. He winced at the bright light coming through the kitchen window but was grateful to find that it brought into focus the glass of water and painkillers that Anela had left for him. Along with a note.

He washed the painkillers down, chugging the entire glass of water before stumbling over the Keurig. With a cup of coffee in hand and his headache fading into a dull throb from the pounding pain he'd woken with, he was finally awake enough to read what Anela had written.

> *Sami,*
>
> *I know you had far too much to drink last night. I'm a terrible influence on you, but you really ought to be more careful about such things. Also, I think we should talk about last night. I'll call you on my lunch break.*
>
> *Love always, A*

He snorted, a small smile gracing his face as he put the note back down on the counter. Always burying the real reason for a message in the middle of things. Last night. He wasn't ready to think about that or what he should do about it. There was no protocol in the books for something like this and, even if there was, he wasn't sure it would apply.

Anela would have an opinion. She usually did when it came to his personal life and, in this instance, her insight would be invaluable.

Samir still couldn't wrap his head around any of it. By his own accounts, Keeler had no interest in the human experience, but Samir was starting to wonder if those words had been less than truthful. He doubted that anything had changed that much. It made no sense to him at all and thinking about it only made his head ache more.

Of course, he also wasn't ready to think about why he hadn't stopped it from happening. As much as blaming alcohol would have been nice, it wasn't the only thing to blame. He'd been drunk, yes, but not that far gone. He'd known that it was not a good idea, but… He sighed, there was always a but. He needed Anela.

He checked the time; it was afternoon and his phone showed no missed calls. Not even a text message. He didn't think it was likely that she'd have forgotten. That wasn't like her. His stomach churned and he didn't think he could blame the hangover.

He dialed her number and it went directly to voicemail. Pacing the kitchen, he did his best to quell the mounting worry that plagued his mind. He tried again with the same results, not bothering to leave a message. She never checked them anyway. If something had happened to her or perhaps simply to her phone, a text would be as useless as calling.

He held out the hope that it had been broken or that she had forgotten to charge it—as unlikely as it seemed. Either way, she could have still called him from there. The likelihood of her forgetting that she wanted to talk to him about last night was next to nil. She never wasted an opportunity to give a hard time about his love life—or lack thereof. He tried the number anyway.

"Good afternoon, Jamieson Insurance Adjusters. Celia speaking," an overly friendly voice trilled at him.

"Hi, may I speak to Anela Masterson, please," Samir said.

"I'm sorry, Ms. Masterson is not in today, can I direct you to another associate?"

"No, thank you." Samir hung up.

She wouldn't have left for work and not shown up. It was a part of their deal for her to be out in the world. She needed to fully integrate and that meant having a job. She would never risk her freedom and the life she had built here. He looked at her note and then back at his phone, willing her to call or text. It remained silent. He tried her number one last time; again, it went straight to voicemail.

His thoughts raced, running through every possible scenario, his coffee growing cold on the counter, forgotten. He took a deep breath and centered his thoughts. It wasn't time to panic—yet. Before he let the worry find a more permanent home in his mind, there was one thing he could try. He hated using it, but this was the one time he was glad that he hadn't fought the Institute about the decision.

Samir turned on the tracker app that, if Anela's phone was on, would tell him where she was. He cursed at the message that popped up. *"No signal found"*. That meant her phone wasn't operating which fell under the column of 'distinctly not 'good'. He looked up her last known location—it was only two blocks from her office.

Samir put the phone down on the counter and leaned against it, head down and eyes closed. He needed to be detached, not emotional. No matter who she was or what she meant to him, this was now a Nergal issue. He should call Liana, but he knew that Anela would curse him profusely if he did so and nothing was actually wrong. She had never liked or approved of his choice in head of security. If he was overreacting, then he would never hear the end of it. Not to mention Liana was in Bucharest visiting family.

Samir glanced back down at the last known location that still displayed on the screen. He'd start there, maybe there was a camera that would tell him something about what happened. Any clue would do right now. He didn't want to move forward without knowing for sure what had gone wrong. There was still a chance he was overreacting, but she didn't work far from here. He could retrace her route and find out what happened.

He caught sight of his reflection in the glass on the microwave and revised his plan. First a quick shower, then go after Anela. Time was of importance, but it would do him little good if he looked like he had just crawled out of a gutter.

The shower helped clear his foggy head, by the time Samir was dressed and heading out the door, he felt ready for almost anything. With the app, tracing her route would be easy enough. Up until the point the signal had stopped, it had followed her normal routine. She may be impulsive in many ways but, when it came to her daily life, she rarely varied in what she did.

Even parking in the same spot whenever possible—and her car was hard to miss. Her custom-painted shimmering pink Mini Cooper with sparkly black racing stripes stood out in a sharp contrast to the boring sedans and SUVs. Samir parked his rental in a free spot and headed towards the next stop.

It was a little place around the corner called 'The Kitschy Coffee Shop', that lived up to its name. Garishly painted walls, and random, dubious 'objets d'art' assaulted his eyes. He would have preferred the hangover to this place—it was easy to see why Anela loved it so much. Samir focused on the young man behind the counter, trying not to look at anything else. When it was his turn, he fixed the barista with his warmest smile. The name tag said 'Chad' and Samir hoped that he had been working earlier. "Hi, Chad, can I get an extra-large Americano?"

"Of course, will that be all?"

"Not quite…" Samir brightened his smile, hoping this was all it would take to get the information he needed. "By any chance do you know Anela? Persian accent, bright purple hair, normally orders a vanilla latte. Did she stop by today? We were supposed to meet for lunch, but she never showed up."

Chad seemed hesitant to answer the question as he rang in the order. Samir knew that pushing emotions was frowned upon unless necessary, but in his mind, it was necessary. He couldn't really afford the energy expenditure, but the coffee would help, and it was an easy enough ritual for him. He didn't have to push hard to convince the barista to answer his questions. "Yeah, I know her. She was in this morning."

"Cool. Thanks." Samir grabbed his drink and made sure to leave a generous tip behind. He poured in more sugar than he liked. It would help with renewing the energy he had spent to get an answer—one that gave him little clue as to what may have happened to her. It had only ruled out that anything might have happened here.

He walked the rest of the way to where his phone had told him was her last known location. Two blocks from her office, he stood on the corner of a busy intersection. If anything had happened here someone would have seen it. There were plenty of cameras to access for surveillance video. It wasn't an ideal location for illegal activities. Too many people and machines would be witness to what happened.

Samir took a moment to take careful stock of his surroundings. Two blocks east, about the middle of the block would be Jamieson Insurance Adjusters. He'd never walked with Anela to work, but her route wasn't a difficult one to follow. He knew she grabbed a coffee and would be at her desk by the time she finished it. He was almost finished with his own drink by now.

Samir walked back half a block to an alley that he had passed. He could see straight through down to her office building from here. Not a lot of women would choose to walk down an alley alone, but Anela would have no need to fear the average predator. If anything, they should fear her. Though her powers were limited, she could take care of herself far better than most humans and it was nearly impossible to catch her off-guard.

Unless, of course, someone knew about her abilities and was prepared for them. It was a thought that sat heavy in the pit of his stomach. It also meant he'd have to consider an official response to the issue, and he'd be forced to stand on the sidelines instead of being in the field. It was the curse of being in his position. He rarely got a chance to leave his desk.

He'd been able to narrow her last location down to this block, the tall buildings making it hard for anything more exact. He searched the area carefully for any sign that she might have been here, and it didn't take long for him to find it. A coffee cup identical to the one he was holding was on the ground and a few steps farther down the alley was what remained of a cell phone that had been smashed.

Samir stared at the broken remains. There was no denying that it had been hers. Not with that rainbow cover she'd had custom-made. It was clear that something bad had happened. The air caught in his throat, and his chest tightened with the realization that there was only one way someone could have gotten the drop on Anela—they knew what she was capable of.

Fighting the panic that threatened to overwhelm him, he focused on what he needed to do next. It was his duty to inform the Institute and involve the Nergal. This put him in a position he had hoped would never happen—do his duty and be sidelined or break all the rules and risk his career to save her himself.

Knowing she was out there and, potentially in danger, scared the hell out of him. She was his closest friend, his family, but using Institute resources would send up more red flags than he could easily dismiss. He could only think of one way to find her that might not trigger too many alarms—and it meant facing Keeler Lim.

Samir wasn't ready to deal with that can of worms, but it was the lesser of two evils. He couldn't simply stand on the sidelines. He only wished he'd had more than a second to think about what had happened, and why. There'd be no time for that now, he had to hurry. Pushing his reservations aside, he searched for any information he could find on Keeler Lim.

There wasn't much to be found on him which seemed strange. Lim might be a common name, but Keeler wasn't, and something should have come up. He chewed on his lip as he tried to think of another way to find him. It didn't help that Samir couldn't fully ignore the dread that filled him at the thought of seeing Keeler again so soon.

Forcing his thoughts back on track, he tried to recall what few personal details he had learned. There wasn't a lot, Keeler hadn't been overly forthcoming about himself. However, Anela did say that he worked only a few blocks away and that they had often met downtown for lunch. That was something to go on. He'd also mentioned something about a company that handled business mergers.

It wasn't a lot, but he gave it a shot. There were only two companies that came up nearby. It was a fifty-fifty chance that he would get it right. He chose the one nearest to his current location, *Nu Business Services*.

He tried not to think about what would happen when he found Keeler. Or if Keeler would even agree to what he was going to ask. It wasn't ideal, showing up at someone's work unannounced, but it would be a public space and that was a small comfort. That meant that he wasn't going to be alone with him, but it also meant that there were certain things he wouldn't be able to discuss.

Samir shoved the worries out of his mind as he followed the directions to the address listed. One problem at a time was how he made it through a lot of things in his life and that was how he would get through this as well.

CHAPTER NINE

Samir stared up at the tall glass building and hoped that this was the right place. He stepped inside and read the list of offices carefully. Near the top was the one he was looking for—Nu Business Services. Samir frowned. He had no idea exactly what Keeler did. He only knew what kind of company he worked for.

Not knowing what to expect when he stepped off the elevator, he wasn't surprised to see an opulent desk with an efficient looking receptionist behind it. He approached the desk and tried to relax. It was fine, everything was going to be fine. All he had to do was ask if Keeler worked here. If he didn't then he would try the other company that Google had told him about.

And if he did work here, then he'd worry about what he was going to say and how to say it. He'd been doing his best not to think about it at all.

"Can I help you, sir?" the receptionist asked, giving him a good look-over and seeming to find him wanting. Samir didn't hold it against her. He hadn't trimmed his beard and he'd grabbed the first thing he could find. Jeans, t-shirt, and scuffed trainers didn't really fit the aesthetic of this place.

"I'm looking for Keeler Lim." Samir flashed her his friendliest smile, but she stiffened at his request as if he had asked for the head of the company itself. He tried not to read too much into her reaction but took some comfort in the fact that he'd gotten the right place on the first try.

"Do you have an appointment?" She gave him a second, harder look over. He tried not to fidget under her intense scrutiny. Anxiety might have a choke hold on him, but he needed to appear as if everything was okay—a balancing act he was normally proficient at.

"Um, no, I'm an acquaintance of his. My name is Samir, Samir Amin." He smiled at her again and she frowned in return.

"Please take a seat over there, sir," she said with a nod at the comfortable chairs that lined one of the walls. "This will only take a moment."

Samir did as he was told and took a seat. As much as he tried to relax, he couldn't stop the nervous tapping of his foot as he waited. He pulled out his phone to stare at so he could pretend he didn't notice the curious glances that the receptionist gave him before she hung up the phone with whoever she had been speaking to. He almost expected that she was going to tell him to leave.

"Mister Amin?" a pleasant-sounding voice asked. Samir fumbled with his phone as he looked up to see a ginger-haired woman in a power suit looking at him with obvious curiosity and amusement as if he were a strange creature that she had never seen before. He smiled at her and shoved his phone back in his pocket as he stood to greet her.

"Yes, hi." Samir could feel the doubts starting to grow in his mind with his anxiety over seeing Keeler. He almost regretted showing up here.

"Hello, Mr. Amin. I'm Jenny McGregor. I'm Mr. Lim's executive assistant. He's currently in a meeting but he said he would like to meet with you as soon as it is finished. If you could please follow me." She smiled at him pleasantly then led the way to the other side of the building and through a set of frosted glass doors. If possible, this waiting area was even more luxurious than the previous one. Samir tried not to feel more self-conscious about his appearance than he already did. He hadn't expected any of this, Keeler had never given any hint that he was doing this well for himself.

"Erm, uh, Jenny, was it?" he asked when the doors shut behind them. He wasn't too sure he wanted anyone else to overhear what he was about to ask. It was bad enough that he'd sound like a fool in front of her right now. "This is going to sound stupid, but what is it that you do here?"

Jenny smiled politely. "We deal with multiple aspects of high-level international business mergers and acquisitions."

"I see." Samir nodded to himself as he took a seat. He still wasn't entirely sure what that meant, but it wasn't as important as the next question. "And um, Keeler, what is his position here?"

Jenny chuckled. It wasn't malicious or derogatory, but she seemed honestly amused by his question. "I'm going to guess that he wasn't overly forthcoming about what he does for a living with anyone he's met so recently, but the fact that you even know where he works shows that he trusts you more than most people. He isn't one to overshare about anything. To answer your question, he owns the company."

"Right." Samir was dying to know more, but he felt awkward asking any further questions about Keeler. It seemed that he was an enigma even to those who worked closely to him, but it was obvious that Jenny knew him well enough.

Jenny leaned against her desk instead of sitting in her chair. She stared at him intently, her head cocked to one side and that look of amusement never leaving her face. Samir waited for her to say something, but her silence forced him into taking the lead. "I'm sorry, is something wrong? Am I missing a joke?"

"Oh, god no. I'm sorry." She laughed and shook her head. "It's just that I don't think Mr. Lim has ever had a personal visit at the office before. I guess I'm curious about who you are, why you're here, and how you know him, but none of that is my business. Unless, of course, you want to tell me."

Samir laughed, relaxing some as he did so. It amused him that he wasn't the only one who found Keeler to be such a mystery. Her entire demeanor put him at ease and gave him something else to focus on instead of what he was going to say when he finally did talk to Keeler. "It's complicated. I met him through a good friend of mine. Sort of a sister to me. How she met him is a whole different complicated story. I've only known him a few days, but something important came up that I need his input on. How long have you worked here for?"

"About five years. He's a strange boss, but a good one. Most of the people who work for this firm as his assistant usually end up in a pretty good job when they leave. Although, to be honest, I'm not sure I really want to work elsewhere. I like it here, but don't tell him that." Jenny winked at Samir and glanced at her watch. "He should be done soon enough."

She smoothed herself out and took a seat behind the desk. Samir guessed that Keeler probably wouldn't be a fan of his assistant gossiping with a visitor, but he couldn't resist one more question. Samir walked over to lean against her desk. He honestly liked her. She had such a sweet disposition. It was refreshing. "Five years is a long time to work for someone and not know about their personal life. Why do you think that is?"

Jenny leaned forward and lowered her voice to a conspiratorial whisper. "I didn't think he even had a private life until a few months ago."

Samir laughed hard. "I think you might be right."

At the creak of the wooden door that led to Keeler's office Jenny's entire manner changed dramatically. She sat up straight in her chair and her face became a professional neutral. Samir took a step back from the desk as weight settled in his chest. He didn't want to be the cause of any issues for her.

Keeler didn't even spare him a glance as he stepped out of the office with two older gentlemen. "My assistant Ms. McGregor will email the necessary documents for you to look over later today or tomorrow. Thank you for your business gentlemen. It has been a pleasure."

His words weren't reflected in his face. It was the same passive neutral that it usually was, and it made Samir's mind flashback to when he smiled last night, and his soft lips—

He pushed the thought out of his head. He didn't have time to think about any of that. It was something that needed to be addressed, but not now. Anela took priority. Finding her and making sure she was safe. Those were the thoughts he needed to keep at the forefront of his mind.

Keeler waited stiffly for the men to be shown out by Jenny before even acknowledging Samir's presence. "Samir, what are you doing here?" He took a step towards him before stopping. His head cocked to one side. "What's wrong? Is this about last night?"

"Um, uh, no." Samir could feel his face grow warm at the mention of last night knowing that Keeler had probably followed the emotional signatures attached to his earlier thoughts. He cleared his throat and focused on what he needed to say. "I'm actually here about Anela. It's important."

"About Anela?" Keeler paused for a second before continuing. "Would you like to talk in my office, in private?"

"Um, yes, that would be a good idea," he agreed as Keeler opened the door for him. The last thing Samir wanted to do was be alone with him, but it was better than having this conversation with an audience. It would not be a good thing for him or Anela if anyone tried to involve the police.

"Jenny, hold my calls." Keeler didn't wait for a response from her before letting the door close and turned to Samir. "What's going on and how can I help?"

"Uh…" Now that he had to say something, Samir found himself at a loss for words. Instead, his mind focused on the one thing he didn't want to think about. He forced his thoughts to slow down, reminding himself this wasn't simply an attractive man that stood before him. He wasn't human and, therefore, entirely off-limits. More importantly, Samir knew it wasn't going to happen again, not here. Keeler would be able to sense his emotions; his worry and concern that overrode all else. "Anela's missing."

"Missing? What do you mean missing?" Keeler managed to look immediately concerned even though he didn't seem to move at all. Samir wondered how he could tell that, but that was something that he could think about later. For now, he would accept what his brain told him as being true. He glanced around the room and his eyes landed on a carafe of water sitting on the desk. Keeler followed his gaze. "We can sit and talk."

He motioned to the chair as he moved around to the other side of the desk. Samir felt a wave of relief that he didn't suggest the couch. It helped him, having this barrier in place. Though, he got the impression that Keeler was relieved at this arrangement as well. He took the glass offered.

He sipped at his water as he organized his thoughts so that he didn't waste too much time explaining things. "She never showed up for work and, when I tried to call this morning, her phone was going straight to voicemail. I know she would never leave the house without it charged. So, I traced her route to the office and found her phone smashed in an alley. I'm worried that something may have happened to her and I need to find her."

"Then why did you come here?" Keeler interrupted, his voice cold and stiff. "You have resources that are intended to find beings like us."

Samir pressed his lips together as he tried to find a way to explain why he came here, but none of the reasons were things that he wanted to admit to in front of a being he didn't know that well. He had no idea exactly how much he knew about the Nergal and how it worked or Samir's position within the organization. He went with the only excuse he could think of, as weak as it was. "Anela is as much a fan of the Nergal as you are. I doubt she would be happy if I called in the troops to find her."

Keeler stared and Samir shifted in his seat. Anela was a darn good lie detector, and he was sure that the same could be said of Keeler. It was why he had gone with a weak version of the truth, hoping that it might slip by unnoticed. He sighed.

Looking away from the piercing gaze, he admitted the one thing he hadn't wanted to consider—one of the other reasons he hadn't followed protocol besides the possibility of being sidelined. "And if something terrible didn't happen, if it is all an accident, I don't want the Nergal to be called in to find her because she values her freedom more than anything. I want to make sure she gets to keep it."

"That doesn't explain why you're here. Whether she likes it or not, your first recourse should be the Nergal," Keeler pointed out and Samir cursed silently. He had been foolish to think that Keeler wouldn't pick up the emotional undertones in what he was suggesting. Even if Keeler didn't wear his emotions on his face, he was as sensitive and proficient as Anela at reading them.

"If I went to them, I would not be allowed to be involved and I care too much about her to allow myself to sit on the sidelines," Samir admitted and looked back up at Keeler. He almost regretted doing so. In those amber eyes, he saw softness that he hadn't expected. He looked away again and started rambling. "It's not that I haven't worked in the field, but I don't anymore. The only reason I am the one in charge of Anela is that she refused to work with anyone else. I can't stand by and wait for someone else to find her when I know I can get to her faster. I don't want to be sidelined on this, I can't be, and I need your help. Please."

"And what do you think I can do?" Keeler continued to stare at him, though the ice in his voice had melted some.

Samir wanted to know what was going on behind those eyes, what he was thinking and feeling. Not only about this, but about last night as well. He wanted very much to understand Keeler, but he kept himself focused. "I was thinking of using your connection with her as usesima to locate her."

"You can do that?" Keeler leaned forward slightly over his desk. "How?"

"Um, if I can get to a secure terminal, there is a ritual that we have on record for finding someone's usesima. I haven't memorized it, or I would suggest we do it now." Samir barely managed to stop himself from babbling on about this little-known ritual. He turned his gaze to stare out the window so he wouldn't have to face Keeler. He had no idea how he was going to get him to agree to what he was going to say next.

"By using this ritual, you are sure you can find her?" Keeler asked softly. Samir was sure the gentle tone was in direct response to the anxiety he was feeling.

"Yes." Samir forced himself to look Keeler in the eyes as he spoke. It was now or never. He had to tell him the truth about what he was actually asking him to do. "This may end up revealing who you are to the Nergal and the Institute. We have to go to one of their main facilities to be able to access the files I need for this ritual. I know it would be asking a lot of you, but I'm worried about her. Please, help."

He hadn't wanted to beg, but he found himself doing so anyway. A part of him was terrified that Keeler would refuse to help him and his only option after this was to follow protocol. To wait in worried silence for someone else to save her and bring her home. It wasn't often that he thought about how much Anela meant to him, but other than his father, that he wasn't that close with, she was his only family. She was the one that had stood by his side during every stage of his life. She was his crazy aunt, mother figure, bratty sister, and best friend all at the same time.

"Please," Samir asked again when he got no response from Keeler who seemed to be weighing all the options with great care.

"You've given me a lot to consider, I need a second to think about it, okay?" Keeler spoke softly. He reached out to take Samir's hand, perhaps to comfort him in his distress, but Samir flinched away from the touch. The flash of emotion—regret or sorrow, it was hard to tell—made him regret his reaction, but he couldn't have helped it.

Keeler leaned back in his chair and closed his eyes tight. Samir waited patiently, trying not to count the passing seconds. It seemed forever before he opened his eyes and looked at Samir. "I'll help."

CHAPTER TEN

Anela opened her eyes to darkness, her head spinning. Attempts to raise her hand met with resistance. She tugged at the binding, surprised that it did not give, and discovered her other limbs to find them similarly bound. Throwing extra effort behind her struggles proved fruitless. She should have had the strength to break them.

"Son of a fucking bitch." She murmured as she gave another tug. Even the chair didn't move which meant it had to be bolted into place. Whoever had done this knew what they were doing. She tried to remember what had happened, but most of it was a blur. She had sensed something that gave her alarm and then there was only blackness.

"I see you're awake now and you do have a mouth on you darling, don't you?" A soft southern accent startled her from her thoughts and attempts at escape. "Now, those bonds were made with your unique abilities in mind. I don't think you're gonna find a way out of them any time soon. However, there are options available to you if you're willing to listen to reason."

"Who the fuck are you?" Anela snapped. She should have sensed that someone was here, but even now there was little to read on the person. She searched for where the voice was coming from; there were no windows in the room, and the only light came from a partially cracked door. It was barely enough for her to see the outline of a man sitting beside it. She focused all her attention on that spot.

"Who I am is hardly important, but you can call me Connor if you wish. What is important is what we're going to do together." He didn't move from where he sat, and there was little sense of any emotion. From beyond this room, nervousness and excitement reached her. There were more people out there, but she had a hard time discerning exactly how many. She narrowed her focus back on the single figure that had addressed her.

"Connor, was it?" She drawled the name as her mind tried to figure out what he could possibly want from her. Over the years people had made attempts to release her but it had been centuries since the last time anyone had tried something so stupid. Since then, the Nergal had been careful to hide most of the rituals that pertained to such things. "And how are you doing today, Connor?"

"I beg your pardon?" His words showed more confusion than his emotions told her. He was an actor by habit, feigning emotions without feeling them. It gave her little clues into his psyche, but nothing that she could work with to manipulate her way out of this place. Not yet, anyway.

"Well, Connor," Anela put as much venom into his name as she could, doing her best to project fear onto a man who might not even feel it, "I wanted to make sure that you're feeling healthy before I rip your fucking throat out with my teeth."

Connor chuckled as if she told a mildly amusing joke instead of threatening to kill him. Her attempts to make him fear her had no effect at all. If he knew about her powers, there was a good chance he had warded himself against any sort of emotional push. "You do have some gumption there, missy. I like that. It bodes well for our working relationship."

He finally stood up, turning on the light as he did so. Anela took in the tall, lanky man before her. Grey-green eyes watched her intently and a small smile played on his handsome face. She tried harder to project any emotion on him, but all she got was another laugh.

"That little trick ain't going to work on me." He walked up to her but stayed carefully out of reach before crouching down to her level. "See, I've done my homework. I know what you can do and how to stop you from doing it. Nice try though."

Anela wanted to spit at him, but it seemed too cliché—even for her. She smiled instead. There was no way he could know everything about her or everything that she could do. He would have needed access to the Nergal archives and that was heavily restricted. Surely, someone would have discovered such a breach of security long before now. "I will burn you from the inside out. You will scream for a mercy that will never come as you feel yourself die slowly until all that remains is a pile of smoking ashes. Although, if I'm feeling generous, I'll disembowel you instead and wear your entrails like a crown when I am done."

"Sure you will, princess." Connor chuckled again. It was infuriating, his entire lack of reaction to her statement. His strongest emotion seemed to be mild amusement. "And that is just the kind of thing I want to hear from you. Nice to see the darkness on the inside is still there despite your appearance."

Anela couldn't do much, but she tried to throw herself towards him anyway, chair and all, not that it did much good. Frustrated she growled at him out of instinct. It was a sound she rarely made, a throwback to her early years. All anger and ferocity, none of the humanity that she learned to embrace. Pinned as she was, it reminded her too much of the days she had hoped to forget.

"Easy there, darling." Connor cooed at her as if she were nothing more than a misbehaving dog. "Easy now. I got a proposition for you. I wasn't convinced you'd be interested earlier, but seeing you like this, knowing that the darkness is still alive within you, perhaps you would like to hear it. I think you might find my offer more than tempting."

Anela bit back her initial response. She still had no idea why he had taken her in the first place. Obviously, he knew more about her than she did about him, but she didn't trust herself to speak. She waited in silence to see what he would say. Not that she had a lot of other options at this point.

"This world is a filthy, disgusting place." Connor stood up and started to pace in front of her. "It's filled with wicked people. Those who take delight in destroying others, destroying this beautiful gift that we've been given. They lie, they cheat, they tear this world apart with their misdeeds and are they the ones who suffer for it? Hell, no! It is the good people of this world who are made to suffer for their sins while the unworthy lay in the lap of luxuries that were gained through the blood of the righteous. They are unworthy of the lives that they have been given. The lives that they have squandered and wasted for passing pleasures. Evil runs rampant in this world."

Anela thought he was ramping up to give her a sermon, but instead, he laughed and shook his head. "But who am I to be telling you about these things? I don't need to convince something like you of how dark the people in this world can be. You know their darkness. It courses through your veins. A bit of an occupational hazard. I've spent so much time shouting at the world about its misdeeds that sometimes I forget who I'm talking to."

Connor brushed his hair back as he crouched down in front of her again. "You know what I'm talking about. You feed off that darkness, those evil souls that pollute the world. They are a delicacy to you, but you can't consume them the way you once did because those fools who summoned you didn't understand what you really are. They underestimated your power and you had to be trapped in this pathetic, useless shell."

She couldn't even begin to deny most of what he said. There was too much truth to it, even the last line about this prison she had been stuck in. Once she had been powerful, an all-consuming darkness feasting on the souls of those it encountered. Their darkness called to her, it still called to her, but now she ignored it—mostly.

Instead, she had chocolate to curb the cravings and lovers to feed that void, to keep her from coming completely undone. Her past, what she had been, it wasn't who she was anymore. She had embraced her humanity, the joy and light of this world. There was more than darkness—in her and the world.

More troubling than these reminders of what she wished to forget, was that she had no idea how he knew any of this. So much of what he alluded to was ancient history, much of it scrubbed clean and hidden away from the public by the Laibiruzi Institute. It was a puzzle that she wanted to figure out, but, more importantly, she needed to know what it was all leading up to. "What do you want?"

"To release you, of course. To show the world what happens to those who are wicked and unworthy. I want to cleanse this world of those who do not deserve her riches." He gave her a lopsided grin. Though his face showed amusement, there was still nothing of the mirth in his emotions. She wondered, a bit belatedly, if he had somehow warded himself against her even sensing him or if he really was this empty. She wasn't sure which thought disturbed her more—that he had emotions and still wanted to destroy the world or that he was an emotionless psychopath with an obvious talent for magic.

"Release me?" Anela grinned widely despite the sinking pit of dread in her stomach. "Well then, reach on over and undo these restraints."

"Oh no, not the shell you're trapped inside of." Connor chuckled and though she could still sense nothing she was sure that he was honestly amused this time, which made her believe that he had managed to ward himself from being sensed. "That prison of yours has been corrupted by the sins of humanity. It would do me no good to let you go still trapped inside, a shell of the greatness that lies within. I need you in your pure form. I need the beast that will consume the darkness of this world and make it clean again. My dear, I want to release the real you."

Anela counted to ten before responding. "You can do that too, but the result would be the same. You would be dead."

"Ah, that is the problem, isn't it?" Connor didn't seem the least bit phased from her continued insistence that she would kill him. "However, there is a solution to this problem, but it might take a few tries to get it right."

"Get what right?" Anela pushed back the fear that threatened to rise in her at the quiet confidence in his statement.

"I am sure you would love to know, darling, but I'm thinking that is one thing that I will be keeping to myself since you seem disinclined to agree to help me. Perhaps you've been a human for a bit too long." Connor stood up and stretched.

"If you play nice, we'll feed you. Try to hurt any of my brothers and you will suffer. I can't kill you, but I can hurt you. Remember that." He walked out of the room and shut off the light on his way, leaving her in complete darkness. Although she knew it was useless, she struggled against the restraints again. They held firm. Anela collapsed forward as far as the straps would let her.

It wasn't the darkness that bothered her. Darkness was something she knew better than most. She now knew what this madman wanted from her and that was what terrified her. Though she could play at being human, those who knew her true nature still feared her. She never begrudged them that fear because she understood it. Ignore it as she might, deny her past all she wanted—that darkness, the need to consume, was still there.

Right now, her only hope was that Samir had realized she was missing already. Anela knew she could count on him to find her. He always came through when she needed him the most. Hopefully, he would be in time to stop this madman from releasing her. The last thing she wanted was for Samir to have to be the one to destroy her.

CHAPTER ELEVEN

Keeler knew he had pushed things too far last night and he regretted it. As much as he would have liked to blame it all on the wine, he knew that it was only an excuse. He'd been surprised by how much it bothered him to have Samir flinch when he had gone to comfort him. There was nothing he could have done about it except the one favor that Samir had asked of him.

Of course, if he was going to do this, there was no way he'd be forced to fly commercial as Samir had suggested. He wasn't a fan of crowds, it reminded him of what he was, how he didn't belong here and, occasionally, it brought back memories of angry mobs that wanted to destroy the monster hiding in their midst.

Thus far, the flight could be best described as awkward. It was hard to ignore the man seated on the opposite side of his private jet, staring silently out a window at the passing clouds and landscape. Samir had said little beside thanking him several times for agreeing to help. His emotions cycling through worry, nervousness, hints of fear.

Keeler sipped at his drink, occasionally stealing glances as he tried to figure out what to do about the situation. He had no idea how to ease the nervousness and uncertainty that were directed towards him. The only thing he could do was keep his distance and give Samir time to work through things on his own. It would do no good to push. Although he was tempted to offer an apology for his behavior last night, he wasn't sure how well that would be received.

The fact that he was even considering apologizing felt strange to Keeler. He couldn't remember the last time he had apologized for anything he'd done or said. A few hundred years at least. He kept his life closed for a reason. It was easier for him that way. Being close to humans never worked out well for anyone involved.

He wanted to blame Anela for even making him consider wanting more out of life than what he had now. He'd been just fine before and, as much as he wished he could, he wouldn't blame her for what had happened. That had been his own choice, his own actions and he should have known better, but it was hard to not want something that tasted so good. An essence and energy that was a siren's call to him.

Worst of it was, though his initial interest in Samir had been based purely on the allure of his essence, he now found himself wanting more than that. He wanted to know the man himself and that confused him. He should hate him for what he was and what he represented, but the more time he spent with Samir, the more curious he became about him. He was unexpected in every way conceivable.

And unexpected was rarely a good thing in his world.

He would get through this, help him find Anela, and then he would back off. It was as simple as that. He could run his business from anywhere in the world that he wanted. He didn't have to be here, and distance would be a good thing. A safe thing. As much as Anela wanted him to try embracing humanity, he wasn't ready to do that again.

Samir shifted in the silence and leaned back in his seat. The movement was enough to catch Keeler's eye. Restlessness had joined the other emotions and Keeler wasn't surprised when Samir pushed out of his seat. He walked over and joined him at the table. Keeler grabbed another glass and Samir shook his head.

Keeler waited for Samir to break the silence as he had no idea what to say. Keeler almost sighed when he recognised the emotional surge that came with the decision to speak. Samir had barely opened his mouth when Keeler held up his hand and shook his head. "Please don't thank me again."

"I wasn't going to—" Samir tried to protest, but Keeler cut him off before he could finish his sentence.

"You were." Keeler looked away from him and stared out the window as he debated over the apology that he knew Samir deserved. If he was going to do it, now seemed like a good time. Whether or not he accepted it would be another thing entirely, but it needed to be done. "I think I owe you an apology. For yesterday. I shouldn't have done what I did. I shouldn't have kissed you."

"Oh. Um. Uh…" Samir stammered, unsure what to say in response to that, before pausing. His mouth twitched in amusement. "Thank you?"

Overtones of amusement and nervousness told him that perhaps Samir hadn't understood why he had apologized. He wasn't sure he wanted to explain all the reasons behind it, but he wanted Samir to know that this wasn't a joke to him. "I mean it, whether or not you think it's necessary, you deserve an apology because I had no right to do that. It's not something I normally do, and you can take it easy, it won't happen again."

Samir relaxed, his amusement from earlier growing a bit more. "Well, at least it was a good kiss."

It was the last thing Keeler had expected him to say and he had no clue how to respond. Instead, he took another sip of his drink and turned the conversation back to more serious matters. "Please tell me how I am not getting detained the moment we walk into any place that is protected against my kind by your people?"

Samir's smile faded. "It'll be fine. I'll take care of it."

"I wish I could say that I find that reassuring." Keeler murmured into his glass. It would have been more reassuring if there still wasn't an edge of nervousness to that statement. He couldn't blame him for being nervous because he was taking a risk. He should be nervous, but it was also Keeler's entire life on the line here.

Samir didn't respond to that statement.

"We land in less than an hour." Keeler poured himself another drink and then pushed it away. Drinking wasn't a solution nor the wisest idea. He would need to be on top of his game walking into somewhere he wasn't welcome with what seemed to be no plan at all. Samir was asking a lot of him and giving him little assurance that it would work out for the best. He needed something more to go on than 'I'll take care of it'.

"I know." Samir smiled at him again. "You don't need to worry. It'll be fine. I promise."

Keeler let it be. Samir was confident, but he needed to be prepared for anything. Confidence was not enough when his freedom was on the line. He wanted to trust Samir, but he didn't know him that well. Most of what he did know was through Anela, and when it came to Samir's position in the organization, she had been vague. He wanted to trust him. He wanted to believe that Samir had everything worked out, but he couldn't take that risk. He'd spent a lifetime being careful and it had done him well until now.

Then again, he had also stayed resolutely uninvolved in the lives of others. It may have been a lonely life, but it had kept him out of the eye of the Nergal. Now he was about to walk right into the lion's den because he had gotten involved. First, Anela had walked into his life as if she had always belonged there. He could hardly imagine being without her in it now, but there was also Samir, which complicated things more than he had ever planned for.

What he couldn't decide on was if lonely was better than complicated. He couldn't deny that there was a part of him that needed more in life than what he'd allowed himself to have. It was the risks involved that caused him to face this stressful choice. History had proven that it wasn't safe for him to inflict his presence on others, even if they were willing to accept the risks involved.

CHAPTER TWELVE

"Here?" Keeler followed Samir through the university campus. He paid no attention to the students milling about, they weren't Nergal and none of them gave him a second look either.

"Surprised?" Samir smirked. "The Laibiruzi Institute funds a lot of research. Universities have so many people going in and out that a small organization like the Nergal can easily go unnoticed. Or did you forget they are funded by the Institute?"

"I didn't forget," Keeler grumbled as they approached a building. It was obvious that this was their destination. A small plaque off to the side stated that the facility was funded by the Institute even though it had been named after no one he'd ever heard of.

"Don't worry." Samir smiled, seemingly at ease in this environment. "It'll be fine. I've got this."

Keeler didn't bother to respond. He was doing his best not to worry. To have a bit of faith in Samir but he struggled with it the closer they got to going inside. He knew that no one would be waiting with weapons bared at the front door, but his imagination told him a different story. It didn't help that he was hesitant to reach out to sense emotions in general due to the sheer number of people that were in their proximity. It would have been too overwhelming.

"Dr. Amin? Is that you?" a young voice called out. Samir turned around at the sound and Keeler followed his gaze to the young man jogging towards them. He was immediately on guard, but there was nothing there but a flush of excitement, joy, and recognition.

"Ash, right? How are your studies going?" Samir smiled politely at the student.

"Great. Decided to do my doctorate thesis on the Egyptians. I just couldn't get it out of my head after our talk." Ash shrugged and gave a lopsided grin. "I'm glad I listened to your advice."

Samir chuckled. "Well, sometimes I have moments of brilliance."

"Are you here to do another lecture? I don't remember seeing anything about it." Ash asked with a side glance at Keeler who continued to ignore him. Although ignore was the right word, he was too busy wrapping his thoughts around the new information he had learned about Samir. It wasn't something he had expected, but he guessed even the Nergal needed day jobs.

"Ah, no. I'm actually here to do some research myself." Samir said. "I'm actually on a bit of a time crunch right now but do be sure to email me and let me know how your thesis goes. I'd love to hear more about it. I might be able to point you to a few lesser-known resources."

"Hey, that would be great. Thanks, Dr. Amin. I'll hopefully see you around later." Ash waved and dashed off in the other direction.

"Dr. Amin?" Keeler asked with a raised eyebrow. Even when he wanted to distance himself, every time he learned something new about Samir it made him want to know more. Most of those he met with titles like that were eager to throw them in the faces of others and Samir hadn't mentioned a thing. It also left him wondering what other things he might not know.

"Um, well, yes, I have a doctorate." Samir's face colored slightly as he shrugged off the question. "But it's not a big deal. Really."

"Right, not a big deal." Keeler agreed. It was hard to keep the amusement out of his voice even if he didn't smile. His ability to read emotions aside, it was clear that Samir felt awkward touting his accomplishments. It was almost as adorable as was his tendency to blush at the slightest embarrassment. Keeler cursed at himself for thinking that and pushed the thoughts from his mind. He did not have time for this, but he couldn't resist one last comment. "We should get moving, doc."

"Shut up," Samir said, redness brightening as stalked towards the entrance of a building. It was enough to distract Keeler from any more comments as they crossed the threshold. He tried to stay open and be ready for any threat, but this was like every other university building that he'd ever been in. It could have been anywhere and not a place where he feared bumping into the Nergal.

Those who were in the building ignored them as they walked through the hallway until Samir stopped before a set of doors that had a keycard lock on it. A sign stated that it was restricted access only. It didn't seem like the location of a secret organization, but that meant nothing. The only way to be a secret organization is to not look like you are one.

Samir glanced up and down the empty hallway. He kept his voice low as he spoke. "Once we cross through here, I would recommend you stay close to me and not say much. If someone talks to you, say you're a new trainee."

"Right." Keeler nodded. As much as he wanted to stay calm, he could feel nervousness coming from Samir that hadn't been there before. "What's wrong?"

"Well, they may have upgraded the security systems here already. I didn't think this place was on the schedule until a few months from now and…" Samir frowned as he fumbled with his wallet and pulled out an unmarked grey card. "It's not that big a deal. I'll handle it, but it may mean a bit of unwanted attention."

"What does it mean if they have upgraded the system?" Keeler wasn't sure he wanted to hear the answer, but he needed to be prepared for what he would find on the other side. He had no idea what Samir meant exactly by the phrase 'unwanted attention', but he was sure any attention past this point would be unwanted.

"It's a system set to pick up any non-human presence almost immediately and send an alarm to the security station." Samir shrugged as if it wasn't that big of a deal. Keeler would have thought he wasn't worried if he couldn't sense his emotions. Samir touched his card to the sensor and the light turned green. He pulled open the door.

Keeler saw nothing different on the other side, but he hesitated anyway. Now that he was here, he was starting to think that this was a terrible idea. He almost took a step back when Samir placed a hand on the small of his back and guided him through the door. No alarms sounded, no one came running.

"You should probably breathe," Samir leaned over and said in a mock whisper, his hand still unthinkingly on Keeler's lower back as they walked down the empty hallway.

"I don't need to." Keeler was aware that Samir probably knew that. It didn't matter. It was something to say. It wasn't enough to distract him from thinking about the sweet taste of energy and essence that was so close to him right now. He had managed to withstand the temptation of it being close but touching, that was an entirely different thing. He hadn't prepared for that and a hunger that shouted for more was a distraction that he couldn't afford. He would have stepped away, but there was nowhere to go, and he didn't want to ask Samir to not touch him. That begged of an awkward conversation and this wasn't the place for that either.

"Right. This way." Samir tapped his card against another sensor beside the door for an elevator. No one was inside it when the door opened. He could feel Samir's concern increase as they stepped inside the doors. His hand dropped away, and Keeler said a silent thanks as Samir moved to stand in front of him. It gave him a chance to breathe and refocus, but the worry that permeated the air was almost as distracting. Samir didn't say anything as the elevator took them far below ground level.

"Let me handle things, okay?" Samir asked quietly. The elevator slowed to a stop.

"Okay," Keeler agreed. The doors opened. No one stood there waiting for them. If they had set off any alarms, then it wasn't evident.

Samir stepped off the elevator to a few curious stares, but no one stopped them as they made their way farther into the facility. Samir paused outside another door. This one had not only the card sensor but the additional security of a retinal scanner. Samir glanced around to make sure no one was close enough to overhear him. "This is a secured area that we are about to go into. Even without the upgraded security, your presence here will be questioned and—"

"Let you handle it. I know." Keeler snapped at him. He hadn't meant to sound that sharp, but he didn't need to be reminded of the same thing again.

"Right." Samir took a deep breath and went through the process of opening the door. This time there were people waiting for them.

"Samir?" A slender black woman with bright red braids stood front and center of their welcoming committee. She drew out his name as she said it, turning a single word into a question. Confusion and suspicion rolled off her in equal measure. Her eyes narrowed as she looked behind him at Keeler. "Who is that?"

"Liana, I thought you were in Bucharest?" Samir smiled at her and Keeler was surprised by the warmth in his words to this woman that he could sense no equal measure of warmth from. Of course, such things might be pressed aside for the more important matter of them having set off the alarm. He wondered exactly at their relationship, but he knew it wasn't any of his business.

"I was, I came back early. That doesn't answer my question about what that thing is doing here with you?" Liana flexed her fingers around a small device that she held. Keeler didn't know what it did, but he was sure he wouldn't like it. It was obvious that Samir had noticed her movement as well as he adjusted his stance to block him from her view.

"He's with me, Liana. It's fine." Samir took a half step forward, but she refused to let him pass. Keeler would have backed away from them all if he weren't worried that any movement on his part might set someone off. Even someone not in tune with the emotions of others would have had no trouble reading the tension in the room.

"It set off the alarms." Even though she lowered her voice when she spoke this time, Keeler heard her clearly. Even more clearly, he felt a wave of disgust that was directed towards him. This was more of what he expected from a Nergal. Not Samir's warmth, but this woman's obvious hate of him without ever knowing who he really was.

"He," Samir emphasized the pronoun, "is with me. I am not being coerced; you know I'm more careful than that. He's a friend and he's here to assist me in a very important matter. Please, step aside."

Keeler had never heard Samir speak with such utter confidence before. Not a stutter or a stammer and, even though his words were polite, his tone of voice made it clear that his request was not optional. He sounded like someone who was used to being in charge. It was a tone and attitude that Keeler knew well, but he had no time to consider the implications of that thought. Right now, his life was on the line and that was more important. He could sense Liana's clear indecision and discomfort. "You know I can't let you bring it in here. It's not allowed."

"Don't make me pull rank on you." Samir stood his ground, his stance stiffening as he stood a little taller. Keeler could sense no bravado, no hint of anything but confidence behind that statement. "You know how much I hate doing that. If this weren't important, I wouldn't have brought him here, but as it stands, I have no other options right now."

He had assumed when Samir had told him that he wouldn't be allowed to go after Anela himself that he wasn't very high ranking, but now he was talking about pulling rank on someone trying to stop them from entering a secured facility. Keeler tried to wrap his head around what was happening. There was only one obvious answer, that he was the person in charge, but that didn't even seem possible. There was no way that this man, this Nergal who had nothing but gentleness and warmth towards others, could be in such a position. It was enough to give him a headache and that shouldn't have been possible either.

Keeler filed it away with every other thought and question that had occurred to him since he had met Samir. It was something that would have to be resolved later. He would ask Samir about it when he had the chance. Maybe there was an explanation beyond the obvious, something he was missing.

"It's against protocol." Liana insisted again, this time she sounded far less confident than before as she took a step back. "I don't like it and the Institute won't like it either."

"Then close your eyes and keep your mouth shut," Samir suggested rather harshly. He reached back and placed a hand on Keeler's shoulder to guide him through the confused guards. As they pushed past them Samir's hand slid down to his lower back again. He tried his best to ignore it and was thankful that the confusion that circled in his mind was enough to keep him distracted from his hunger. He didn't say a word as he was guided to a small office down the hall. One that had Samir's name on it. Proof that he had severely underestimated the situation.

As soon as the door was closed and locked behind him, Samir relaxed, his hand finally dropped away again for which Keeler was grateful.

Samir walked over to his desk, leaned against it, and laughed. "Almost thought she might not stand down there. A good soldier, Liana, but sometimes a little too fixated on the rules."

"That door has your name on it," Keeler stated the obvious as he tried to wrap his mind around everything that had transpired since they had arrived here. He'd already come to his own conclusions, but he wanted to hear it from Samir. "What did you mean by pull rank?"

"It's not important." Samir pushed himself off the desk and walked around to sit in the chair.

"Not important," Keeler mumbled and took one of the other chairs in the office. He glanced at the door, wondering if Liana might change her mind about letting him pass as Samir opened the computer that was sitting on a desk. "Just like having a doctorate isn't that big a deal."

Samir ignored him as his fingers played across the keyboard. Keeler was sure that he had been heard and it bothered him that Samir didn't think him worth answers. Or perhaps, much like the doctorate, he didn't want to make a big deal about his accomplishments. Still, it dawned on Keeler that had he known Samir's true position within the Nergal, he would have left that lunch meeting no matter how insistent Anela had been. Now it was just another fact about Samir that made him want to understand even more what made the man tick.

"This'll only take a minute. I wish I could access some of this information from the outside, but there is no outside access to anything this highly classified. There's a lot of stuff that we've gone to pains to keep out of the hands of people. Like the exact nature and physics of how magic works." Samir didn't look up from his computer.

Keeler sat and studied the understated office in silence as Samir worked. There was nothing here designed to impress, it was all meant to be functional. Even the few personal touches, a handful of pictures that sat on the desk told the story of someone who put little importance in his status. He was finally starting to understand why Anela liked him so much. And as much as he hated to admit it, he was starting to like the mystery that was Samir. He couldn't deny that his interest in the man had moved well beyond his initial attraction to his essence. He wanted to deny it, but he had never been a fan of lying to himself.

Though he could read emotions, he still didn't know exactly how Samir felt towards him—except confusion—and Keeler wasn't ready for him to know how he felt. He forced himself to think about Anela instead. It was her that was more important than anything else.

"Ha. Found it." Samir cried out and then smiled sheepishly at Keeler. "Sorry, didn't mean to shout, but that took me a bit longer than I had expected. I had to do a bit of following the links in the reference material to be confident that this was the right one."

"Can you do it?" Keeler pushed himself to the edge of his seat. It was one of the few reservations that Samir had expressed about this ritual beyond the need to come here to gain access to it.

"I think so and we have everything that I need to be able to do this." Samir leaned back to grab a sheet of paper off the printer behind him. "Good thing too because anything printed in here can't leave the facility for security reasons. Not sure I'd have time to memorize this."

"What does this ritual require?" Keeler asked. Samir hadn't told him much about it since he couldn't remember the details, only that it existed.

"Something the other half of the usesima has used their powers on and the half of the pair that is present." Samir grinned.

"What has she used her powers on here?" Keeler glanced around the room that contained little other than the two of them. Anela had talked about her revolving door of lovers before. It was, after all, the easiest way to connect with humans. To feed that hunger that they both had, but he highly doubted any of her lovers would be found here.

"Oh, that would be me," Samir told him as he distractedly read through instructions again. Keeler kept his thoughts to himself. There was more than one reason for her to have used her powers on him other than the first thing that came to mind. He couldn't think of any right now and Anela had admitted to rarely trying to extend her abilities beyond the basics.

"When and where are we doing this then?" Keeler focused his thoughts back to the matter at hand. Everything else, all the questions and confusion that were brewing in the back of his mind had no place in the now. If it were still relevant later, he'd take the time to pick it all apart and try to understand what was going on. For now, there was the ritual and finding Anela.

"Here and now." Samir put the sheet of paper down. "It would be easier with more people, but I should be able to handle it. I think. It's a little unclear on exactly how much energy this is going to take and, from what I understand, it's usually done by at least three or more people..."

"More people?" Keeler was a little unsure about the idea of involving more people. He knew that some humans had managed to tap into the power required to do magic to a limited extent. Many, but not all the Nergal, had learned how to use the near-infinite well of energy that every being contained, but something about the connection drained them, left them exhausted and weakened. He'd seen it once or twice over his lifetime. "Are you sure you can handle it?"

"I don't really have a lot of other options. I sure as hell don't want anyone else knowing what we're doing." Samir held out his hand. "Let's get this done."

"What can I expect?" Keeler stood up and moved to stand beside Samir, though he was hesitant to take the offered hand. He knew that it was easy to project any emotion he was feeling from touch when energy mingled like it might in something like this. However, not doing so meant they couldn't go forward, so he took it.

"I'll focus on the ritual. You focus on Anela. Find any trace of her essence in me and use that to track it back to her and," Samir turned his computer to face Keeler, "we're updating things a bit. I figured Google maps might be a better idea than trying to find a paper map in this place."

"Right…" Keeler walked closer to the desk to look at the map that Samir had brought up. He had zoomed it out to show most of North America. "And how does that work?

"Ideally, as soon as you feel a strong connection with her, touch the map and it'll…" Samir looked down at the sheet of paper again. "Um, it'll show us where she is."

"Right." Keeler took a deep breath and took Samir's hand. "And not potentially torch the computer in the process?"

"Then I guess we would have to try again with a paper map." Samir laughed and gripped Keeler's hand a little tighter. "Ready for this?"

"Not at all." Keeler tried to ignore the allure of Samir's presence. As much as he wanted to allow himself to taste that sweetness, to let it wash over him and merge with his own, he knew that this was not the time. It was getting harder to hold back from doing so the more he was forced to be in such close contact with him. To be that near without giving into the hunger was nearing torture. He regretted not having brought any chocolate with him. He would have to rely on willpower alone because this time Samir would be aware of the connection. If he wasn't careful, he would broadcast everything. He turned his thoughts from what he wanted and focused on Anela.

Samir looked down at the words on the sheet and mumbled them. Keeler could sense his own focus was wavering slightly, though he refused to read into it. Instead he listened to what was being said in a language that even he didn't know. As Samir repeated the words over and over until a rhythm formed.

Connected as they were for this ritual, it wasn't exactly the same as the other night. He could taste the wonderful essence as Samir stared at the words on the sheet and mumbled them to himself. Now that he could feel their energy mingle, it was harder for Keeler to stay focused with this intimate echo to what had occurred the other night.

That tingle, the light touch and taste deepened. Emotions and energy crept in on him. He tried to ignore them, but it was stronger, more intense than anything he had expected from him for this ritual. Keeler pushed against the hunger that called to him, begged him to dive in deeper.

It was tempting to let it carry him away, but he couldn't allow himself to lose the focus on his part of the ritual. Samir's energy was waning, and he felt a pull, as if Samir were drawing from him. He had no idea how he was doing it. As far as he knew, it wasn't even possible.

His thoughts on it were distracted as his connection to Anela jumped into focus. He could feel her presence again. Hoping this would work, he reached out to touch the screen of the computer. A small spark leapt from his finger to the screen. It blurred until a single building stood out boldly.

Ritual complete, Samir let himself slump back in his chair, too tired to do anything but close his eyes.

Keeler released Samir's hand reluctantly. He quickly made a note of the address in case something happened before turning his attention to Samir.

"Are you okay? Do you need anything?" Keeler asked, concerned at how exhausted and worn Samir looked. It surprised him that any human could draw power from one of his kind, as far as he knew it shouldn't have been possible, but he wondered if it could be done again—this time to restore Samir's strength. He'd never tried it before, but it could work.

On the other hand, it might be too much temptation no matter what he had promised Samir. After that moment of closeness, another taste of what he was missing, he was hungrier than ever. Except, he still had no idea where Samir stood on the subject.

"Yeah, I'm fine." Samir took a deep breath, but he hadn't bothered to open his eyes or even attempt to sit up. Fine seemed to be an overstatement to Keeler. "It worked. That is what's important. It doesn't take much to regain energy."

Samir fumbled blindly in one of the drawers and pulled out two chocolate bars. He pushed one across the desk that Keeler happily took. He needed the chocolate, wanted the chocolate. He had been working so hard to restrain himself but today had left him wanting more than he knew he could have. More than he probably deserved.

"Now what?" Keeler asked.

"We make a plan and then we go get Anela." He attempted to push himself out of the chair and promptly crashed back into it. "Tomorrow."

Keeler placed a hand on Samir's shoulder and gave it a squeeze, trying to comfort him slightly. "It's fine. From what I can tell she's not hurt. Take your time."

"Good. Okay." Samir sighed. "I need to see if we have people in the area to do some reconnaissance. Once we have an idea of what we're dealing with we ought to be able to handle it effectively."

"I thought you didn't want to involve the Institute. You were worried about not being allowed to be involved. Did something change?"

"They don't need to know why." Samir opened his eyes and smiled at Keeler. "Grab a seat."

Keeler dragged the extra chair over to sit beside him, still worried about how wearied Samir looked. He didn't like it, but at least he was sitting up instead of lying limply in the chair like a ragdoll.

Samir picked up the phone on his desk. "Can you page Liana to my office, please and thank you."

CHAPTER THIRTEEN

Liana took a moment to gather herself before walking into Samir's office. She'd been working with him for almost eight years now and, as strange as some of his decisions were, she'd never had cause to question him. Today, though, she couldn't understand what could have prompted him into such an extreme breach of protocol. He'd never even brought Anela here before, not that she would have been willing to come in here under her own volition.

Liana did her best not to let her thoughts run away on her. There was likely to be a reasonable explanation. She walked into Samir's office in hopes that she would find that explanation, but instead, she found him sitting far too close for comfort beside that thing he had dragged in here. She tried not to read too much into it. Samir may have a soft spot for those creatures, but she didn't think he'd put his entire career on the line for one of them, not even Anela. As much as she respected Samir, she had always been concerned about how much he seemed to care about those things.

Before she had a chance to say anything, Keeler looked up at her and she swore she could read hatred in its eyes. If she had her way, it would be in a cell right now and waiting to be exiled back to wherever it came from. She turned to meet Samir's far warmer gaze instead.

"Liana." Samir smiled. He looked exhausted, even though she knew she shouldn't have been monitoring the internal systems, it told her that he'd expended a huge amount of energy. More than he could have possibly done alone. She was curious about what he was up to, but it wasn't her place to ask. "I was wondering who we had in the Dallas area that might be available for a training exercise."

Liana didn't leave the doorway as she considered what he might be asking. A training exercise was a lie, she knew that much. She was the person who handled most of the training for recruits as well as for their seasoned troops. Whatever he wanted wasn't going to be a training exercise or he would have consulted with her beforehand. She pursed her lips and crossed her arms. "I think we have a couple of people down that way. But a training exercise? Do you expect me to believe that?"

"This isn't up for discussion or debate." Samir avoided her gaze and she wondered whether she should push for a more acceptable answer. She glanced at the creature that sat too closely next to him, then back to Samir. Even someone as experienced as him could make a mistake that could cause him to be compromised.

"You can't ask that of me because 'I was following orders' does not remove culpability." She lifted her chin and stared him down. She had already let him through, but she wasn't putting her career at risk for anyone—not even Samir.

He took a deep breath, letting it out slowly. "No, it doesn't. One of the many reasons I chose to promote you to your current rank, is the fact you do know that. If this weren't critical, I wouldn't ask it of you."

"If it's a personal thing, using Institute resources is frowned upon, but you already know that." Liana hesitated as she wondered if she should ask him if it had anything to do with that thing beside him but decided to hold her tongue for now. She spared a glance at Keeler before looking back at Samir. "I'm not going to authorize anything without knowing why. These are my field agents too; I am responsible for them."

Samir sighed. "I understand, but this is a private matter."

"Right, private, but somehow involving that thing," Liana sneered. She hadn't meant to say that, but she didn't regret it either.

"Liana, don't." Samir's tone of voice carried a warning in it that she'd heard him use before. As nice and cheerful as he always seemed to be, she'd seen him get truly angry only twice before. She didn't care if she was treading on thin ice here. Samir was technically her superior but there was little he could do to her without approval from the council.

"Don't what? Do my job properly? The job you trained me to do," Liana snapped back at him. "I don't care how fond you are of Anela and whoever the hell this is. I don't see any reason why I should put my job at risk because of some mysterious personal matter. Unlike you, I don't have connections in the council. I don't have a family legacy here to protect my precious reputation."

Samir's jaw tensed for a second and then he relaxed, his voice softening. "Fair enough."

"So, tell me why you need people on the ground in Texas," Liana demanded.

"Could you come in here and close the door behind you?" Samir asked. "I'm definitely not going to talk to you about confidential matters with my door open, shouting across the room at you."

"La dracu…" Liana mumbled as she walked over to the desk, banging the door behind her as she did so.

Keeler pushed out of his chair, leaned over the desk towards Liana, and slammed his hands down on top of it. Samir jumped at the unexpected outburst. "Arată niște a-și ține rangul."

Liana stopped where she was and glared at Keeler. His pronunciation and word choice weren't perfect, but she understood perfectly what he was trying to say to her. She stayed standing halfway between the door and the desk. "Who said you could speak to me?"

She saw that another flash of hatred in his eyes though his expression didn't change at all. It was disturbing. "I don't need permission to voice my opinion. I stand by what I said."

"You aren't human. You have no rights, and no one gives a shit what you think. Least of all me." Liana glared at it and then turned to Samir. "Keep your pet on a leash or I won't give a fuck if he's here with your permission. I will detain him by myself if I have to."

"Căţea." Keeler growled at her, refusing to stand down. She couldn't believe the audacity of this creature, or perhaps it was putting faith in Samir to keep it safe.

"Enough, both of you!" Samir bellowed and grabbed Keeler's arm to drag him back down into his seat. Liana jumped back at the sound. Samir was not one who was prone to shouting and she hadn't expected him to yell at them both.

He motioned to the chair across the desk from him and she reluctantly sat down. "Now, if you two could behave for a second that would be great."

Liana crossed her arms again and fixed her deadliest glare on that thing. Deciding it was best not to push things, she kept her mouth shut out of respect for Samir. Though, if she had half the chance, she wouldn't think twice about trying to take that creature out.

"Okay then." Samir leaned casually over the desk and smiled at Liana. "It's Anela and I know what the damned protocol is, but I would like to keep this a private matter. I'm not sure if this has to do with her specific nature or something more general. I would like to find that out and, if it is the former, then I swear I'll pass the matter on to your division entirely."

"I can't authorize that. When it comes to her, you're only allowed to monitor and report. You're not allowed to be in the field." Liana tried to keep her voice soft out of respect for his feelings towards Anela. She would have loved to flat out refuse the request and then storm out to tell the council what was happening, but that wasn't her style. And she was fond of him despite his unfortunate choices of association.

"Liana, I know I've asked a lot of you already today, but can you please do this for me?"

She wanted to tell him no, but the word caught in her throat and her uncertain thoughts slowly wavered over to the side of acceptance. He had promised that if it weren't a simple, standard matter he would let her take point. But still… That thought trailed off unfinished as her anger dulled. She would have to trust him with this, and Samir wasn't one to be dishonest without a good cause. With a sigh, Liana threw her arms up in surrender. "Fine, but if this comes back at us then

I'm throwing you under the bus, mentor or not. I won't take the fall for this."

"Thanks, Liana." Samir smiled at her. "As always, I owe you one."

"Sau ceva…" Liana pushed out of her chair. "I'll make sure you get the reports and I'll have the crew aware that their assistance might be needed on your arrival. Don't do anything stupid."

"Thanks again."

CHAPTER FOURTEEN

Liana stormed out of the office, the door rattling in the frame with the force she put behind closing it. Keeler followed the emotional resonance of the retreating woman—her anger already starting to drown everything else out. He was still trying to sort out what had just happened. The intensity of the emotions had been projected—compliance, acceptance, and gentle calmness that bordered on becoming an emotional sedative— was almost enough to make Keeler wonder if Samir had mastered a talent he didn't think possible for humans. Except the Nergal were warded against such attempts at influence.

Keeler was half-tempted to ask Samir *"What the fuck?"* right then but decided that it could wait for later with the rest of the questions he had. Except for the most important one. "And now?"

"Guess we should call it a night and head out to Dallas tomorrow?" Samir closed his eyes and leaned back in his chair. Looking as though he was ready to fall asleep where he was.

"I'm guessing you would be opposed to spending the night in the dorms here?"

"Rather intensely." Keeler tried not to shudder at the thought. He wanted nothing more than to get out of here. "I can get a hotel and meet you in the morning. It's not a big deal."

Samir chuckled and grinned at Keeler. "I would say 'don't waste your money', but I doubt that's much of a consideration for you. I have a small apartment near here, off-campus of course. I'm out this way often enough and I guest lecture here frequently, so it seemed like a good investment. It's not much, but the couch is comfortable, and you are more than welcome to it."

"Right." Keeler nodded as he tried to decide if he wanted to take Samir up on that offer. A night alone was almost too tempting for him to resist, which was exactly why he knew he ought to say no, but on the other side of the coin, it would give them a chance to talk. "I'd hate to put you out."

He was hesitating, searching for anything to help him decide what to do. He wished that chocolate worked better but it barely seemed to have much of an impact when it came to Samir. All he had left to rely on was willpower—and that seemed to be growing weaker the longer he was near. This would have been an easier decision if not for all the questions that he longed to have answered.

"If it were an imposition, I wouldn't have offered." Samir insisted as he pushed himself up from his chair and fell right back down into it. He took a deep breath and managed to shove himself to his feet. Keeler debated on reaching out to help him but held back as Samir steadied himself against the desk. He trembled as he closed his eyes, his lips pressed together in a thin line.

"Do you need a hand?" Keeler asked. He didn't like how pale Samir looked nor how he swayed where he stood. It was obvious he'd overexerted himself. He didn't want to have to tempt himself further by being in such close contact with Samir, but he wasn't sure he'd make it out of here without the help.

"Uh, no." Samir smiled weakly. "I'll be fine. Just give me a few minutes."

Keeler shook his head. "No, I don't think so."

Before Samir could protest, he wrapped an arm around his waist and pulled Samir's arm over his shoulders. There was no resistance. "You will be fine later but lean on me for now"

It wasn't until Keeler reached to open his office door that Samir pulled away even though he could barely support himself. He slumped against the wall and Keeler wasn't sure how he even managed to keep from falling down. "I do appreciate this, but I can't be leaning on you on the way out. People might get the wrong idea."

"Samir, you can barely stand." Keeler gave him a once over and debated on a different option to help Samir out. It wasn't one he wanted to do, it was pushing boundaries that he knew he shouldn't be crossing, but he couldn't think of anything else that would work. "If I can't help you walk out of here physically there is another solution. Maybe."

"Maybe?"

"When you were doing that ritual, you were able to draw energy from me. Maybe I can try giving you some? It's just that..." Keeler let the sentence trail off as he tried to figure out the best way to phrase it. He could think of nothing other than to blurt it out. "Well, it's going to be a bit similar to the other night and I promised you I wouldn't do that again. I mean, I shouldn't have to kiss, um, well, you know, but it'll be similar.

Of course, we can sit here and wait until you're strong enough to walk out of here on your own?"

"Oh, I'm sure I'll be fine." Samir said, his face near scarlet. He pushed himself away from the wall and Keeler rushed to grab him before he fell. "Or maybe we'll try your thing. I guess I exerted myself more than I thought today."

"Maybe." Keeler tried not to let the proximity distract him, but with Samir agreeing to his suggestion he was even more hesitant to try it. Too close, too much, too soon were the words that ran through his mind. He wasn't even sure it would work; it was only a guess on his part. He lowered Samir to the floor where he could lean more comfortably against the wall again. "Ready?"

"Not at all," Samir smirked as he mimicked the same words that Keeler had used earlier.

"Leave yourself open as you would for performing any ritual. I need you to be able to pull from me rather than me doing anything." Keeler did his best to push away the hunger and the feelings that he needed to hide. If he could keep it constrained, then he might get through this without doing anything he'd regret.

Steadying himself emotionally, he reached out and placed a hand against Samir's cheek. Carefully, he allowed a gentle spark of energy to flow out from him.

Unlike the first time he had done this, Samir was open and receptive. This wasn't coming as a surprise and, as much as he wanted to hold back, he could tell that Samir wasn't getting enough from him to be able to recover. He needed to be more open and the thought terrified him. A little at a time, he lowered the barrier he had created to keep all of his emotions at bay.

It was a balancing act between opening up and keeping everything hidden. During the ritual there had been something else to focus on, to keep him in check. This time, there was only Samir and it would be too easy to get carried away. Still, it didn't seem to be enough. With a small mental curse, he relaxed and allowed himself to be as that gentle, cool energy to flow over him.

Like the floodgates opening on a dam, a sudden overwhelming wealth of emotions flowed out of him. He knew Samir could feel it all, he saw the look of surprise wash over his face. Keeler closed his eyes, struggling to pull back, to make it stop—his efforts were as successful as using a bucket to empty an ocean.

Even his hunger was exposed, a hunger for both an emotional and physical connection. Strong and driving, Keeler ignored all else and tried to push away only the hunger. He couldn't lose control even as it demanded that he take as much as he was giving. For him, Samir may be an infinite well, but he had promised. Curiosity filled him as Samir reached out to touch that emotion.

"No," Keeler gasped, letting the connection break. He collapsed, nearly curling into a fetal position from where he kneeled. Too close. Dangerously so. He shuddered at the thought of what would have happened if Samir's essence had touched it and taken that hunger in only for it to be reflected back at him.

Even without that happening, he could feel the hunger raging inside, having been so close to what it wanted and being denied. He had tried to keep it restrained, but it hadn't been possible. Though the connection hadn't lasted long, it was enough to awaken that need that he had been trying to hold back and it was proving harder to push those thoughts and desires away. "That's not... That isn't..."

He clenched his fists determined to shove it all away, to not break any promises. He didn't want to look up, didn't want to know how much Samir understood everything that he had felt, but he couldn't stay here. He had to at least pretend that he wasn't some monster that couldn't control his more basic instincts.

Keeler steadied himself and tried to clear his mind of every thought and emotion. Sitting up, he finally looked at Samir who was watching him intently. Smoothing back his hair, he took a deep breath. He had no idea how he was going to make it through another minute with Samir, let alone an entire night. "Are you feeling better?"

Samir stood and smiled at Keeler. "I'd say yes."

Keeler nodded, and got to his feet as well, being careful to stay at least a foot away from Samir. It wasn't much, but it would have to do. "Shall we get going then?"

CHAPTER FIFTEEN

Samir chose to say nothing about what had happened in his office which made for a silent, awkward trip to his apartment. He was still trying to understand everything himself. There was a lot to unpack from the last two days—though it felt like it had been so much longer than that.

Whatever Keeler had done to help him regain his energy, this close, he could still feel a hint of that connection. It made it nearly impossible to ignore the overwhelming worry and concern that were directed towards him, nor the battle Keeler was still waging to contain his hunger. It had surprised Samir that he hadn't insisted on returning home but had continued to stay with him.

Leaving the complex, he'd ignored the glances cast in his direction. His only concern was what rumors were going to flow after this incident—and if those rumors would land on the wrong ears. He wasn't overly worried. His family legacy was one of the few reasons his liberal views and relationship with Anela had been tolerated for so long. Anyone else would most likely have been ex-communicated from the organization. He was more than aware of his status, as well as where the lines stood that even he couldn't cross without repercussions.

And he was treading perilously close to that point now.

What he had done to Liana, if anyone found out, definitely crossed the line. He had hoped that he could have avoided pushing her emotions as he had. However, if he'd gone behind her back and called for surveillance without her knowledge and consent, she'd not only be angry but insulted as well. She took a lot of pride in her ability to do her job properly. Maybe too much. Samir had foolishly hoped that she might be a bit more flexible for once in her life.

It was all a mess. Everything. He stared at the back of Keeler's head reflected in his window. Samir didn't take offence in the fact that he had squished himself up against the door, trying to stay as far away as possible. Closing his eyes, he focused on that fading bit of connection. It was still strong enough for him to tell that the fight against the hunger inside of Keeler was being won. He hoped the extra chocolate he had insisted on grabbing for them both had helped.

He tried not to let his own worries, fears and insecurities get to him. Everything that had transpired, all the moments he had yet to pick apart and examine. There would be time for it later. For now, there was rescuing Anela. Other things could wait. Though, watching Keeler come so close to breaking down had affected Samir in a way that he couldn't even begin to explain—another coin to toss into the pot of 'think about it later'.

What he had felt of Keeler's emotions, especially that hunger, was beyond anything in Samir's knowledge. Those few times he had performed rituals with others created a closeness between the people involved. In those times, he had often gotten a vague sense of the things they were thinking and feeling, but this had been more than that. It was stronger, more intense than anything he had felt before.

Even ignoring the hunger, there were all those emotions that he was still trying to sort through and understand. He knew they belonged to Keeler, because there was something about them that struck him as being uniquely non-human, though also familiar in the way the hunger was familiar. Desire, wonder, compassion, fear. Some of them were easily identifiable if surprising. Others were complex, impossible to understand, a reminder of the vast difference between them.

Though, some of the feelings brought up were frighteningly similar to his own. It was something that he didn't know how to deal with, one of the things he still needed to sort through in his own mind. He stole another glance, wondering if Keeler was following the flow of his emotions and what he thought about it. He would have asked, but he was afraid to know the answer.

"We're here." Samir announced unnecessarily as the taxi came to a stop. He paid for it, as Keeler got out of the cab as quickly as he could without breaking that calm exterior attitude. A part of him wondered why Keeler hadn't insisted on staying at a hotel after the incident, but he wasn't going to push the issue.

He couldn't get his mind off the other night, comparing those sensations with the two rituals. All the similarities and differences. He couldn't deny that a part of him wanted to explore that more. Anela had told him the pleasure effect of those connections before, how it had been what helped her discover the best way to feed her hunger. He'd never experienced it—until now.

He unlocked the lobby door and led the way to his little apartment. He hadn't had much time to sort it all out in his own mind. He probably should have used the time on the flight doing that, but instead, he had spent most of it being nervous.

Wisdom told him that he'd be better contemplating these things without the object of his contemplations so close at hand, but he was enjoying Keeler's company. Sometimes he forgot how good it was to have someone that he could relax around—well almost relax around. He smiled at Keeler, no longer able to feel that connection anymore was almost a relief. "If you're not comfortable staying here, I'll understand."

Keeler stood a few feet away from him, still keeping a careful distance. He didn't say anything for a few seconds and Samir gave him the time to mull over his response. "No, it's fine. I can keep my promise to you and my hands to myself."

"Alright, if you're sure you'll be okay." Samir smiled, not sure if he was happy or slightly disappointed at that statement. He opened the door and stepped inside. "Welcome to my very humble abode."

CHAPTER SIXTEEN

Keeler glanced around the small apartment. It was tidy and simple but felt very much like a home—no matter how much Samir insisted that he didn't spend a lot of time here. Only one thing stood out as a problem to Keeler, it was only a bachelor suite with the bed clearly in view. He didn't spend too much time thinking about that as he flopped down on the couch. "This is nice."

"Thanks." Samir walked over to the fridge. He pulled out a couple of beers and offered Keeler one. "Are you hungry? I'm hungry. I'd love some Chinese. Uh. I mean, um, take-out. There's a place around the corner."

Keeler couldn't help but laugh at his awkwardness, especially after the tension on the ride over here. "That sounds fine."

"You laughed." Samir stared at him as if he had suddenly grown a second head.

"Yes, I suppose I did." Keeler shrugged as if it was nothing but in truth, he was surprised at himself as well. He didn't remember the last time he had laughed.

"Um, so, I'll go down and grab some food?" Samir offered. "Anything you don't like?"

"It's all fine." Keeler sipped his beer and watched Samir leave. He glanced around the apartment, tempted by the thought of checking things out. He had a lot of questions, but he doubted any of them would be answered by snooping. However, it would pass some time and perhaps he could learn a thing or two. It was better than simply sitting here and sipping at his beer in silence.

He got up and walked about the small apartment. He stopped at a bookcase filled with old textbooks interspersed with pictures. Keeler had little interest in the historical texts, but the pictures he studied. Most of them were older, pictures of a young Samir with his parents. One or two that looked like they dated back to college. He was surprised by how many of them had Anela in them.

He was beginning to see why she considered Samir her family. She had been a part of his life for a long time—though both had said as much he'd found it hard to believe. He picked up a formal picture from college or university. He didn't look overly different from how he did now. A few more wrinkles, nicer beard, and better hair, but still that same adorable grin and kind eyes.

He put it back and grabbed a different one—a formal family portrait. He guessed Samir to be maybe nine or ten years old. An only child standing in front of his parents. It was easy to see that he got his smile and fairer skin from his mother, but he looked far more like his father in every other aspect.

"I love that one." Samir's voice came from behind him. Keeler had been so absorbed in studying the picture that he hadn't noticed he was no longer alone. Samir placed a hand on his back as he leaned over to look at it. Keeler did his best to stay focused and not think about how close Samir was standing.

"Of course, I almost threw a fit that 'Auntie Annie' wasn't allowed to be in it with us." Samir chuckled as he took the picture from Keeler and placed it back on the shelf. "They only got me to smile by telling me that they would do one with Anela in it later. They never said how much later."

Keeler turned to face Samir. He relaxed as the hand dropped away and Samir took the food to the kitchen. He longed to know what Samir was feeling, but he was doing his best to stay detached. That meant not even reading his emotions, no matter how much he wanted to try and understand what was going through his head.

Samir picked up one of the containers and a pair of chopsticks. "Still, hungry?"

"Yeah…" Keeler grabbed one of the containers. He didn't open it until he was sitting down on the couch.

"Want to watch something? I think I can throw on a movie or something." Samir asked. Keeler repressed a grin at how much it sounded like a date at this point. Dinner and a movie. He pushed that thought away. "I don't have a lot to choose from."

"I've never been much into watching movies." Keeler took a bite of the less-than-authentic Chinese food.

"Ah, um, okay." Samir stammered. He opened his own food in silence and dug into it.

Keeler ate a few bites as he watched Samir who seemed overly intent on staring at his meal. It was almost enough to make him smile seeing the way he was awkwardly holding the chopsticks.

Samir must have felt him staring because he stopped with food midway to his mouth and looked up. "What?"

"That's not how you do that." Keeler put his own food down.

Samir lowered his hand as he tried to figure out what Keeler could possibly be talking about. "What?"

"You're holding your chopsticks wrong." Keeler grabbed his own and held up his hand. "Hold them like this."

Samir looked at how Keeler was holding his and then looked at his own hand. "That is how I'm holding them."

Keeler shook his head and shifted closer to Samir. Taking his hand, Keeler moved his fingers on the chopsticks until they were in the right position, doing his best to ignore the familiar tingle at the touch. "Like this."

Samir attempted to pick up a bit of food and immediately dropped it. He laughed as he tried again with the same result. "I think my wrong way worked better."

Keeler hid his smirk by picking up his own food and shoving some in his mouth. It wasn't much of a distraction, but it gave him something else to focus his attention on. He didn't mind the silence, but he could think of no better time to ask a few of the questions that were weighing on his mind. "Can I ask you something?"

"Hmmm?" Samir raised an eyebrow and swallowed the mouthful of food. "What's up?"

"How high ranking are you within the Nergal?" Keeler kept his eyes on his own food instead of looking at Samir. He broke his own rule at the emotional spike that he couldn't ignore if he wanted to. Indecision and awkwardness at the question filled the space between them. He'd expected it since that always seemed to be Samir's reaction to personal questions.

"Does it matter?" he asked. Keeler wasn't sure if it did, but he still wanted to know. He had yet to figure out the conundrum that was Samir. Every bit of information was important to him. He wanted to know everything, but he didn't know how to say that. Samir sighed at his continued silence. "Director of North American Operations, which is a fancy way of saying that I am nothing more than an administrator. I answer directly to the council and no one else. Does that answer your question?"

Keeler thought about what that might mean and decided that it wasn't overly important. He had known he was high-up from everything he'd learned today, but that was a bit more important of a position than he had thought. "That would explain the name on the door."

Samir chuckled. "Is that why you were curious?"

"You're a mystery to me. You're not what I would expect from the Nergal, but you're one of the highest-ranking members." Keeler shrugged and stared down at his food, it seemed strange to admit that he wanted to know about this man. It had been a long time since he'd wanted to know more about any one person. "I'm trying to understand you."

"Understand me?" Samir put his food down. He turned to face Keeler, his brow furrowed. "There really isn't that much to understand. I'm me, there's no mystery here."

"Isn't there?" Keeler spoke without thinking about what he was saying. "You're different."

"You've said that before." Samir frowned. "I'm not sure what you mean by that."

"Oh." Keeler hadn't intended to bring that up with him. He wasn't even sure if Samir knew how different he was from other people. "I've never met anyone who was anything like you, and I've met a lot of people in my time here."

"Um, thanks?" He shifted uncomfortably in his seat.

"Can I ask something else?" Keeler said, wanting to move on to a slightly different topic.

"Sure?" Samir said it hesitantly as if he were dreading the question. It was almost enough to make him rethink his question, but he forged on with what he was going to say anyway.

"I thought I felt you try to force Liana's emotional response to your request, but the last I knew humans couldn't do that." Keeler regretted his decision when he felt a wave of guilt coming from Samir.

"I was raised in the Nergal. It's been my entire life and my experiences within it are different from those of most. I started learning these things at a younger age and I have access to older texts and rituals than the majority of the Nergal do." Samir shifted in his seat again as he picked his food back up. Keeler was sure it was a signal that he wanted to end the conversation. "So, you're right, most people can't do that."

"But you can? How?" Keeler pushed the point anyway. He couldn't help but be curious since it was an unusual thing for any human to be able to do.

Samir swallowed the food he had shoved in his mouth. "It's not easy and I don't like doing it. I shouldn't have done it to her, but I didn't think she was going to agree without the push. No one should have their emotions manipulated like that, it's not right."

"No, it's not, but a nudge here and there goes a long way to making a life like mine a little..." Keeler wasn't sure where he was going with that statement. A little easier, maybe. He didn't do it often, but there was an occasion when it had been necessary. Although, he wasn't sure Samir would believe him considering what he had done out of desperation when they'd first met. He didn't bother to finish what he was going to say in his own defense, but he had one last question on the topic that was bothering him. "I thought Nergal were warded against emotional pushes like that?"

Samir grinned at that question, his guilt dissipating like the clouds after a sudden mountain storm. "We are, but against the energy signature of non-humans. So, while you can't do it to me, without being in physical contact to override it, I can do it to another human."

"Have you ever tried doing it to a non-human?" Keeler considered the possibilities. It might be easier to forget the hunger if he could get someone to push it away again. Except, he couldn't ask that. It would be far too awkward a conversation.

"I've never tried. No." Samir grinned at him. "Want to know what it's like on the other side of something like that?"

"Hmmm. Maybe another time." Keeler considered his next question carefully. "What do those wards look like? I've heard of them, but never been close enough to a Nergal to see anything."

Samir made a face that Keeler wasn't sure how to interpret and the emotions that went with it were layered and confusing. "You can't see them. They're not a physical thing. Although there is one that I might be able to show you, but, um, well, I'll need to ask you to do something to be able to see it."

"Sure," Keeler agreed, curious as to what this involved that would bring that hint of color back to Samir's face. His unasked question was answered when Samir pulled off his t-shirt. He placed it aside before turning so that his back was to

Keeler who was doing his best not to read anything into it besides an answer to his question. Other than a few scars there was nothing to be seen there. "Am I supposed to be able to see something?"

To his surprise, Samir laughed as he shifted in his seat and sat up straighter. "I'm sorry I should have explained first. One of the most common powers we come across has to do with lightning or electricity. Anela isn't able to do it well, but if you are, try a small electric shock or something similar to that."

Keeler saw no harm in doing as asked. He was fully capable of creating something similar to an electric shock. He reached out, stopping short of actually touching Samir's back, and released a small arc of lightning from his fingers. He watched as a strange symbol glowed palely. He tried a slightly more significant zap and this time he could see the shape more clearly. "That's interesting."

"Not good for anything too strong, but it'll help mitigate the damage. Also works for more mundane sources of electricity as well. So, I could always consider a career as an electrician." Samir laughed and reached for his shirt. He paused as Keeler ran his hands gently over his shoulders.

Keeler couldn't resist, tracing the symbol with his fingers, wondering if he could see it more clearly. He hadn't even thought about what he was doing until that undeniable sweetness touched his mind and woke the hunger that he had barely gotten under control earlier. He pushed back at it, sending out a shock stronger than the last two.

Samir gasped, and Keeler removed his hands immediately. He held them to his chest and looked away. He knew it wasn't enough to hurt Samir, he would have sensed that pain, and what he felt wasn't that. He grabbed his food, to keep his hands occupied. "Sorry."

He filled his mouth. It wasn't chocolate, but it would have to do. A distraction, a way to keep him from rambling or saying something without thinking. This was the second apology today that he had been forced to give to Samir and he still had another one that he needed to do once he was under control.

"Um. Uh. That was interesting," Samir stammered as he put his shirt back on and picked up his own meal. He didn't look up either, but Keeler could still see the redness in his face out of the corner of his eye.

Silence filled the small apartment so heavily that Keeler, who normally relished it, was desperate to say something. He only had one thing he needed to say though. "Before I forget, I need to apologize for one more thing."

"Apologize?" Samir's brow furrowed in confusion. "I don't understand. What are you apologizing for this time?"

"For earlier, with Liana." Keeler wished he were more prone to showing emotion, but he hoped that Samir would understand the sincerity of his apology. "I shouldn't have spoken out as I did and if that makes things difficult for you, I'm sorry."

Samir snorted and smiled. "I know what you both said. I've spent enough time kicking around to pick up a few words of Romanian. Not enough to even be partially fluent, but I do appreciate you sticking up for me. It was sweet and, if I had been upset, I would have stopped you both sooner than I did."

"Oh." Keeler hadn't expected that, and he had no idea how to respond. He was used to people respecting him, not talking back, but he was in a business where people wanted his services and most of his employees feared and respected him. He had no idea why or how Samir would let disrespect like that go uncommented. "Still, I am sorry."

Samir placed his food aside and took Keeler's from him as well—a move far more reminiscent of the other night with the roles reversed. Only this time, all that happened was Samir taking his hands and staring him in the eyes so hard that Keeler wondered if he was trying to see the creature that wore this prison of flesh.

"Remember when you told me to stop thanking you? Stop apologizing to me. I appreciate it, especially for…" That blush returned even deeper and Keeler didn't need to hear the rest of the sentence to know what he was talking about. "I understand that this can't be easy for you. How about instead of apologizing you ask me if I am okay with what happened first. If I'm not, then you can grovel all you want."

"Thank you." There was little else Keeler could say to that as he broke that intense gaze. He wasn't sure if he was ever going to understand this man, but he did know that if he hadn't broken that stare, he would have broken his promise and be forced to consider an apology yet again. He'd already said sorry today more than he had in the last few thousand years. It was the most conclusive proof he had of how much Anela and Samir's arrival in his life had changed things in such a short time.

He was almost terrified at the idea that things might continue to change outside of his control—and he wasn't sure if it would be for better or worse. He let out a near silent sigh of relief as Samir let go of his hands, only to find his face being lifted by a gentle touch and those warm brown eyes far too close to his.

"I mean it. It's going to be okay." Samir leaned forward. Keeler wasn't sure why; perhaps it was supposed to be a kiss on the cheek, but he jumped as Samir moved closer and a gentle kiss landed on his lips.

Samir sat back, surprise registering strongly despite the fact the Keeler's mind was clouded with other thoughts. "Um, we should probably call it a night. Early day tomorrow."

CHAPTER SEVENTEEN

Keeler stared out the window as Samir drove through the city. He had no idea exactly where they were going or what the plan was, and he wasn't too sure how much he wanted to press Samir for more answers. It had been an awkward flight here. All Samir had told him was that he was working on a plan and nothing more. He decided he was better off not asking questions at this point. Samir would tell him what he needed to know when he was ready to do so.

He could feel a lot of emotional turmoil directed towards him as well as worry for Anela. There was a lot going on in his head and Keeler left him to his thoughts, doing the best he could to tune out the emotions that were being broadcast. Besides, he had his own problems to deal with; like how the longer he stayed around Samir, the harder it was for him to not give into the hunger and longing that tortured him and what he would do after this was all over. He still hadn't made a firm decision on that yet.

Eventually, Samir pulled into the parking lot of a nondescript warehouse in a light industrial area. He sat in the car, stared at the building, and said nothing. Eventually, he sighed and turned to Keeler. "This is one of our warehouses where we monitor activity for intrusions. I have no idea what Liana would have said to them, if anything, about you or this situation."

Keeler nodded. He had expected this. "So, keep my mouth shut and don't give anything away. I know the routine."

Samir grinned and his expression softened a little. "No, if you have something to say, please say it. However, maybe don't tell them what you are. I know for a fact that these outer warehouses are last on the list for upgrades so unless Liana told them, no one here knows."

"Okay." Keeler tried not to read into the change in attitude, but he was more than happy to have a voice in things. He wanted to find Anela as much as Samir did. Since he'd found her it had been like reuniting with a part of himself that he had never known was missing before—and now he didn't want to live without that. He also wanted this to be over as soon as possible and he wasn't going to do anything to jeopardize it.

He followed Samir inside. It didn't look like anything special, but the perky blonde with the wary emotions behind the counter gave everything away to him. Her smile was professional, but it became far more natural when he felt her spark of recognition on seeing Samir.

"Dr. Amin." A young blonde woman stiffened to the point that Keeler thought she might salute Samir. She spared only a quick glance at Keeler before focusing her attention fully on Samir. "Pleasure to meet you, sir."

"Please, call me Samir." He smiled warmly at her and Keeler felt all tension in the room melt away. He understood the effect that smile could have on someone because it had a similar effect on him. "And what's your name?"

"Megan Sanderson, sir." She looked at Samir with the wide-eyed admiration of someone meeting their hero for the first time. Keeler wondered if it was because of his position or if it were something else that he didn't know about.

"Nice to meet you, Megan." Samir shook her hand. "I take it there is a room in the back where we can sit down and chat about what you discovered during your surveillance?"

"Yes, sir." Megan used a keycard to allow them access into the back. Keeler followed in silence taking it all in. There weren't a lot of people here, but the security looked no less extensive than the university complex. "We still have someone out that way to keep an eye on things. We would prefer at least forty-eight hours worth of observation if not more, but Ms. Na'im said that this was a priority project."

Keeler could hear the curiosity in her voice, and he was sure that Samir couldn't have failed to notice it. He smiled and nodded in agreement. "Yes, it is a priority."

Megan glanced back at Keeler who was following them in silence. She had yet to ask about him, but since Samir had not introduced him, she was uncomfortable asking. Keeler was okay with that. He didn't need anyone in the Nergal knowing his name. Knowing his name meant they would be able to find him easier. Not that names weren't changeable, but he happened to like this one.

"Right in here, sir." She opened a door to a smaller room with a table and several chairs. Megan let the door click closed behind them. "This is a secure location. No one specified the security level of this project, so we've been using high-security protocols as a precaution."

"That's appreciated and a good move. Are you in charge of this facility?" Samir asked as he took a seat.

"Oh, no. I'm not." Megan beamed at Samir's comment. "That would be Mr. Colin Reilly, sir. He's on days off. Will this room do for the review?"

"This'll do great." Samir leaned back in the chair and pushed one out for Keeler. He sat down beside him and waited to see what came next. "So, what do we know, Megan? Can you break it down for me?"

"Yes, sir. Definitely." Megan sounded more confident as she focused on her work. She picked up the remote that sat on the table. Lights dimmed and a picture popped up on the wall opposite them. "We haven't identified anyone as there hasn't been time to do a proper search of the databases. We have determined that there are three or four people occupying the building, although we have only been able to catch the images of two of them. We haven't seen much in the way of weapons other than personal handguns. There have been some indications of magic usage at a lower level. Possibly the most basic of rituals, nothing that would normally even show up on our radar."

"I see, what sort of rituals are we thinking?" Samir frowned as he studied the few images that had been taken of the people coming in and out of the building. Keeler studied them as well. Neatly if not well dressed, they looked average, but he couldn't miss that spark of recognition that came from Samir.

"Hard to say." Megan shrugged. "It really is that faint of a trace. Unless they warded the place, but that's not common knowledge."

Samir pressed his lips together as he studied the images and Keeler watched him closely. He looked lost in his own thoughts, and not the most pleasant ones either.

"Sir?" Megan seemed to be waiting for him to say something, anything in response to the information she had presented.

"Can you give us a second?" Samir asked stiffly, all pleasantness gone from his voice.

"Sure, I'll wait outside the door." Megan walked briskly out of the room. Samir waited until it had clicked firmly behind her before he slumped down in his chair and put his hands on his head.

"You're worried you made a mistake?" Keeler asked even though he knew that was exactly how Samir felt. It was written all over him, there was no need to read his emotions. He didn't like seeing him look like this, but he had no idea how to make things better.

"Yeah." Samir let his head drop to the table. "It could all be coincidence, but my gut tells me that it's not. There is more going on here then I initially thought. I don't know if we should engage help or call in civil authorities or what. I have no idea what to do."

"What do you want to do?"

Samir turned his head to the side to look at Keeler. He seemed defeated as he spoke. "I want to charge in there like a reckless idiot and save Anela. Which would probably get me killed."

"I wouldn't let that happen to you." Keeler knew it was foolish to make such claims. He was only capable of so much. He could heal wounds when he had to, not that he'd done it often, but he couldn't save Samir from death if he didn't get there in time. He'd tried once before and failed.

"Thanks." Samir's smile was weak as he sighed and closed his eyes. "I wish I could figure out what to do. Normally, I would have had a plan by now. I didn't rise through the ranks on charm and my family name."

"I didn't think you had, but you do have some resources that you wouldn't normally have. I don't have a lot of power, being trapped in this form doesn't make it easy to do much, but I have worked at expanding my abilities. We've got this going for us." Keeler let a small arc of blue electricity jump from his hand to Samir's as a reminder of what he could do. "It's not much but it is something."

"It is something but maybe I'm no longer cut out for fieldwork." Samir sat up with a sigh. Leaning back, he stared up at the ceiling instead. "Fuck."

Keeler reached out and turned Samir's head so he could look him in the eye. "Don't doubt yourself. Tell me your concerns. We'll figure this out."

Samir took his hand and gave it a squeeze. "Thanks for the vote of confidence. Self-pity isn't going to do me any good. I need to think this through logically."

He didn't let go of Keeler's hand, but held it tightly he closed his eyes to think. "Okay, we have no clear idea of entry or the number of people we're going up against or what their abilities are. I don't like going in blind even in better situations than this."

"And the risks of bringing a couple of your people with us?" Keeler forced himself to keep his mind on the conversation instead of letting himself be drawn into what he wanted. Whether it was intentional or not, it didn't matter. It was as enjoyable a sensation as it was confusing for him.

"They'll report back about what you are if you blow your cover." Samir sighed. "You've risked enough to help already. It isn't fair to ask for anything more."

"That is hardly the end of anyone's world. No one here knows who I am, and I think my cover as an ordinary human was already blown back at the university." Keeler gave Samir's hand a little squeeze. "Although your concern is touching."

"A small force then? Two extra people, to help handle things?" Samir let his hand drop away and Keeler tried not to be disappointed—no matter how hard it made things for him. He was starting to enjoy the simple sensation of physical touch. "We're still going in blind."

"Is more time worth the risk?" Keeler saw no point in beating around the bush with his questions.

"Not sure it will be." Samir stood up. There was a firmness in his mind that told Keeler he had made his decision. He opened the door to find Megan standing stiffly beside it. "We've decided that we're going to go in early in the morning. If you have a couple of people to spare that would be great."

"Yeah, we do." Megan nodded her agreement. "I can go in myself. I have field training and I think we have one or two other people that would be available on short notice in the area."

"Great." Samir held the door open for her to come back into the room. "Here are the details. We're going in blind and we need to be prepared for standard as well as for a possible supernatural response. This is a rescue mission. There is a being in there that is being held captive. She is not to be harmed."

Samir dug out his phone and, after flipping through it for a few seconds, showed it to Megan. "This is the person that they are holding captive."

"Wait, I know that face…" She frowned as she stared at the picture.

"You would. That is Anela Masterson." Samir said.

"Oh, okay." Megan nodded and made no other comments.

Samir continued telling her the few things he had figured out so far of his plan and Keeler listened intently. "We'll go in at 0400 hours. This isn't an area I'm familiar with, so I need to rely on you and your people to choose the location we're going in from and the exact plan. You're in charge."

"Me?" Megan's eyes widened at that statement. "I never… I mean, thank you, sir. I won't let you down."

Samir chuckled. "Don't be shocked. You have an impressive resumé, lots of field experience and it's about time someone gave you a chance. How else are you going to prove yourself?"

"Thank you, sir. I won't let you down." For a moment Keeler was sure she might either salute him or hug him. He was happy when she did neither and held out her hand to shake Samir's instead.

"I know you won't." Samir smiled and shook her hand. "Email me the details and we'll see you in the morning."

They headed back out to the car. Samir stopped to look at his phone when it dinged for his attention. He shoved it back into his pocket, annoyance tinged the action strong enough to be noticed. Keeler wanted to dig deeper, but the last thing he needed to do was submerge himself in Samir.

They got into the car, but Samir made no effort to go anywhere. He sat there in silence and Keeler gave him the time to think. The silence grew to discomfort, even for Keeler who was used to spending days not talking to anyone. He could read the uncertainty that filled him over the decision he'd made, but now there was an unease that went far deeper.

Eventually, he couldn't keep waiting for Samir to do something. He broke down and asked, "What's wrong?"

"Nothing." Samir started the car and drove out of the parking lot. "Just thinking."

"Sure." Keeler didn't want to read anything into the sudden nervousness that popped up when he spoke. He did his best to not invade Samir's privacy as they drove off. He had no idea where they were going or what was bothering Samir this much. After a few more minutes of silence as Samir drove in what seemed to be no particular direction, Keeler needed to say something to ease the tension.

"If it helps, I think you made the right decision," Keeler said, hazarding a guess at what was bothering him. The problem with reading emotions was that he had no idea what the reason behind those emotions were. His best guess was that Samir was worried about tomorrow, but his words did nothing to ease the tension in the car.

"We need to figure out where we're staying tonight," Samir stated the obvious.

"I know a nice place. I stay there often when I am in town working. I'll pay for it, the hotel." Keeler offered. He shifted in his seat as he watched the city move by them without any answer from Samir. Some of it seemed familiar as if they were driving in circles and it was getting harder to ignore the tension. He wanted to convince himself that it was all in his head, but it was more than that.

"That's not necessary. I can get my own room" Samir said, irritation and worry weighing heavily in each word.

Keeler didn't respond immediately. He didn't want to argue too strongly against that in case Samir read too much into his protests. He had no problem with paying for things and, despite the difficulties it presented for him, he enjoyed spending time with Samir. He still wasn't sure what he would do after this but for now, he was determined to enjoy the time he had with him. "I know, but you don't have to."

Samir spared a glance at Keeler. As short as it was, it was intense—as though Samir were trying to read his emotions. He wasn't entirely sure that the man beside him might not be capable of doing so.

Samir drove on, his eyes darting from side to side, his discomfort and indecision growing stronger by the second. They fought with other emotions that Keeler shied away from examining too closely. It was hard not to do so when he was being met with only silence.

"Don't make me argue the point." Keeler insisted after a while of driving. "Find somewhere nice and I can book a suite."

"A suite." Samir repeated.

"Yes." Keeler pushed the point in hopes that he could convince Samir to see things from his point of view. "I have spent enough of this existence not having a comfortable place to lay my head and I'm not about to lower my standards for anyone."

Samir smiled wanly at that, but still didn't respond.

"It's been a long few days. We both need to get some good rest. Choose somewhere nice, please." Keeler turned to face out the window. Nothing he had said had improved Samir's emotional state. He was starting to think he had made things worse by insisting on this one thing, but he was getting tired of driving around this city.

"You're right." Samir said. "A shower, time to relax and a chance to figure a few things out would make all the difference in the world."

"There." Keeler pointed at a hotel he knew well. It was more than decent, it was one of the best places to stay in the city—in his opinion anyway.

"I can't afford that." Samir protested even as he drove towards it.

"Then it's a good thing you don't have to." Keeler stared at Samir. It had dawned on him that the emotional confusion that he was sensing wasn't about tomorrow. This was one of those moments where he desperately wished for the ability to read thoughts instead.

"You've done more than enough. I can't let you pay for the hotel." Samir's unease increased; his eyes fixed on the road in front of them as he turned into the parking lot. He nearly jumped when Keeler reached out and put a hand on his leg to get his attention.

"Please, let me do this. I haven't asked you for much." He made it sound like Samir was doing him the favor by letting him pay for the hotel.

Samir did as he was told and stood in silence as Keeler booked the suite that he had insisted on. Two separate bedrooms connected by a shared area.

"Your room, sirs." A bellhop said as he showed them into an opulent suite. Keeler tipped the bellhop and flopped back onto one of the couches with a sigh.

"This place is nice. I enjoy staying here on the few occasions I have to be down this way." Keeler raised his eyebrows at Samir who still stood near the entrance. "Are you okay?"

"Um, yeah." Samir wandered a little bit farther into the room. "This is a bit much to take in."

"I don't know about you, but I could use a nice long soak and something to drink."

"Yeah, that sounds nice." Samir looked around and saw one of the rooms. "I need to make a phone call. Do you care which room I take?"

"Take your pick." Keeler shrugged. He watched as Samir, his mind weighed down with worry and that unshakeable uncertainty, disappeared into one of the rooms. He wished he could do something, anything to take that away, but he wasn't sure such an offer would be welcome. Instead, he ordered some room service and went to have a soak in his own room. He would wait for Samir to come to him.

CHAPTER EIGHTEEN

Samir flopped down onto the bed with a sigh and stared at the ceiling, not knowing which of his two immediate problems he should deal with first: his father or Keeler.

He had almost felt confident leaving the warehouse, but that message from his father had thrown him off. It was short, but unexpected.

We need to talk. Call me.

He had an idea what it would be about, but it was only a guess. It was an innocuous enough message for the most part, but it was more that his father rarely messaged him. They had been close once, but he highly disapproved of a lot that Samir did. He hoped that it was nothing, but the timing was off. His father still had connections within the Nergal even though he had long ago retired.

He would have to respond, and he wasn't convinced he would like what his father was going to say. He checked the time in London as he stared at his phone. It was late, but not excessively. Not that it mattered, his father would pretend he was awake no matter what time a phone call came in.

He debated on not calling. There was nothing his father could say that would help with being able to concentrate on tomorrow and he couldn't afford that kind of distraction. On the other hand, putting it off wasn't going to make things any easier on him either. Which answered which problem he had to deal with first. Keeler wasn't about to go anywhere.

He hit dial and waited for the overseas call to connect. It rang several times and he was hopeful that his dad wouldn't answer, but his luck didn't hold out.

"Samir." His father, Hamid, sounded like his normal stiff self. No warmth, no hello, right down to business. "You took your time calling. I was starting to think you were avoiding it. I had been expecting your call a couple of hours ago."

"I was busy. With work." Samir was sure his dad knew exactly what he had been up to and what city he was in, but it wasn't a total lie. He wasn't about to admit that he didn't want to call.

"So, I've heard." Every word dripped with disapproval. Samir needed no more proof than those three words that this had to do with recent events. That tone of voice was a familiar one. Having heard it often over the years, it still made him cringe knowing the lecture that was likely to come.

"What did you want to talk about?" There was no reason to put off the inevitable. He might as well get it over with.

"Talk. Yes." His father hesitated and that was unlike him. Samir sat up, wondering what could possibly give his dad cause to pause. He was always so sure of himself, of his own opinions that he gave out freely. "Samir, you know I'm proud of your success within the Nergal even though we've had our differences of opinions, right?"

Samir lifted his phone from his ear and stared at the screen for a second to make sure that he had dialed the right number. His father wasn't one to beat around the bush when it came to his disapproval. He was starting to wonder if there was something more than this unsanctioned mission that had come to his father's attention. "Um, yes, why?"

"I'm concerned about your behavior lately. I had a call from an old colleague of mine about an incident at the university yesterday." Another pause and Samir almost groaned aloud, knowing where this might be going. He could only imagine what his father had been hearing or assuming with the lack of any actual facts. Of course, the facts might not completely exonerate him of some things his father might be thinking. "You showed up there with an undocumented being that you were described as 'close with', which is highly unusual and against protocol. I know you're not foolish enough to let one of them get near enough to manipulate you. I'm hoping there is a reasonable explanation for this apparently foolish behavior."

There it was—the accusation that he'd been waiting for. It could have been worse and, as far as disapproving dad talks went, this didn't rank among the worst of them. His mind flashed back to college and the first time he ever brought a guy home to meet his family. His mother had been more than willing to accept things, but his father had a harder time adjusting to the idea. He was still uncomfortable with it, although Samir had to give him some credit for trying.

It had been a dad talk for the books, ranking right up there with the one when he decided to move in with Tommy after university. That one had also included the all-too-familiar warning of putting his job at risk moving in with someone who wasn't a part of the organization. Unfortunately, that time his father had been right that it was a bad idea: it had ended in heartbreak, though not in terms of work.

Samir forced his mind back on the current argument. "There is, and it's a particularly delicate situation. I would explain it to you if it wasn't a breach of security protocol."

"Right." Samir could tell that his dad didn't believe a word of it. "And how close are you to this being?"

"Dad, it's not like that, I swear. This is work related, not personal." Samir wasn't a fan of lying to his dad. Keeler was definitely one of those firm lines in the sand that would cost him everything. He could never allow himself to have more than a casual friendship. His job, what he was trying to accomplish with the Nergal, was far too important to risk. No matter what he thought he might be feeling.

"Work related even though he's undocumented and the council hasn't sanctioned anything like what you're doing?" He knew his dad would press on about this until he was sure that Samir wasn't lying. He was too well informed to be fooled by simple falsehoods or half-truths. "Tell me the truth, Samir."

"I'd rather not talk about it," Samir mumbled. He was almost forty and he still felt awkward talking to his dad about his life. Even if he hadn't been insinuating at anything more than a friendship, this was pushing things too far for him. More importantly, he didn't know what it was like or what was going on between him and Keeler, but he wasn't going to talk to his dad about that. He was the last person who needed to know those kinds of details about his life.

"Whether or not you want to talk about it, I need to know that you are not out there doing something foolish, Samir." Hamid insisted. "What is going on between you two?"

"Nothing." Samir gritted his teeth and tried to calm his anger. If anything ever triggered his temper, it would be his father and he was determined this call wasn't going to end in a one-way shouting match or him saying something he might regret later.

"Is it?" Hamid pushed the issue. "I know how you can be sometimes. You know your closeness with Anela is frowned upon by the council. Are you really willing to put your whole career at risk for that thing?"

"I think you know me better than that. I know the job comes first. I've never forgotten that." Samir tried to keep the bitterness out of his voice, but it was hard to do. His response was met by a long pause.

"Not intentionally, no." Hamid's voice softened some, but not enough that Samir would be able to accuse him of actually sounding like he was honestly concerned. "But you sometimes let your emotions get the best of you."

"I won't, but it's been a long couple of days. Perhaps we can discuss this when I am not on assignment?" Samir wanted off this call more than ever. All it was doing was slamming home the fact that he needed to deal with the other issue: Keeler. He needed some time to himself to sort all of that out.

"Please do take care to remember what he is and what that means for your life if you choose to do something less than wise. Protocols and procedures exist for a reason." Samir wasn't sure if his dad was referring to Keeler's undocumented status or something else, but it was a far gentler reminder than he had expected.

"Thanks, Dad. I know." Samir sighed, flopped back down, and stared up at the ceiling. "I appreciate your concern."

"I do worry about you. You've always had radical ideas and the Nergal, the Laibiruzi, they are not going to change easily or accept those whose ideals do not align with their own." He did sound genuinely concerned which surprised Samir. His father wasn't the best at emoting. "Be careful and I will see you for the holidays?"

"Yeah, wouldn't miss a wonderfully rainy winter in London. Highlight of the year." Samir smirked as he said it. He did enjoy visiting his dad in London for the winter holidays. Even the rain didn't bother him that much — it was better than the snow. "I'll talk to you later. Promise."

"Right. Bye then."

"Bye." Samir hung up his phone before his father could get another goodbye in. Sometimes hanging up the phone was the hardest part of a call. He wondered who had told his dad about Keeler. He didn't think they had appeared that close, but he knew that sometimes he wasn't always careful with maintaining a neutral distance with people. He had always been overly affectionate even in his most platonic relationships.

Except there was more going on here than a platonic relationship and that was part of what was bothering him. He liked Keeler, but he had no idea how much of it was friendship and how much was more than that. There was too much going on, too many uncertainties and, no matter what he thought he might feel, there was the undeniable fact that Keeler was not human.

He had even tried to insist on finding his own hotel, which he knew was ridiculous, but he wasn't sure that he wanted to spend another night alone with Keeler. Not tonight, not when his own emotional state was precarious and the chances of him doing something he could regret were higher. And after last night, he was more confused than ever about his feelings towards Keeler.

He knew that Keeler had feelings for him to some extent. It was the one thing he had picked up clearly beyond the hunger when he'd shared his energy. How deep those emotions ran, he wasn't sure. Besides that hint of something more, all he had to go on was that kiss at Anela's, and the accidental one last night. They'd barely known each other when Keeler first kissed him and, whatever Keeler's feelings were towards him, he wasn't interested in being one in a long line of lovers.

Samir frowned at the ceiling as he thought about it. He wasn't going to resolve anything today. There wasn't much to do until tomorrow morning other than wait for the email for Megan about where they were meeting. Everything they needed would be supplied by the field office. There was nothing else to do but worry and hang out with Keeler.

Hang out with Keeler who could read all of his emotions even if he had no idea what caused them. Samir had no doubt that he had felt every emotion that had gone through him as he had talked to his father. Not that it mattered, he was used to that with Anela. It was simply a fact of his life.

Leaving the room, he found Keeler standing on the balcony with a drink in his hand as he stared out over the city. It was the first time Samir had seen him with his hair literally down. It reached halfway to his waist. He turned as Samir approached.

"Trying to give me some privacy?" Samir asked as he walked out onto the balcony with him.

"It seemed appropriate." Keeler shrugged and took a sip from his glass.

"My dad asked me to call him." Samir contemplated the whiskey Keeler was sipping at but decided against it. He was not in the mood to drink. "It wasn't a pleasant conversation, but I didn't expect it to be."

"Ah. Did you want to talk about it?" Keeler sipped at his drink again.

"No, it's fine." Samir appreciated the offer. He hadn't thought that Keeler was someone who liked to talk things through like that. Right now, all he could think of was his father's warning. Even if it had to do with friendship to a being whose status was undocumented, it was a fair warning for not becoming more emotionally invested in him than he already was.

"Okay, if you change your mind…" Keeler didn't finish the sentence as he turned to stare back out at the city as if that were the end of the conversation. "It's a beautiful view from here."

Samir wasn't even sure if he was saying it more to himself or as a way of keeping the conversation flowing. He walked out to join him, and much like had Keeler had done the other night, he kept his distance.

As much as he hated when his father was right, it had been the reminder he needed. He couldn't risk it all on something happening here that wasn't likely to last anyway.

CHAPTER NINETEEN

Keeler had no idea what to say. He could feel Samir pull back from him, physically and emotionally. He didn't know exactly the reason for the change in behavior, but he wished he could change it. He had been enjoying the closeness of someone in his life and, even if he didn't want to admit, he did like Samir as a person. Being around him was easy—if not for the hunger, but he was getting better at controlling that too— he could relax around him which was a rare thing.

They stood in silence as they stared out over the city. A knock on the door made Samir jump, and the small spike in fear he sensed worried Keeler. He didn't know what there was to be scared of here.

"Sorry, I ordered room service. I thought you might be hungry." Keeler walked briskly to the door to let the waiter wheel in the trolley of food for them. He glanced at the champagne and wondered if that had been one step too far. It was too late to send it back now. "I wasn't sure what you would like. We've never really talked about it, but I thought something simple might be nice. They have a good menu here."

"Right." Samir didn't sound too enthusiastic, and his mood was a heavy blanket that even dampened Keeler's slight nervousness.

"I didn't know what you liked so I may have over ordered." Keeler lifted a few lids off some of the platters and smiled when he heard Samir laugh. It didn't even matter why he was laughing, but it had lightened the mood in the room. He reconstructed his mask before turning to face Samir. "What?"

"I'm sorry. That's just a lot of food." Samir walked over and grabbed a grape off one of the platters. He popped it into his mouth. "But I'm starving, and I'll definitely need energy for tomorrow. Thank you."

Keeler's mouth twitched as he worked to keep his face neutral, not wanting to give Samir any reason to move away. It was a wasted effort as he took a half step back and attempted to cover it up by lifting the lid from another platter. "This looks great."

"Do you want to eat on the couch, we can talk or watch a movie or…" Keeler left the suggestions hanging in the air for Samir to choose, knowing it was all too similar a situation to last night.

"What movies are there?" Samir asked as he walked over to the couch, dragging the trolley behind him as he did so. He spread the platters out on the table, grinning again at the amount of the food that covered it. Keeler walked over and picked up a sheet from the table, studying that instead of Samir.

"These are the movies we can order." He passed it over, not really seeing anything that called to him. He hadn't expected that he would. He rarely consumed media of any sort. His life had been only work before this. "You choose."

Samir studied it, his frown increasing the farther down the list his eyes travelled. He plopped down on the couch and grabbed a prawn from one of the platters. He nibbled on it as he stared at the list for a bit longer. "I can't decide. Maybe just the news or something?"

Keeler agreed with that, not caring what they watched, but wishing he could do something—anything really—to lighten Samir's mood. The best he could do was respect the distance he seemed to want, by taking a seat in one of the chairs instead and waiting for him to start the conversation.

They watched the news in silence, followed by some mundane program as they both picked at the food until they were full. Keeler tried not to follow Samir's shifting moods, but he couldn't help himself. He wanted to understand what was going on. It wasn't until Samir had picked up the remote and flipped twice through all the channels that Keeler decided it was time to say something.

He reached over and took the remote away from Samir who didn't bother to resist. He shut the TV off and dropped the remote on the table between them. "Somehow, I don't think this channel flipping has anything to do with not knowing what you want to watch."

"I'm worried about Anela and it's been a long couple of days." It was the truth, for the most part, but there was more— Keeler could sense that easily.

"It has been a long couple of days." Keeler agreed, hoping that sympathy would help ease the conversation forward. It was true, even for him—he'd never had two days be both so long and too short at the same time. He waited to see if Samir would expand on what he had said, perhaps tell him what else was going on in his mind, but he stayed silent.

Keeler picked the remote back up and started flipping through the channels again. If this was what Samir wanted, then this is what he would do. Flip through everything until they both decided it was time to call it a night.

"I'm sorry," Samir said, halfway through the sixth round of channel flipping. He dropped his head into his hands and stared at the floor.

"It's okay," Keeler said, remembering their conversation from last night as he shut the TV off. "You don't owe me anything, I understand that you haven't known me that long, it's been an intense couple of days, and you've had to make compromises with your job. That cannot be easy on anyone. There is no need to apologize."

"I…" Samir let the single word trail off with a sigh.

Keeler waited to see if he would say anything else, but that single word seemed to be all he was getting in response. There was so much confusion there and a hint of anger submerged within it. He wanted to reach out, to touch Samir and assure him that everything was going to be okay, that he was here if needed in a way that words could never fully communicate. But he wasn't sure it would be welcome. His hand twitched but stayed where it was and he looked away from Samir, tightened his senses until there was nothing but his own thoughts for company.

He contemplated escape, an excuse to give Samir the space he seemed to want, but it was too early to feign tiredness and he had no idea what else to do.

"I'm sorry I'm not good company," Samir apologized again.

"It's fine." Keeler took the verbal interaction as a sign that, perhaps, Samir didn't want him to leave. He took a chance, hoping to find a clue as to what was wanted of him in Samir's emotions. He wasn't good with people, he didn't spend enough time around them, but beyond that near perpetual confusion there were currents of loneliness and longing. He wished he knew why, and for what. "Do you need me to leave?"

Samir didn't even raise his head at the question. Silence stretched to the point that Keeler assumed that this was his answer. He stood to leave, not bothering to say anything. There was nothing to be said that words could communicate. Had it not been for the slight emotional surge that preceded it, he would have been surprised when Samir reached out and grabbed his hand.

He froze, not sure what to do. Still, Samir stayed silent and, though Keeler didn't look, he was sure his face would be bright red. There were no clues as to what was wanted from him and he didn't want to overstep any boundaries. Not again. A slight tug prompted him to look down, but Samir hadn't lifted his head.

"Oh, okay." Keeler didn't know how else to respond but sat down beside him and continued to hold his hand. Sitting here, like this, made it harder not to crave more and it took a concentrated effort for him to do nothing. It was hard not to read Samir's emotions this close and it made him want to find a way to make him feel better. To take away the confusion, the worry, the fear—all those negative emotions and then some— and replace them with something better. Such things were possible, but he wasn't sure they would be welcome.

Not knowing what else to do, he went with a human

reaction that was meant to comfort and console. His nearest arm was still free, so he wrapped it lightly over Samir's shoulders. He wasn't sure what sort of reaction it would get, but he was happy when Samir leaned into him. It didn't take away the uneasiness or indecision, but he relaxed a little. Keeler moved slightly, wanting to be sure they were both more comfortable and Samir adjusted with him still not saying anything.

He pulled Samir a little tighter against him and refused to read any further into the situation. He knew that humans often craved basic physical comfort. He'd found himself wanting that on occasion—though he rarely indulged those human cravings. This was something he could do for Samir and, somehow, it made him feel a bit better too.

Even if he wasn't willing to admit to anyone else, he was worried about tomorrow. He could feel Anela. She was scared and angry, but it was indistinct and fuzzy. He guessed it was from the wards that Samir had mentioned earlier.

And he was worried about Samir, about what was happening between them. As much as he was enjoying the comfort of having someone in his life there were things that he had refused to let himself think about the last few days. Every time one of those thoughts or memories surfaced, he pushed it away with more determination than he did his hunger. He wanted, more than anything, to live in these small moments.

Although, he more than understood some of the confusion and uncertainty that Samir was feeling because it was the same for him. In six thousand years he'd experienced a lot of things, and every day seemed to pass faster than the last, but these last couple of days had lingered for him. He wanted them to continue to crawl.

He didn't want to face reality after it was over when he could have this right now. Warmth, comfort, companionship. These were things he never had before, and he wanted it to last.

CHAPTER TWENTY

Connor slammed the binder down on the small table with a frustrated cry sending paper cups and half-finished containers of takeout tumbling to the ground. He'd worked straight through the night, trying to get this done. It was only a matter of time before the Nergal realized that the vessel in which Zi-Asbu was trapped had been taken.

He needed this to be done before it was too late. All his plans, everything he had worked for, hinged on this happening now. There was no back-up plan, no time for a second chance. Based on his research, he had given himself two days before they came for her and he wanted to be long gone by then. They could have the vessel, Zi-Asbu would have no use of it when he was done.

"I told you, it's impossible. Give up. Let me go and I promise I won't let you suffer when I kill you. Not too much anyway," Anela taunted, though her voice was weak and hoarse.

Connor ignored her and took a deep breath, her comments nothing more than water off a duck's back. His attention was on the sheet of paper in front of him; a terrible photocopy of an old fax and nearly impossible to read. He ran a hand through his hair as he tried to make sense of a language he only partially understood. As much as he had studied all the ancient texts and forbidden rituals that he could get his hands on, there were subtleties to it that eluded him still. He was sure that it was those little details that made the difference between success and failure.

He made a few more notes as he squinted at the blurred writing, trying to guess at what a few of those symbols might be. He was close, his last attempt had allowed him to feel the chains that kept the darkness trapped within. There was a vital fury in it that he was overjoyed to discover, but not all that bound it, he had learned, were created by those who had come before the Nergal.

Unfortunately, Zi-Asbu had been corrupted by the vessel as well. It was a complication he had not expected or even considered possible. It was a mystery how something as pathetic could affect something so powerful, but it had. Not that it mattered how many bindings or what kinds were on it. Releasing was the part he had already figured out.

Controlling the darkness once released was the most difficult part of his plan. It was where those who had come before him had failed. He had no intention of failing, but the unexpected changes effected on that powerful creature by something so ridiculous as this vessel was vexing him. He'd get it though. He just needed a little more time.

"Hey, um, Connor?" He looked up to see David standing by the door, looking as if he were about to be beat.

"I told you not to bother me while I was working," Connor grumbled. He made another couple of notes before turning to look at David, taking the opportunity to stretch as he did so. "What is so important that you feel the need to disturb me now?"

"I think we're being watched." David took a step back as he spoke.

"They're coming for me and they're gonna stop you," Anela said. "I told you this would happen."

"Don't worry about it, we're almost done here." Connor continued to ignore her as if she weren't even in the room. He waved a hand dismissively as he went back to deciphering the blurry words on the page before him. He was sure that if he combined this ritual with another that he might be able to do something no one else had done.

The Nergal had moved faster than expected. He would have liked more time, but he was close. So close. Once he figured out this page, he would be one step closer to having control of the darkness. Once he had that, nothing could stop him. All he had to do was wait for the right time, for everything to be in alignment and then the Earth would be cleansed.

He guessed that he had the night, two if he was lucky before they barged in. He'd stayed as far off their radar as he could, but he'd always known they would cross paths eventually. He'd done his homework, studied what he could find of their fighting style and tactics. Preparation was the key to success, and he was prepared.

"Alright let's try this one again." Connor picked up the copper dagger that still had a few drops of blood clinging to the blade. He casually wiped them off on his jeans as he approached Anela. There was no need to rush, that would only lead to mistakes and mistakes led to failure. "This will only hurt a lot if you can even feel pain. A monster like you, one can never be sure."

Anela didn't respond.

Connor was careful as he reached out with the dagger to slice into her arm. He kept pressing into her skin until blood covered the blade. Her arm healed quickly, but the blood on her skin stayed, a telltale sign. Connor walked back to the table. He held the knife as he read over the instructions one last time. Blood dripped down onto the table, but he barely even noticed it. "I'm thinking that I can see where I went wrong on this last time. It's a longer ritual than I had thought. We're in for a night, darling, but I think it's worth one last try before we move to the next best option."

Anela growled at him, a feral sound that always made him smile a little. There was the darkness that wanted to consume. It was there, no matter what the weak and willful vessel insisted. He walked around her, slowly chanting, getting into the rhythm. He flicked the knife, splattering the vessel. Another slice, another splash of blood. Eight times, eight cuts.

Now it was his turn. He gritted his teeth and cut deeply into his own arm with the still bloody knife before repeating the ritual again. Eight wounds upon his arms to match the ones on hers. He continued the chant until her scream pierced through his trance, and then he switched to a new rhythm, one that he had created himself.

This time, it had to work.

CHAPTER TWENTY-ONE

An insistent beeping broke into Samir's pleasant dreams and interrupted everything. He groaned as the real world tried to intrude, wanting to go back to the dream. It was easier there, warm and safe, but… the waking world was also warm. Arms wrapped around him making him feel safe and comfortable. He wanted to stay right here forever, and the rest of the world could disappear. He closed his eyes, ignoring the demand of the alarm as best he could.

"Morning." Keeler's whisper came from somewhere nearby and he sounded entirely too awake.

It took him a few moments to figure out why. He had fallen asleep on the couch wrapped up in Keeler's arms—or was that part of the dream. He should have been sore if he'd slept in such an awkward position, but he felt better than normal.

"Time to go rescue Anela." That struck a chord, but he couldn't remember why she would need his help. It seemed important though.

"Eerrmmmm." Samir struggled to make the words form, but he had nothing yet. It was too early for words. Too early for even logical thought as he pushed in closer to Keeler, the beeping finally having worn itself out. "Five more minutes."

Whether a full five minutes had passed or not, Samir wasn't sure, but it was enough for the hazy veil between dreams and reality to lift. Anela needed him, he had to go save her, but first, he had to get up and moving. He opened his eyes and froze when the feeling of arms holding him didn't disappear as well.

Samir looked up into amber eyes. Keeler didn't seem to be bothered that he was lying on top of him. His mind flashed images that he wasn't sure had actually happened or not, but his father's words drifted to him as well. That was real. Panic shot through him and Keeler's arms tightened, keeping him from flailing and falling.

"Easy there." Soothing warmth surrounded him, calm clouded his panicked mind. Samir knew the emotions were coming from Keeler, but he gave into them willingly.

"I'm okay now." He took a deep breath and slowly released it. "Thank you."

Keeler nodded, his eyes smiling though his face did not. He didn't say anything, he simply watched Samir who did his best to stave off the blush he could feel rising. That stare reminded him too much of dreams that weren't fading quick enough.

"We should get ready to go." Samir averted his gaze as he pushed himself away from the warmth and off the couch, the familiar tingle of Keeler's touch dissipating.

"We should," Keeler agreed.

Samir made a beeline for what was supposed to have been his room and the ensuite attached to it. He wasted no time getting into the shower in hopes that the water would wash away the last of the cobwebs and dream fragments from his mind. He tried to keep his thoughts focused on the day ahead, but it was nearly impossible to do.

It had been nice waking up in someone's arms—it had been too long since that had happened. And Keeler… With a sigh he leaned against the wall. He needed to get it out of his head. No matter how much he had enjoyed waking up with someone, that particular someone was firmly out of bounds.

"Not human," he muttered, eyes squeezed tight as he lightly pounded a fist against the tile in time to his words. "Get him out of your head and focus on your job."

Except it was easier said than done. No matter how hard he tried, he couldn't force those thoughts and images from his mind. It was a distraction he couldn't afford to have today even as he kept comparing the man he first met in the restaurant that had refused to speak to him and the man who had been with him last night, showing him understanding and compassion.

It was amazing how much could change in such a short time, including for him. He turned the temperature to cold and gritted his teeth. It didn't help much.

"Focus." He told himself again in the mirror. "Today is about Anela. You know the speech you give to first-time field operatives. If you can't keep your mind in the game, then you need to walk away. Anela needs your help, so you need to fucking focus, Samir. She is too important to leave her fate in the hands of others."

He dressed quickly and joined Keeler in the main room feeling refreshed. Samir still found himself unable to look him in the eyes yet. "Ready?"

"Yes." Keeler gave a quick nod of his head and opened the door for Samir. "Let's bring her back."

It didn't take them long to get to the rendezvous point, though it felt longer than it was with the silence in the car. Samir was happy to see Megan and another operative were already waiting for them to arrive. They had equipment waiting and ready for them. Samir wasted no time gearing up and then helped Keeler get equipped as well. He didn't push the issue when he turned down carrying any weapons—even for appearances sake.

"All right, it's been pretty quiet for the last few hours," Megan spoke in hushed tones even though their meeting spot was more than a block away from the building. "We've set up standard excuses with local law enforcement, so we expect no issues there. There are two entrances to the building that we're aware of. Fehr and I will take the back door and you and your associate can cover the front."

Samir nodded in appreciation that she made it an order and not a question despite the fact that he outranked her. He wanted her to take lead and she did it without apology; he made a mental note of that for later. No matter how things went, she deserved to be rewarded for her competence.

He turned his attention to the diagram as she covered the details of the plan. Everything seemed in order and well thought out. He was glad that he had chosen her to lead this excursion. She had covered nearly every detail that he could think of.

"Looks perfect." Samir glanced back at Keeler who nodded silently in agreement. "Be careful you two. Don't take any chances. This is not an official mission. Do remember that, but if you can, take them down so this doesn't happen again. Understood?"

"Yes, sir." Both agreed in unison. Samir smiled at them. They stayed close to the shadows, moving with cautious silence. They split as they approached the building. Samir made a point of staying in front of Keeler as they edged closer to the front entrance.

He paused beside the door. It wasn't often he found himself in the situation of going after other humans. Albeit humans who had kidnapped his friend and were doing things that might be less than ethical. He was comfortable enough with guns, but they weren't his favorite tool of the trade.

He placed the shaped charges around the door and waited for the word from Megan to bust through. Chaos was their friend in this situation, but it had to be organized chaos. It would take the people in there a few minutes to figure out that they weren't with the local authorities. That was usually enough to give most humans significant pause.

"Go time," Megan's voice rang confidently in his ear and Samir set off the charge. He wasted no time in charging through the door. Smoke and debris filled the air with shouts of those inside as well as his own crew. His own voice bellowed automatically. "Hands in the air! Down on your knees!"

No one inside had enough time to react before they had them subdued. Guns or not, it was obvious they hadn't expected anyone to come busting the door shortly after four in the morning. However, Anela was nowhere to be seen.

Keeler pointed towards a half-open door off to the side. Samir nodded his agreement. Anyone on the other side of that door would be ready for them now. They lacked the element of surprise, but there wasn't time to waste. He motioned for Megan and her colleague to stay put as he made his way cautiously to the door. Keeler stood, unarmed behind him.

Samir gave a small nod and kicked the door fully open. Keeler ran in first. If someone were waiting and ready, they both knew that he would survive, but Samir might not.

A bright flash of light blinded Samir and he threw his hands up to protect his face. There was no bang, no sound that went with it and he had no idea what had happened, but he wasn't going to abandon Keeler.

Samir dashed in through the door, his gun at the ready, and stopped short at the sight of Anela. She was slumped over, only the bindings that held her to a chair kept her from falling to the floor. A tall, dark-haired man stood calmly and confidently in front of her. Keeler lay prone on the floor, somehow unconscious.

Samir took aim at the man. Despite his anger and fear, he kept his voice even. "Get down on your knees, hands behind your head."

The man didn't budge an inch from where he stood, but Samir could see his lips moving.

"I told you to get down on your knees and hands behind your head. Do it now!" he commanded, his unease growing as he noticed the wards that he had suspected were in place. Some of them were more advanced than anything he had ever used before and a few were completely unknown to him.

Still, the man continued to silently mumble to himself, his lips moving faster than before. It slowly sunk in that, whoever this man was, he had power that even many of the Nergal did not. Between that and the fact that Keeler was out for the count, Samir had to do something. He fired, not aiming for the kill, but enough to distract and injure.

Even though he was sure his aim had been good, the bullet hit the wall behind the man—if he was a man. With both Keeler and Anela in the room, any device he had for detecting interdimensional intrusions was useless. They overwhelmed the sensors. Samir's instincts screamed that this was a human, but what he was doing shouldn't have been possible.

Samir fired again, even though he didn't think it would do any good. He was right. It was useless, but in that short time the man stopped his mumbling and smiled. An invisible wall struck Samir and sent him flying backwards. He landed hard back in the other room. His head bounced against the cement floor. He was thankful for his helmet and the fact that he'd been standing near the door. He didn't even want to think what would have happened had he hit the wall at that velocity.

"Get out of here. Now!" he yelled at Megan and Fehr as he rolled back to his feet. He didn't wait to see if they listened, but he didn't need anyone getting injured on an unsanctioned mission. His life and safety, on the other hand, were his to risk and he was getting Anela out of here—no matter what it took.

It was obvious that traditional methods weren't going to work here. He dropped most of his weapons, keeping only what he needed to protect himself. He tried to think about every ritual or spell that he had ever learned in hopes he might be able to fight back. There had to be something in his limited arsenal that might work against that man. He was advanced, but Samir had a few tricks up his sleeve, and—at this point— he wasn't willing to hold anything back.

Charging into the room at full speed, he launched himself at the man who had his back turned. He was busy unstrapping Anela from the chair. Samir threw his arms in front of him and focused all his energy on a single point. Normally, this was used as a defensive spell, but he'd adapted it similarly before against an intrusion.

Samir was pushed backwards by the force of the blow, but he had prepared for that. He rolled across the floor, sliding to a stop a couple of yards away. The man slammed into the opposite wall hard enough to leave a dent. His strike had been enough to even tear the chair from where it had been bolted to the floor and it had skidded across the room with Anela still strapped to it.

Samir managed to get into a kneeling position, his energy exhausted. He had put everything into the blow. He cursed silently as the man struggled to gain his feet, using the wall as support. That strike would have killed most people, but this man was proving to be more resilient or better prepared than he had imagined.

The man hesitated, his gaze jumping from Anela back to Samir. His shakiness the only sign that he had been affected by the blow. Samir took that time to find his own feet as his hand reaching for the rarely — and nearly forgotten — gun.

His movement didn't go unnoticed. The man grabbed a piece of metal pipe that was on the ground. It wasn't a large pipe, but Samir grinned. Energy or not, he was damned if he would go down without a fight and he had always excelled in hand to hand combat. His grin faded as the man threw it up into the air instead and struck out with his other hand, not to hit the pipe but to accelerate it.

Exhaustion more than surprise slowed Samir's reaction time as he tried to dodge it. The piece of pipe slammed straight through his lower abdomen and clattered to the ground behind him. Between one blink and the next, he found himself back on the cement floor, staring across at Anela. Her eyelids fluttered open as his closed.

CHAPTER TWENTY-TWO

"Sami!" It was Anela's cry that broke through the fog that surrounded Keeler's thoughts. He tried to remember where he was and why, but the answers danced out of reach. Something was wrong, but he wasn't sure what. Everything, every thought was a deliberate effort. He opened his eyes slowly as his sluggish mind worked to catch up with what was happening. The first thing he saw was Anela wrestling her arm loose from its binding as she called out again. "Samir!"

He watched her as she struggled harder to free her hand. She yanked and pulled, managing to free her limb from the constraints, though it looked all the worse for it. She called out again louder. "Samir! Wake up, please!"

His mind searched for the sweetness and found it. Weakened, but still there. He didn't understand why or what had happened. It was like watching a grainy old moving at half speed as he watched Anela reach around to yank at the restraint that still held her other arm tightly to the chair. He didn't know how she had so much energy as he struggled to pull his thoughts together. Slowly, it came back to him. He tried to move, but his body felt as though it were made of sand, heavy and limp.

He had charged in here and seen a man standing over an unconscious Anela. Before he could do anything, the man had turned to see him, anger and frustration dominated his emotions. Then something had hit him like a ton of bricks. Whatever he'd done, hadn't been directed at her, but only him. He'd been useless—or worse, a hazard for the person he had sworn he'd protect.

He closed his eyes, disappointment washing over him, drowning out everything else. Once again he had failed, and it brought back memories of other humans he had been unable to protect. Those few and far between that had managed to reach out to him only for their kindness and compassion to be the source of their death.

Except, Samir was still alive. He could sense him, he had to be okay. Everything would turn out fine because unlike so many others, Samir was accustomed to non-corporeals. This time was different. Except, Keeler couldn't help but wonder why he wasn't answering Anela's cries. He inched his hand towards his temple and attempted to rub away the headache that plagued him. It was a new and strange sensation. He needed to get it together so he could find Samir and make sure he was alright.

He opened his eyes as the sensation of pain faded. Anela wasn't looking at him, but her eyes were focused on another spot. He followed her gaze to see Samir lying nearby—and far too still—in a pool of dark liquid. It took a second for the dots to connect. It was blood. Fear gripped him harder than it ever had before as he stared at Samir's chest, waiting for it to move.

It was shallow, but the movement was there and that meant he was still alive.

It was only a small relief as he reached out with his senses. The life that Samir clung to was fading. He needed to do something, he had to get to him.

"Samir…" It was barely more than a hoarse whisper as Keeler pushed himself to his knees, fighting against a lethargy that was determined to weigh him down.

"Keeler!" Anela's cry brought his attention back to her. "Can you get to him? I can't get these bonds off. Please, please, help him."

He didn't waste the energy on trying to reply. Slowly, his strength was returning, and he dragged himself over to Samir. Though it was not far, these few feet seemed like miles. With each inch, though, he could feel his strength returned and hoped it would be enough as he reached Samir's prone body.

He studied the wound. The bleeding was slowing, but that didn't mean anything. He'd seen wounds like this before and they were never good. He tried to push himself up, his head spinning from whatever that guy had done to him but, like the weakness, the dizziness was fading quickly.

Not that it mattered, he'd have fought death itself to save Samir. He pressed his hands over the wound and tried to focus on what he needed to do. Healing him would mean diving deep into the one thing he wanted the most. That wonderfully sweet and cool essence of Samir he had resisted for so long. There was no other option.

For a second, he hesitated, worried that doing this would leave him unable to fight that driving need any longer or if doing this would make it easier on him. Not that it mattered, he would deal with the outcome when he was there. Right now, saving Samir was the priority. Everything else, his own problems, paled in comparison.

Keeler relaxed and allowed his warmth to mix with Samir's brilliant icy pureness. Like the first time, it was overwhelming for him, drawing him deeper, not only feeding his hunger but making him crave more and more. He tried to ignore it, but the pleasure he sent out to dull the pain reflected back at him. It was more alluring than anything, it made him want to stay right in this moment forever.

He pushed through it. There was little time to spare in healing this wound, in saving Samir. If he ever wanted even the slightest chance for more, he had to focus on healing and repairing the damage that had been done by the pipe.

Seconds inched by and he could feel Samir's pulse strengthen, his breathing become more regular. He held onto that connection, giving as much of himself as he could. Knowing that Samir needed it more than he did. It also gave him a chance to stay more deeply connected for a little bit longer.

When he could no longer convince himself that he was doing this for Samir, Keeler pulled back from a feeling that he wanted to spend forever exploring. There was no time for that, and he had done this without permission, but he was sure that Samir would understand.

Breathing heavily more from the exhilaration of everything he had felt than from exertion, Keeler opened his eyes to look down at Samir whose eyes were still closed but he could see only healing skin and no more gaping wound. It was a step in the right direction. He rested his hand against Samir's face.

"Wake up." He pleaded quietly. If Samir could hear him, he wasn't able to respond yet. Forgetting Anela, ignoring his own promise, Keeler kissed him gently on the lips. "Please."

"Is he..." Anela didn't finish the question, her emotions were enough for him to know what she was asking, though he cursed her intrusion on his thoughts.

"I hope so." He rested a hand on Samir's chest, keeping track of his heart beats, as he waited for Samir to wake up.

CHAPTER TWENTY-THREE

Warmth and light washed through Samir, demanding his attention even as it soothed away his aches and pains. Almost everything beyond that feeling, the gentle touch drifting over his body, faded away. His skin tingled in the most beautiful way where he was touched. Keeping his eyes closed, he luxuriated in the feeling even if he didn't know where the sensations were coming from.

From somewhere in the distance, Keeler's voice called to him, asking him to wake up, but he wanted to stay here where he was, floating in the pleasure of this moment. He didn't want to leave behind the warmth this time. He'd already done that once today and it hadn't turned out well.

A burning sensation flushed through his lips and set him on fire. If this was what it felt like to be consumed in flames, he would do it a million times over. Then there was Keeler again, a single word, that could mean anything, but there was so much pain there that it took all the pleasure away.

He opened his eyes to find Keeler's face only inches from his, amber eyes full of concern and worry.

"Thank you," Keeler whispered as if he had done something more important than waking up. He tried to move and felt a twinge in his side. He remembered the pipe and relaxed back as Keeler continued to cradle his head. "You had me worried that I was too late."

"Anela?" Samir asked.

"I'm here!" she called out. "Are you alright, Sami, darling?"

Samir smiled at the familiar sound of her accented English. She sounded as if nothing unusual had happened. It could have been any ordinary day. "I'm okay. I think."

"You should be, just take it easy." Keeler leaned back up, watching him with that same intense look. Samir tried to move, but his entire midsection screamed at him with each attempt.

"Can you help me up?" Samir asked. Even with Keeler doing most of the work to get him into a sitting position, he could still feel the slight twinges, like a pulled muscle, in his side. Whatever the damage that had been done by that pipe, it had been fixed, he assumed, by Keeler. He would have to find a way to thank him for that later. For now, he had to get them all out of here.

He looked around, doing his best to ignore the pool of blood that surrounded him. He noticed a door that was opened a crack, enough to allow the streetlight to shine into the building. He wanted to curse that the man had gotten away, but his anger was mitigated by the fact that Anela was safe now.

"Are you okay? Does it hurt?" Keeler asked.

"A little, it's fine. Help me to my feet? I want to see if Anela is okay." It was more a full lift than any work on his part. Every time he tried to use any of his core muscles, the pain shot through his body as if he were being impaled on that pipe all over again. He leaned on Keeler, letting him more or less carry him over to where Anela still lay attached to the chair.

She had managed to get both her arms freed, but the damage she had done to accomplish that was incredible. Samir shook his head as he examined the injury, knowing that it was already healing. "Taking your hands off isn't a good idea no matter how desperate you are to escape."

"I will live. I was more worried about you." Anela said, reaching out to wrap her wounded hand around Samir's. "I will live for a long, long time and I don't want yours to come to an end so soon. You are my family, my friend. I would move mountains if that is what it took to make sure you were okay."

"Let me take a look at those other restraints." Samir acted exasperated to cover up how much her words had touched him. He ran his hands over the remaining restraints. It was a basic enchantment, something he could normally deal with easily, but he was tired. Too tired to even do the most basic spell. He would need help. He looked up at Keeler and wondered if it was too much to ask of him after what he had done already.

He swallowed back his awkwardness and asked anyway. "I can break the enchantment on these, but I don't have the energy to do it. I'm tired."

"You almost died." Keeler pointed out, stiffening beside him.

"Please?" Samir pleaded, pushing the point. He knew they were both exhausted from everything that had happened.

"Okay." Keeler said, not looking Samir in the eyes. Samir wondered what was going through his head, but that was something he could ask about later—if he could find the courage to do so.

Samir focused his attention on breaking the basic enchantment instead. It wasn't hard, but he was tired. Even with Keeler helping him he could feel it draining him quickly. He leaned back against Keeler as he finished the spell and the enchantment broke. Even though the spell was complete, Samir couldn't stop himself from borrowing a little bit more energy.

He knew that Keeler was holding something back from him. Last time, he had felt so much more, but this time there had been a wall. A barrier between him and Keeler's emotions that saddened him, made him feel unwanted which was silly.

He didn't have the energy to waste on trying to figure out what any of it meant. All he wanted to do now was rest in the warmth and pleasure that he had left behind when he'd woken.

"Everything okay in here?" Samir let his eyes close again as he heard Megan's voice.

"All clear. We lost the suspect but Anela is safe." Footsteps came towards him, but even if he wanted to, he couldn't force his eyes to open. Everything outside faded and he fell asleep trying to find that place again. To become an island in a sea of warmth.

But there was only the empty darkness.

CHAPTER TWENTY-FOUR

Anela regretted having to leave the shower behind. It was another of those wonderful human things that she had always enjoyed. She wrapped herself in the big fluffy bathrobe and her hair in a towel before prancing into the main room of the suite to find Keeler staring morosely out the window.

"You seem unhappy for someone who had such an exciting day." Anela poured herself a generous helping of coffee from the trolley room service and adulterated it with three generous spoonfuls of sugar and a dollop of heavy cream. Samir was resting in one of the rooms and she was surprised that Keeler hadn't done the same. He looked exhausted.

"I'm fine." He didn't turn to look at her.

"Something is bothering you." Anela elbowed him gently in the ribs. "You can hide a lot of things, but you cannot hide everything from me. In many ways, we are one. Do not make me have to be a pest about this because I can be."

Keeler sighed but didn't look at her. "Why is he like that?"

"What?" Anela hadn't expected that question. She knew what he was asking but it was something that she had never talked about. It would mean admitting to what she had done, what others had asked of her when they shouldn't have. It could have been bad for Samir if it got out, but Keeler was safe. She doubted that he would run and tell the Nergal or Institute.

"That is a long story," Anela said, her normally breezy voice subdued and her demeanor unusually serious. "We should sit."

Keeler sat down at the table and sipped his tea. Anela nursed her coffee as she figured out where to start with the story. She doubted that there had been much time for him to learn a lot of Samir's past and he needed to know that before he could understand.

"Before Samir, his parents were the agents assigned to watch over me as I learned to transition into a normal human life," Anela said. "I have known Samir since he was a little child. His parents raised him with the expectations that, one day, he would also choose to join the Nergal.

"His mother was far more liberal in her leanings than his father, but they had been working with me for near a decade before I ever met him. I watched him grow and become a wonderful, if somewhat wild, young man. He seemed to be always chasing the next high, charging towards the next great adventure. His parents were at their wits end with him more often than not." Anela laughed warmly at the memories that came to mind.

"I can see you doubt that, but like most humans, he had the same nature of duality. Dark and light, sweet and spicy. I think that the dark side of his nature drove his behavior a lot of the time. It was not a truly dark side; he was still a good person, but he had that streak in him." Anela smiled at the memory. "Maybe that was my influence. Who is to say?"

"And then what happened?" Keeler prompted.

Guilt flushed through Anela as she stared into her coffee cup. It had been nice thinking about Samir, running around and doing everything he could to irk his parents. More often than once, getting dragged home by the police. She always wondered what would have happened to him had things not gone the way they did.

"There was an accident. A bad one. He had been driving too fast in poor conditions. Foolish boy. Ended up wrapped around a light post. Thankfully, no one else was injured." Anela sipped at her coffee. "There was little the doctors could do. He lay in the hospital with his life fading away with each passing day. Hamid and Kate were distraught and desperate. They asked for my help, to see if there was anything I could do to save their only child."

Anela sighed and stared into the depths of her half-empty mug. It wasn't quite the truth, but it didn't matter the details of who had asked her. Or any of the problems that resulted from that one incident. This was about Samir, not his parents. "I agreed, of course. They were my family. As close as I had ever come to having one anyway. I couldn't say no, but I had never done anything like that before. Expanding my abilities has always been frowned on by the Nergal and the most I had ever healed were little cuts and scrapes."

Anela pressed her lips together and tried to push away the images of a Samir in that sterile room. Uncaring machines monitoring him and reporting the details of his slow and terrible death. She still remembered seeing him like that as if it were only yesterday. It was her nightmare knowing that one day she would be back in a room like that having to watch him leave her for good.

"I could feel him dying. Each breath weakened him, each second that passed was one more second closer to the end. There was no hope he could heal on his own. I had to try to do something I'd never done before." Anela looked up at Keeler and smiled unexpectedly. "It is amazing how much I have learned about healing since those days. Ah, but ignorance is not always a good thing. I did the best I could and, as you can tell, I succeeded."

Keeler waited for her to tell the rest of the story, but she remained silent. This was what she hadn't wanted to admit to, but this was what he had been asking of her. She wasn't surprised when he asked his question again. "And why is he like that?"

"I was terrified that pouring so much of my energy into him would leave a mark, would darken his soul. I couldn't have lived with myself if he lived but became darker than he ever should have been." Anela sighed and pushed the mug away from her. She had long cursed her naivety, though she wasn't sure if what had happened was a bad thing or not. It was something only time could tell her. "I know, now, that isn't how it works, but back then I didn't. I was so ignorant of so many things."

"When you pulled out, you took all the darkness with you, even his own, didn't you?" Keeler asked, his question gently instead of accusing.

Anela nodded. "Like a soul filter. Some of it has come back, here and there, but apparently, when the balance is that far out it never really recovers. Everyone attributed the changes in him to the accident being a wake-up call."

"How old was he?"

"Seventeen." Anela pursed her lips in thought for a moment. "I don't think I have even told his parents why he changed. I didn't know how to tell them, and it took time for me to figure it out myself."

"He doesn't know either, does he?" Keeler glanced back at the door to the room where Samir still slept soundly, entirely unaware of how unique he was.

"No, how do you begin to tell someone something like that?" Anela shook her head and wrapped her hands around her mug of coffee, enjoying the warmth of it. "No, he doesn't need to know. It's been more than twenty years and there have been no serious consequences that I have seen. He is a good man, the best man, and that isn't a bad thing."

Keeler leaned back in his chair and tapped his fingers on the table. Anela gave him time to process this new information. He picked up his own tea, took a sip and made a face. Anela hid a smirk at his reaction.

"Let me ask you something now." Anela interrupted his contemplation. She had told him her secret, and now it was only fair for him to be honest with her.

"What?"

"Why are you hiding your feelings from him?" She leaned forward and glared at him, her voice once again taking on its typically playful tone. "I can see the way you look at him even if he cannot see it. And, as much as you try to hide it, I can sense those feelings you are burying. You're in love with him."

"Don't be absurd." Keeler protested quietly.

"Am I being absurd?" Anela grinned at him. "Tell me what I missed. How did this happen? I need all the intimate details."

"There is nothing to talk about." Keeler insisted.

"Like the fact that you kissed him?" Even that light jab did nothing to get the reaction she wanted. Instead, he stared down at the table and his hands. She changed her tact, teasing might have worked well with Samir, but Keeler was a different story. "But I want to talk about it. I have been telling you since we met that you need to learn to embrace the humanness of your existence. I would prefer for your experience to be with someone else but skipping from simply liking someone to loving them is a huge step."

"It doesn't matter." Keeler sighed. "Nothing can become of it. I'm not human. He is and he's a Nergal. It would be close to insanity for me to consider attempting to experience my 'human existence' with him. I am better off as I was before."

"Cold, unfeeling, and lonely?" Anela asked, knowing Keeler couldn't deny any of those things. She could still sense that aching loneliness within him, only slightly diminished from when they had first met.

"Samir, he is special." Anela continued, taking his silence as permission to keep talking. "He has never dated much, not since the accident. He has always been the pursued and rarely the pursuer. His focus has always been on his job. I have tried hard to find someone to bring his life balance without success. I'm far better at temporary distraction than I ever have been at seeking life partners."

Anela snorted. "Not that a life partner would ever be allowed or would mean the same if I found a human that I wanted to keep around that long. However, my failings aside, he does need more in his life than work. I have been telling him that for so long, but that man is so focused."

Telling was too weak of a word. Fighting would have been a better word. She appreciated so much what he wanted to do, but she had always thought his task near impossible. There was no changing the ingrained attitudes and false beliefs that had created the rules that ran her life. He was one man against thousands of years of stigma and bias.

"I am sure you've been charming, but have you tried just being human?" Anela snickered at the thought. "I have told you since day one that embracing humanity would make you happier."

"I do remember your human bodies, human life, human needs talk with some pain," Keeler grumbled.

"Good. Try it. Just remember one tiny thing." Anela pushed herself forward to lean over the table closer to Keeler. "He is family. If you hurt him, I swear by everything I am that I will tear you into pieces. I don't care how connected we are, I will find a way to make you pay for it. Okay?"

Although she kept her voice light, her emotions were anything but friendly. Samir was everything to her and she meant every word she said. Keeler nodded his agreement. "I will keep that in mind. For now, I am going to go get some rest. You should too."

"Yes, rest." Anela flopped back into her chair with a little laugh. "Or you can take the time to think about what I said. Not the threats, but about being human. Finding something that makes you happy, it is always worth the effort, even if it scares you to do so. I won't say you are wrong, I know the challenges and it is likely that he will never put his job aside long enough for there to be any chance for either of you, but you would have tried. The worst thing you can ever do is to give up on something without ever trying to make it work."

Keeler didn't bother to answer her as he wandered off to the other room. Anela finished her coffee and wondered what might come of her advice. Samir needed someone in his life that could simply be there for him, who could show him the love and affection he deserved. All he had now was her.

The way he was going, he would end up just like his father. That wasn't necessarily a bad thing, she understood and respected Hamid, but she didn't want that life for Samir.

CHAPTER TWENTY-FIVE

Samir's phone buzzed for his attention and he glanced down to see another message from his dad. *"Call me"*. He resolutely ignored it. He'd received several messages and calls from his father over the last few days and he had no interest in having one more person tell him how badly he'd fucked up—he knew he'd made a mess of things.

What he wanted to avoid the most were the questions his father would ask, ones the council would never consider. He would have to face him eventually but for now, he'd rather hide his head in the sand.

As soon as he had suspected there were wards in place, he should have turned the entire thing over to Liana who would have brought in a full tactical team. For now, he was safe from any serious consequences since, other than the man they had now identified as Connor Yates escaping, things had turned out mostly okay. The only person who had been injured was him, and he'd done a decent job of keeping that concealed.

If it weren't for his family legacy, Samir had no doubt the consequences would have been far more dire. As it was, he sat at one step below full administrative leave, under orders to stay here to keep an eye on Anela. It was nothing more than glorified babysitting and it irked him. He felt useless, sitting here and watching her go about her normal life. He would have preferred doing something to help keep her safe, but he was going to have to follow orders and toe the line if he wanted to keep his job.

He turned back to busying himself in the kitchen. It was one of the few things he could do to try to get his mind off everything as others did their best to track down Connor. Baking was something that had always been relaxing for him, it reminded Samir of his mom. She had often joked that sugar was good for the soul. He knew it wasn't true, but he still baked when he was stressed.

Today he was making cookies, but it wasn't really doing the trick to keep his mind off everything. It wasn't simply the job, it was Keeler too. He hadn't seen or heard from him since they had gotten back. Samir wasn't sure if that was a good or a bad thing. He needed the space, the time to think about things. Except he'd been avoiding thinking about it.

He considered making something more complex and, therefore, more distracting. He grabbed a recipe book off the shelf and started flipping through the pages to find something that would work. Something suitably complex to distract him for more than five minutes. Another five minutes of not thinking about anything.

With a sigh, he closed the book and leaned on the counter. Avoidance was only going to get him so far. He needed someone to talk to besides Anela. He knew all her opinions well. Screw the Nergal, it didn't matter, he should just run off and have a happy little life. It was a tempting thought, but he wanted the chance for Anela to have that future too. For that to happen, he needed to keep working towards change.

"Are you expecting an army?" Keeler's voice asked unexpectedly. Samir whipped around to see him leaning in the doorway as if he had every right to be there. For a second, he wondered if it were wishful thinking, a response to the thoughts he hadn't wanted to acknowledge.

Samir tried to smile, the muscles refusing to make that happen as his emotions ran an exhausting marathon from angry to elated and back to where he had been before being interrupted: wallowing in self-pity. "I… uh… I find baking to be, um, relaxing."

Keeler walked over and rested a far too familiar hand on his back as he reached for one of the chocolate chip cookies. "And delicious. I'm surprised to see you here. I thought you'd be busy with work."

Samir tried to focus on his anger, how much it had hurt that Keeler simply disappeared from his life before they could ever talk about anything that had happened, but that wonderful warmth spreading from where his hand rested was too distracting. It was so similar to that tantalizing tingle when Keeler had touched his leg that first night.

"Liana is taking care of things in the field and office. I've been placed on what amounts to babysitting duty," Samir explained, his voice bitter as he tried to ignore the pleasure in that touch. It was hard to do with the way Keeler stared at him as he nibbled on the stolen cookie and Samir wished he knew what was going on behind those mesmerizing amber eyes. "Why are you here?"

He almost regretted the biting tone in the question when Keeler let his hand drop away. He leaned back against the counter beside Samir and gave a little shrug. "I wanted to see how Anela was doing, but she doesn't appear to be here."

"She went back to work against my advice." Samir grabbed the cookbook to put it away. It was a legitimate enough excuse to not have to look at Keeler. He had no idea why he would have expected a different answer, but he was annoyed anyway. "She'll be home at five if you want to come back then."

"I wish I could. Work's been busy. I don't normally take time off." Keeler stole another cookie; Samir could see that out of the corner of his eye, but he kept his gaze fixed on the counter in front him. "I don't have much time, but I'm glad you're here."

"Are you really?" Samir knew he shouldn't be so snarky towards Keeler. It wasn't fair. They'd all been busy. He noticed the eggs on the counter and went to return them to the fridge, his interest in baking suddenly waning. He closed the fridge and turned to find Keeler standing right behind him. His breath caught in his throat.

"Yes." It was a soft whisper, one that carried the familiar scent reminiscent of vanilla and cloves. It was the same smell that had nearly worn off the shirt he had been wearing when he'd fallen asleep in Keeler's arms back in the hotel. The shirt he had avoided washing because he didn't want that smell to be gone so quickly.

Samir closed his eyes. Dreams were one thing, reality was a different story. It always was. What he wanted and what he could have were vastly different things. He needed to say something, stop anything from happening before it was too late, but his tongue froze in his mouth as fingers brushed across his forehead.

It was a soft, gentle touch, no ethereal warmth, no hint of the pleasure that it could cause, but a shiver ran down his spine anyway. Keeler traced a line down his temple, across his cheek and his lips which parted in response. He opened his eyes as the touch disappeared to find Keeler's face, and those mesmerizing amber eyes, only inches from his.

Samir had tried to explain away the closeness that had grown between them in the previous days. He'd dismissed it as the high emotions of the situation and nothing more. Staring into those eyes, he knew how weak those excuses sounded. This wasn't some passing flight of fancy—not for him—and, knowing he could never have this, was a knife in his chest.

Samir took a step back but there was nowhere to go with the fridge behind him. His mind grasped at the reality of the hard surface. It was enough to remind him that there was a reason he had been trying to push it all away. "Keeler, I can't."

"Why not?" It was an innocent question, but Samir had no idea how to answer it. He took a chance and pushed Keeler back a step so that he could have the space to think clearly. He didn't resist and Samir left his hand resting on Keeler's chest. Telling himself it would help keep the distance between them, knowing that he was doing it because he wasn't ready to let go.

"This isn't a good time. It's too complicated." Both were worthless justifications that meant nothing, and he knew it. He had no idea how to tell him the real reason why he couldn't do this without hurting him and he didn't want to do that.

Keeler's intense eyes held him captive and Samir knew that he was likely reading every emotion. He wished he could know what Keeler was thinking, what he was feeling, but there were no clues to be found in his expressionless face.

"I'm not good at this. At being close to people," Keeler said it slowly, not breaking his intense stare. "But I'm willing to try. Don't you think it's worth it? To try?"

Samir could feel Keeler's heart pounding as hard as his own. He didn't know how to answer that question honestly without giving him false hope. If things were different, he would want to see if there was something more here, if it could go somewhere, but no matter what his feelings were, it wasn't enough to risk everything. His career, his life, he was already on thin ice as it was.

Keeler reached out, cupping Samir's face much as he had that first time, though there was none of that same blissful pleasure beyond the normal warmth of his touch. Samir knew he should say something as Keeler closed the distance between them. He gave no resistance, didn't try to stop him, though his hand stayed firmly where it was against Keeler's chest.

Keeler didn't hesitate as he leaned in to kiss Samir. Those soft, sweet lips pressed against his. No hint of the power he could wield, not a touch of the ethereal warmth that Samir longed for. There was nothing here beyond ordinary passion and he could feel the same desire, a longing for more than this rise within.

Without thinking, Samir reached around and pulled Keeler closer, pressing hard against him. As he lost himself in this simple kiss, he ignored the thoughts in the back of his mind. His worries of what the council would say if they knew. In this moment, he didn't care. All he wanted, all he cared about, was this beautiful warmth spreading through him and he allowed himself to be submerged by the otherworldly sense of pleasure that filled him.

Like a wildfire, the warmth and desire grew and spread. It stemmed not only from where their lips met but it surrounded him, carried him away on a tidal wave. It made him forget everything, driving him to yearn for more. His head spun as Keeler pulled away taking all the incredible sensations that he had created with him, except for a slight tingle of ethereal pleasure that still burned on his lips.

"Sorry," Keeler whispered. "I don't know how to do this and not…"

"Not?" Samir prompted him to continue. An apology was one of the last things he'd expected. Not for something that he wasn't even sure could fully be controlled. He could read the struggle in Keeler's eyes as he tried to find words to explain something that he may never have described before. Samir knew this couldn't be easy for him.

"And not get carried away." It was barely more than a breathy whisper, his face betraying none of the emotion that Samir could feel coming from him and his heart broke a little more. Until now, he hadn't realized how much lay behind that mask that Keeler wore. Knowing what he had to do made this knowledge that much more painful.

"It's okay." He tucked a loose strand of hair behind Keeler's ear. Samir leaned in and kissed him. Gentle, soft, and undemanding. He knew he probably shouldn't, but he couldn't resist one last chance to be this close. "But I mean it, Kees. I can't do this even if I wanted to."

"Do you want to?"

"It doesn't matter if I did." Samir sighed and pushed past him to stand on the other side of the kitchen. He needed some space between them, to cool his head and his body. That close to Keeler and he found it hard to think straight. He needed to keep a level head. "My job…"

"Your job isn't you." Keeler was quick to point out, annoyance tinged his voice. "You deserve more in your life than your job. You deserve the same happiness every other person deserves."

"I know I do, and I wish I could, but I can't." Samir didn't want to have to state the obvious. He knew if he tried to say it that it would come out all wrong.

"Why not?" Keeler pushed the issue. "It's a part of being human, why deny yourself a chance to have a relationship?"

"Because I can't risk everything I've accomplished on a relationship with you." Samir winced as he said those words. They sounded even harsher in reality than they had in his head, but it needed to be out there so that there were no misunderstandings. It was the cold, cruel truth that he couldn't avoid no matter how much he wished he could.

"I see." Those two words put a chill in the air between them that couldn't be ignored. "It's because I'm not human, isn't it?"

Samir looked away, not able to answer. He wanted desperately to say that it didn't matter, and if things were different, he wouldn't have cared.

"I can look past what you do for a living. Can't you look past that?"

"I..." Samir swallowed back the words he wished he could say and spat out the ones that he wished he didn't have to. "I can't."

He didn't look up as he spoke, regretting the words the moment they left his mouth. It felt like the temperature in the room dropped several more degrees. He waited for a response, another impassioned plea, but that wasn't what he got. Instead, he heard the front door slam without another word.

Samir winced at the sound and looked at the now empty kitchen. He wondered if he had made a mistake. He'd spent his entire life dedicated to his job. His life was the job as far as he was concerned and to say yes to what Keeler was proposing would mean the end of his career. The end of everything he had spent his entire life working towards. It wasn't fair of Keeler to ask that of him.

A timer buzzed and Samir jumped at the unexpected sound. He rushed to take the last batch of the cookies out of the oven. His mind still clouded with indecision. There was no amount of baking in the world that would calm him now. He wished his mom were still around to talk to. She would have known what to do. She had always been good with advice. He already knew what his father would say if he asked him. Don't give up on what you've worked so hard for.

Theoretical advice wasn't going to help now, but he knew one thing. He didn't want to leave it like this, but he didn't know how to fix it either.

CHAPTER TWENTY-SIX

Anela came home to find Samir curled up on the couch watching Casablanca. It was an immediate tip-off that something was more wrong than usual. He only ever watched it when he was upset, and baking wasn't enough to take his mind off of whatever was wrong. Last time he'd binged on it was after Kate, his mother, had passed.

Normally, she didn't intrude on his emotions, but she wanted to know what she was walking in on. She sampled carefully and considered what he was feeling. Remorse, sadness, anger, longing, hopelessness. So many sad emotions and she knew not all of it could stem from the situation with his job. He was too wrapped up in the movie that he never noticed her until she leaned over the couch to wrap her arms around him. "What is wrong, my dear Sami?"

Samir paused the movie. "Nothing."

"That is not a 'nothing happened' movie. That is a 'my heart is breaking, and I don't know how to handle it' movie."

Anela let go and walked around the couch to sit beside him. "Talk to me, tell me all about it."

Samir looked away from her. "I'd really rather not talk about it."

Anela wrapped her arms around him and snuggled in closer. "Yes, you do. Don't make me have to give you a lecture. I don't like having to lecture anyone, not even you. Tell your Auntie Annie what's wrong."

Samir smiled at that reference, though it was a pale ghost of his usual cheery grin. She rarely referred to herself as 'Auntie Annie' anymore. He hadn't even called her that since he was a little kid. He leaned into her embrace. He'd always come to her for advice and comfort, now was no different except that he had only talked to her about his job. She had been hoping he would bring up the topic of Keeler on his own, but so far that hadn't happened. "It's just, I don't know, complicated."

"Does this have to do with your feelings for Keeler or did you finally talk to your father?" Anela asked knowing those were two things he was avoiding the most that might have set him off. She always had a way of getting right to the source of a problem even when he had been trying to keep things secret. She even had him convinced as a child that she was psychic.

"I don't have feelings for him." Samir said though his face made it clear to her that he did. There was no need to read his emotions for that.

"Of all things you could choose to do, you lie about your emotions to me?" Anela tutted. She was mildly surprised that he hadn't jumped on the easier option of claiming he had spoken with Hamid. That was bound to be an upsetting conversation, but his mind must have been too consumed with thoughts of Keeler to even try for subterfuge over an outright lie. "You ought to know better than that."

"Anela, please, I really don't want to talk about it." Samir raised the remote to start the movie again and she snatched it out of his hand. She'd had enough with his sulking this week. She understood that he was going through a lot, but a week was plenty of time. He needed to get his shit together and deal with it.

"But I do want to talk about it," Anela insisted, "you have been distracted and since the disciplinary hearing, and that turned out better than it could have. Now, this. I don't like it."

"You don't have to like it," Samir muttered as he tried half-heartedly to wrestle the remote away from her, but she was more agile and far more determined to get her way.

"I'm worried about you." Anela chucked the remote across the room and yanked Samir back down when he tried to get up to go get it. One way or another, she was going to make him listen and talk to her. "I know the job thing is a shit deal and I appreciate what you did for me. Things don't look so great right now, and maybe that's for the best. You can focus on other aspects of your life instead."

"Anela, I am not in the mood. I want to watch my movie." Samir insisted, though he didn't try to retrieve the remote this time. Instead, he crossed his arms and leaned back on the couch. His eyes fixed on the frozen screen in front of him. She sighed, he was as stubborn and bullheaded as his father—not that she'd ever say that to him.

"Do we start with your job? How you're avoiding your father's calls? Or do we talk about your feelings for Keeler and why they are suddenly an issue?" Anela poked Samir hard enough in the ribs to make him wince. She hated hurting him, but she wanted to make sure she had his attention. "I'm thinking the last one judging by that spike of guilt and regret. What happened and you are going to talk to me about it?"

"I'm done here." He tried to get up again and this time she was sure he meant to leave the room. She was done trying to be nice. Anela grabbed his arm but didn't try to pull him back down. It had been a long time since she'd used her powers like this, but that made no difference. Where Keeler's touch was pleasurable to most, hers caused pain and she sent it coursing through him. His legs gave way and he crumpled back onto the couch.

"I'm not playing around, Samir." Anela glared at him as she slowly loosened her grip on his arm. "We're talking about this."

"What the fuck, Anela?" He rubbed at his chest as he tried to catch his breath. "When did you learn to do that?"

"Doesn't matter when I learned that, but I will do it again if you don't talk about what's going on," Anela said. He tried to stare her down, but that was not a game he would win at either. It was killing her a little to be so forceful when everything inside her screamed to protect him. To hug away his pain, but she could do that later—when he had stopped acting like an idiot.

"Fine. Whatever." Samir crossed his arms again and went back to staring at the stilled frame on the screen, Ingrid Bergman holding a gun on her former lover.

Anela weighed her words carefully. None of her previous tactics had worked. Logic, sympathy, cajoling or even using brute force as she had just now, it was all met with excuses, avoidance, or silence. She needed to try something new.

"Some humans never grow up do they?" Anela rolled her eyes, her voice relaxing back to its normally playful tones. "You are no exception. You used to do the same thing when you were eight years old. I would have hoped you'd have progressed past this in thirty years."

"I told you that I didn't want to talk about it. Can't you just let things be this once? It's like the blind dates you keep trying to set me up on." Samir turned to face her. "My life was fine the way it was, whether you agreed with it or not. I had a goal, a raison d'etre. Why do you think you need to keep interfering?"

"Oh, is it that old argument?" Anela shook her head and sighed. "That is not a life. Maybe you think I don't know what it means to be human because I'm not one, but I think I have learned to embrace humanity more than most of your race. Your lives are short, a burst of light in the endless night sky of this universe, and you waste your little time chasing after all the wrong things."

"You're telling me that trying to change the policies and opinions of the Nergal on your people is a useless endeavor?" Samir raised an eyebrow at her. "That your freedom and rights are not worth my time?"

"It's a noble goal, I won't argue that, but it isn't enough for you to give up every chance of a life outside of your job." Anela leaned in, her nose nearly touching his as she tapped a finger against his chest with each word to emphasize her point. "You. Are. Not. Your. Job."

"You sound like him." Samir looked down at his lap.

"Him, who?" She was sure she knew the answer to that question. His father would never say such a thing. Hamid had driven everyone away because his job was always his priority. She was the closest thing he had left to a personal confidant, and even then, he never told her everything. She didn't want that for Samir, he deserved so much more. Hamid had the chance for more, but it had been destroyed—not by him, but by the same circumstances that had driven him to focus only on his work.

Samir glared at her but didn't answer. He was still trying to avoid the topic, but his silence was answer enough for her.

"Ah. So, this is about Keeler." Anela smirked. "Is all this time off making you miss his company? Longing for a little something more than playing my happy little housewife?"

"Anela, space." Samir reminded her. She had never been good at remembering that there was such a thing as personal space. She moved away, choosing to snuggle up beside him on the couch once again, both her arms wrapped around one of his.

"That does not answer my question though." Anela waited for him to say something. Samir knew she would outwait him with ease. She had the patience of an eternal being. "Why is it that every time I say Keeler's name you suddenly have a surge of guilt? Those emotions weren't there the other day."

"It's not fair for you to read my emotions."

"You should be used to that by now." Anela studied his face, trying to figure out what may have happened between yesterday and today. She sat up sharply as the thought occurred to her. "He was here, wasn't he? What happened? What foolish, stupid thing did you say to him?"

Samir hung his head, refusing to look at her. All that guilt, regret, and so much pain. She felt bad for him, but that didn't mean she would back off until she got the truth. She softened her voice. "My darling, tell me what happened."

"He was here. He told me he liked me. I told him it couldn't work."

"Is that all?" She doubted it was as simple as he was saying—it rarely ever was.

"More or less," Samir mumbled. "Honestly, I want to put it behind me."

"You once spent two days agonizing over the fact that you may have accidentally offended a stranger." Anela wasn't about to let him sit here and torture himself in silence. She knew him too well. If he didn't talk about it or find a way to put his guilt to rest, he'd never stop obsessing over it. "Putting things behind you is not a strength. You are a good man, Samir, but you are not good at leaving your trespasses behind."

"No, maybe I'm not but… I don't know. I shouldn't have said what I said, but what else could I have said?" Samir looked at her, his emotions begging her for answers.

"Maybe if you told me what you said I can tell you how you should have said it better." Anela relaxed back against Samir now that she knew he wasn't going to keep avoiding the subject. She hated to see him so upset.

"He asked if I could look past the fact that he wasn't human, and I told him that I couldn't. I didn't mean it the way he took it, but he didn't let me explain that to him." Samir sighed. "I don't know if he realizes that asking me to give him a chance could mean my job and everything I've been working so hard for."

"Do you honestly still think you can create a kinder, more understanding Nergal?" Anela frowned. "You've been the director for five years now and every time you try to push through modified policies, you're blocked. The Laibiruzi Institute is stuck in its ways and, one day, you will have to come to terms with that reality."

"That's not true," Samir argued. "I've had some minor successes. Not everything has been a fruitless struggle."

"But each time it's been an uphill battle." Anela hugged him tighter. "I appreciate that you want to change things, but that isn't what this is about. You need to realize that eventually you will be forced to make a decision between doing what is right for you or doing what your job demands of you."

"I can't have it both ways forever, can I?"

"No, you can't. No one ever can, look at your parents as an example." Samir winced at that reminder. Anela knew that it wasn't just the job that had gotten between Hamid and Kate, but that was the final straw in the camel's back. Though he was out of the house when the split came, it had hurt him deeply. It was there, she was sure, that the rift between him and his father became irreparable, but she used that wedge to her advantage now. "Do you want to end up like your father?"

"He's respected." Samir replied. Anela raised an eyebrow at that. It was true, but that wasn't enough, not even close.

"Sami, darling, you are better than that. You deserve more than the job." Anela kept her voice soft and gentle. They'd had this conversation a thousand times in a thousand different ways. She always hoped that he would come to see it from her point of view one day.

"I know, but I still think I can make a difference. Not to mention if I were to step down it would likely be Liana who would take my place." Samir frowned. "She's good at the job, but she has never learned how to bend. It's always the rules with her and, as much as I like her, she isn't the best choice. With her in charge, everything that I have worked so hard for will disappear."

"It'll always be something, won't it?" Anela asked. She couldn't argue his point. She agreed with him, but she'd been through worse directors than what Liana would be.

"Not forever, no." Samir smiled at her.

"No, because eventually, you will pass on as all other mortals do." Anela couldn't keep the pain out of her voice as she said it. She had no idea what she would do after Samir was gone. He had no family for her to adopt in the future. She would be alone, mostly. She did have Keeler now, but that wasn't the same.

"I am sure I will find time for a life before that day." Samir nudged her. "Don't be sad. I've got a long life left to live."

"That is what all of you say." Anela didn't bother to point out the risks that came with his job on top of the already dangerous venture of being a person. "Please, don't leave it too long."

"I won't, I promise," Samir said.

"And apologize to Keeler. I am sure if you explained it gently then he will understand your position." Anela wasn't sure he would understand, but she hoped that he would.

"I will." Samir pushed himself up from the couch to go get the remote.

"Promise?" Anela asked.

"Yes, I promise." Samir flopped back on the couch and cuddled up with her again. "Can I finish the movie now?"

"Yes." Anela wiggled into a more comfortable position. "Let's watch your silly little movie until you feel better."

CHAPTER TWENTY-SEVEN

One week. It was all he could take of Anela's constant pestering before he gave in and forced himself to go see Keeler. His stomach was doing somersaults when he stepped on the elevator and the ride to the top took a century.

When the doors opened to let him out, his feet stuck to the floor. They started to slide closed, his hand shot out to stop them. It was sheer willpower that got him to move before the doors tried to close again. He stepped into the reception area, feeling as though almost all the air had been sucked from the room, leaving him struggling to breathe.

This shouldn't be so hard.

He couldn't bear the thought of waiting around the way he had the last time he'd come here. The thought of Keeler refusing to see him, not giving him a chance to say his apology drove him forward. With the main receptionist busy on the phone, he marched right past and towards the back of the building.

He could hear her shouting something, and he broke into a run. He needed to get this over with and move on with things. He pushed through the frosted glass doors. Jenny had already shot to her feet, her mouth agape as she stared at him. It took a few seconds of her staring at him before she spoke. "Samir?"

"Oh, um, Jenny, right? Hi. I, um…" Samir stood in the center of the room, his eyes fixed on the doors to Keeler's office and not the young woman who had addressed him. He was so close, that door was all that stood between him and the apology that he had been putting off. He didn't even know if Keeler would be willing to see him or would listen to what he had to say. Not that it mattered, he was going to say his piece one way or another.

"Yes, did reception let you in because—" Jenny's words were cut off by the doors slamming open to reveal two security officers. They immediately zoned in on Samir and grabbed him. He didn't fight them; he wasn't willing to cause that kind of scene to get Keeler's attention.

"It's alright," Jenny said, her voice calm, even, and full of authority. Samir admired her ability to keep her wits about her, but that was probably why she managed to be in the position she was. He had no doubt that Keeler had no time for people who couldn't handle themselves when things got tough. "He can stay, and I'll be sure to apprise him on proper protocol for future visits."

"Yes, ma'am." One of the security guards nodded her head at Jenny before letting go of Samir. Jenny and Samir both stood in silence until the doors closed on the guards.

"Well, that would explain why I wasn't buzzed." Jenny chuckled. "Here to see Mr. Lim on personal business again? Not planning to run away for several days on some mysterious trip, I hope. We've barely got things back on a normal schedule again."

"Yes, erm, no. I mean. We're not going anywhere, but I would like to talk to him if he's willing to see me. Is he busy?" Samir grimaced as he realized that he would almost prefer for Keeler to be busy than to know that he had outright refused to see him.

"He is on a conference call right now, but he should be finished shortly." Jenny took her seat and motioned for him to take a seat as well. Samir glanced at the offered seat and found that he didn't want to sit. He was too wound up, too nervous. He would have paced if he didn't feel so awkward doing so with an audience. He forced himself to pretend to act normal as he perched on the edge of one of the chairs, his foot tapping incessantly against the floor.

His mind circled, thoughts crowded in on each other, worry and fear battled for dominance inside his head. It was too much. He needed a distraction, almost anything would do now, but he couldn't sit here silently and let his own brain torture him more than anyone else ever could.

"So, how have you been?" Samir asked. He didn't know her well enough to ask her anything else.

"I'm fine, thanks." She looked perplexed as he pulled his chair towards her desk. "Are you okay?"

Samir had no idea how to even answer that. He wasn't okay and he wanted nothing more than to run away, to avoid this confrontation, despite his rational mind insisting that it wouldn't be so bad. "Yeah, I just... I..."

"You're nervous about something. I get it. If it makes you feel better, then you can sit there." She started typing again and stopped after a few keystrokes. "You know what? I need to ask you something personal."

"Uh, okay."

"He's never had a personal visit from anyone ever. You show up and he disappears for several days, dropping a lot of work in my lap." She glanced at a glowing light on the phone before looking back at Samir. "He came back exhausted and distracted but, for him, strangely happy."

"Oh." Samir tried not to read into that as he waited for her to ask the question she was leading up to.

"Now, for the last week or so, he's been withdrawn and almost irritable. I know, he generally isn't the most communicative person, but this is extreme. I am dying to find out what happened, but it's not my place to ask." She raised her eyebrows in lieu of the question she insisted that she wasn't going to say aloud.

Had he been in a better mood, Samir would have laughed. He enjoyed her inquisitive nature and her roundabout way of asking a question without asking a question. He considered his answer carefully, but he had no idea how to answer it without being overly evasive. "It's complicated."

"Complicated?" Jenny grinned and leaned over the desk. "Not my place to ask, but are you dating? You don't have to answer that, but when you work for a man like Mr. Lim you start to wonder about things. I am sure doing more than quiet contemplation of such things has ended many a career here, so I rarely express my curiosity. Besides, I wasn't hired to help keep his personal life in order, I was hired to make sure his job ran smoothly."

This time Samir did chuckle, he had been right. She was just the distraction he needed to keep his thoughts from spiralling. She seemed so intensely intrigued about the possibility that this man that had no personal life might be dating anyone. He wasn't even sure how to answer the question other than with the basic truth. "No, we're not dating."

"Oh." She seemed a little disappointed, but it didn't last long as she gave him a good look over. "So, are you seeing anyone?"

"I, uh… Well…" Samir stammered and shifted in his seat. Even if he were interested in dating her, he didn't think it would have been a wise idea. He decided to be honest with her and hoped that she wouldn't press for a more concrete answer. "I don't think that would be a, um, a good idea."

"Ah, sorry." She smiled professionally and glanced back at the glowing light. He wondered how much longer the phone call would last. He thought about leaving before Keeler was finished, but that would mean facing Anela. "He's done now, shall I let him know you're here?"

"Sure." Samir swallowed back the lump in his throat and tried to go over the speech he had prepared. He was sure he would forget something or say it all wrong. That was only if Keeler would listen to him.

Jenny raised an eyebrow and jerked her head towards the wall where the chair belonged. Samir got the picture and put the chair back. He stayed standing though but was sure to stay a respectful distance away from Jenny's desk. He listened closely to every word and wished he could hear the other end of the conversation as well.

"Samir Amin is here to see you."

…

"I'm sorry, sir, what?"

…

"Um, okay." Jenny hung up the phone looking perplexed. "He said he'd be right out."

"Okay." Samir cleared his throat and ran through the speech for what may have been the millionth time. It was simple enough, all he had to do was apologize for what he said and explain why he couldn't look past what Keeler was. Anela had made it seem so simple and he tried to focus on everything she had told him to say.

But he still couldn't escape the feeling that he was going to fuck it up all over again.

Keeler opened the door and leaned against the frame. He didn't step into the waiting area as he stared at Samir with a cold, hard look. He could see the anger from their argument simmering in his eyes. He tried to remember the words he had prepared, but they were lost. Coming here had been a mistake. He wasn't ready to face Keeler yet.

"What?" It was a single, terse word that held so much meaning behind it. Samir knew he couldn't keep standing here and staring in silence. He had come here for a reason. He needed to say something to him, but his tongue refused to form words.

Keeler turned to go back into his office and Samir knew his only chance to say anything was slipping away.

"I'm sorry," He blurted out. No build up, no 'can we talk in private'. That was all he had, the best he could do at this moment. Keeler turned back to face him but stayed silent though his eyebrow raised slightly. It was obvious that he was waiting for a more specific apology. Samir gave his head a shake and took a deep breath. "Can we talk in your office?"

"No." Keeler crossed his arms, not giving him anything to work with. Samir glanced at Jenny then back at Keeler. He hadn't been prepared to do this with an audience. Slowly, some of what he had wanted to say was coming back to him, but none of it was the sort of thing he could say in front of others. He would have to choose his words carefully.

"I'm sorry about what I said the other day." Samir's face wrinkled as he struggled to find the right words. "It was uncalled for, for me to say what I did to you and I should have done a better job of explaining myself. I am so sorry that I hurt you. Can you please forgive me, and can we talk about it?"

Silence stretched long enough that Samir wished the floor would open up and swallow him whole. He was sure he deserved this punishment, waiting for any sort of response, the only positive being the Keeler hadn't left and slammed the door in his face—not yet anyway.

"I don't know if I'm ready to hear what you have to say." It was a fair answer. Samir wasn't sure he was ready to say it either, but it had to be now.

"Kees, please. I want to explain myself," Samir pleaded. He took a chance and walked halfway to him. "Give me a chance to explain."

"A chance…" Keeler repeated hesitantly, letting those two words hang in the air for what seemed like forever. "Tell me, why should I do that?"

"You owe me that much," Samir said, not sure if he believed that. In truth, he was the one who owed Keeler for saving his life, for trying to be so understanding when they were searching for Anela. For simply trusting him when he could have never taken the risks he did. He needed to find a way to explain everything without hurting him, again. "Maybe not. I don't know. Tell me what I can do to convince you."

He was terrified the answer would be 'nothing', that all this worry and stress would be for naught. All he wanted was not to leave this legacy of pain behind him. Keeler deserved so much more than the harsh words he'd received.

Perhaps Anela was right in that he deserved more too, but that wasn't what mattered as he waited for an answer.

CHAPTER TWENTY-EIGHT

Keeler could feel the truth of every word Samir said, but he wasn't sure what to do with it. There was still that indecision and fear. He could feel so many emotions, but none of them told him that Samir was ready to give him more than friendship—if even that. He knew he should give him a chance to explain his side of things, but it was easier to be angry.

And to use it as a knife to sever the ties that bound him to this man. To cut away the longing for what had been denied to him.

Even though he wanted to hold onto the anger, he knew what had been said hadn't been in anger, and it wasn't a lie. It was his problem that the truth hurt, not Samir's. Staring into those warm eyes, feeling the fear, the insecurity and the quiet panic that were there, he knew he needed to do something other than keep staring in silence. He could either turn away and close the door or take the time to talk about things like Samir wanted.

Or he could do what he wanted to do if Samir would let him. One last goodbye because he didn't think there would ever be another chance for this. "On one condition…"

Keeler closed the distance between them, his movements slow and careful. He stopped less than a foot from Samir. He wondered if this was a mistake, but being this close to that sweet essence, knowing that it was only half the attraction, he knew that it didn't matter to him. He reached up and kissed Samir.

Samir reacted much like he had in the kitchen. Pulling Keeler closer, allowing himself to be open to everything that Keeler was, letting him dive into that sweetness and touch a soul that he wanted to never part with. That tender touch, a passion that melted through him and surrounded Keeler. He wanted more of this and it killed him that he couldn't have it. All he could ever have would be the memories of these stolen moments.

"Shit!" Jenny cried as her coffee spread across the desk. She jumped up and moved the papers out of the way, her reaction breaking the mood and the intimacy of the moment. Samir pulled away. Had he even known how; Keeler might have cried but that was a human reaction he had never learned, and he had no idea how to even begin to express that pain that carved a hole through him.

"Kees, I can't."

The words were so full of remorse. It broke Keeler's heart to hear it, but he understood that it needed to be said. He couldn't let himself get carried away again. Samir had come here to apologize and explain, not ignite the flame of passion that barely had a chance to even exist.

"I know. Let's talk." Keeler glanced over at Jenny who was desperately trying to sop up the coffee. He took Samir by the hand and led him into the office. "Please hold my calls."

"Right, yes," Jenny stuttered as the door closed on her, cutting off the rest of what she was trying to say.

Keeler brought him over to the couch and took a seat. Samir hesitated before sitting beside him, still holding his hand. Keeler broke the awkwardness of the moment. "I appreciate you apologizing and I'm sorry that I may have overreacted."

"No, I said it all wrong. I want you to understand why I can't say yes to this." Samir took a deep breath before continuing. "I have spent my time with the Nergal working towards changes in policy and attitude. It's been a hard, uphill battle to affect any of the changes I long to make, but it's my life's work. If I were to..."

Samir took another deep breath. Even without the ability to read emotions, Keeler knew how hard this had to be on him. He waited patiently, giving his hand a little squeeze of encouragement even though he wished he could do more than that.

"If I were to pursue a relationship with you then I would be putting all of that at risk. I want to be able to say, 'to hell with it' and give in to my emotions, but that isn't something I can do. When you asked me to look past what you are, you were asking me to give up on a lifelong goal." Samir averted his eyes.

The silence grew, but Keeler didn't pull his hands away. His mind tried to give him ideas of how it could work, reasons and impassioned pleas to convince Samir to change his mind. He wasn't going to do any of that. Samir deserved that from him, respect and acceptance of the decision he had made.

Samir looked back up at him, and Keeler still struggled to find the words that he needed to say. He wasn't sure how much longer that Samir would be able to deal with this lack of response. He wasn't at a point where he was able to simply accept and walk away.

"You still deserve more than that." Keeler insisted quietly.

"Maybe I do, but this is the way things are." Samir stared down at their intertwined hands and Keeler was glad he hadn't pulled away completely yet. A slow release, as torturous as it could be, was easier to deal with. "As long as I am a part of the Nergal, there is no chance for us."

Keeler heard that slight break in Samir's voice on the word 'us'. In another sentence, it could have been beautiful. "And after that?

"After that?" Samir sounded confused, as if he hadn't considered the possibility of ever not being with the Nergal. "I can't say 'never' because I have feelings for you and I wish I had the freedom to explore them, but I don't have that right now."

"You can't say 'never'…" Keeler repeated those words and let them roll through his mind as he considered what it meant. It reflected much of what he had felt when he kissed Samir. He was happy that he hadn't been wrong. This was, in a small way, a step forward.

"Not never, just not now. It's all I can offer you." Samir tried to smile, but it was nothing more than a pale approximation that did nothing to hide the sadness in his eyes. "I wish I had more."

"And what if they didn't need to know?" Keeler offered. It was a long shot, he knew that, but there was never harm in trying.

"If only that were possible." Samir shook his head. "There is no way I could hide something like this from them. Even if I thought I could hide it, there is a chance that they would find out. If that happened, it would be my job and your freedom. I can't take the risk."

Keeler nodded and reached out to cup Samir's face, wishing for more than this. He had time. It was the one thing he had too much to spare. He wanted to ardently beg, but it wasn't in his nature and he didn't think it would make any difference. He could feel the resolve behind the words even if they were colored with pain and sadness.

"Then I guess there is nothing more to say?" Keeler wasn't sure what he should be feeling. Too many emotions vied for dominance, none of which he was accustomed to dealing with. He didn't even know how to explain that to Samir, to tell him that he had brought light to a long dark life. He didn't have the words to begin a conversation like that.

"No, there's not." Samir lifted Keeler's hand and kissed his palm before letting go. "I should leave."

"I—" Keeler wasn't sure what he was going to say, only that he didn't want Samir to leave yet. He needed more time to say goodbye, this wasn't enough, but the world spun as a strange sensation washed through him, and the world blurred.

"Kees?" Samir reached for him and quickly drew back as an arc of lightning stuck out from him. "Keeler?"

Keeler could hear Samir, could feel his concern more sharply than he had ever felt another's emotions before. He closed his eyes and tried to focus on forming the words he needed to say. Energy surged forth, filling the body that had been his home for so long. It took everything he had to keep it from exploding outward and hurting Samir. He had to say something, but words were becoming harder to form as the seconds passed. He pushed one simple word from his uncooperative body, not sure how clearly it would be heard.

"Go."

Keeler was losing his fight. He could feel the energy burst forth from this vessel. There was nothing he could do. The one thing he had longed for, he now wanted to avoid.

He was being released.

CHAPTER TWENTY-NINE

Samir had seen a lot of things in his career and it took more than a few moments for him to realize what was happening. This was an uncontrolled release. He ducked as a bolt of lightning struck a lamp nearby. He backed away as he tried to think of any spell or ritual that might help contain Keeler, but there was nothing he could do. Not at this point and not without help.

Another bolt struck near his feet and charred the floor. It was a reminder that there were energy levels his ward could not save him from, and he was sure that if one of those bolts struck him, he would not survive. Samir dived out the door, thankful that this one was of a more solid construction than the frosted glass one for the outer office.

"What the hell is going on?" Jenny shouted as Samir charged into the outer office and slammed the door closed behind him. It wasn't soon enough to stop a bolt of lightning from coming through after him. It struck a plant by the desk which immediately caught fire. "Holy shit!"

Samir darted behind the desk and hauled her to the ground. "No time to explain. Get down."

"What the hell was that? Where's Mr. Lim?" She tried to stand up again, but Samir yanked her back down. Jenny stayed down when a loud crash shook the office and a blinding white light poured out through the cracks of the door. Samir waited until everything was still but the dust drifting down from the ceiling tiles.

Samir peered over the desk to see the door to Keeler's office sitting crooked on its hinges, intense light still pouring through. He ducked back down and saw a fire extinguisher under Jenny's desk. He grabbed it and pressed it in her hands "You wouldn't understand, but it should be okay now. Take care of the shrub fire and can you go make sure security doesn't interfere? I don't have time for that kind of damage control."

"What wouldn't I understand? What is going on?" She crawled out from under the desk and squinted at the bright light that spilled out through the door into the inner office. "What was that?"

"I'll explain later. First, fire and security." Samir gave her a gentle shove towards the glass doors where he could see the shadowy forms of people that were gathering on the other side. "Please, keep everyone out of here while I deal with this."

Jenny narrowed her eyes and pursed her lips as she took precious seconds to think about what he was asking before she jogged over to the doors. She turned the bolt, locking them before turning back, putting out the fire that used to be her ficus, and faced Samir. "Explain before someone gets the bright idea to break the door because my patience is wearing thin and I do not like being asked to do things without a damned good reason to be doing them."

Explaining to Jenny that her boss wasn't a human but a six-thousand-year-old being with god-like powers that had been released from his human prison wasn't an easy thing to do. He had no ready lies to tell her, nothing to make it easier, and he wanted to get into the room to find out what had happened in there. "Jenny, I want to tell you, but this isn't something that can be explained with a few easy words. What do you want me to tell you?"

They both jumped when someone banged on the door, followed by the faint sound of a voice asking if everything was okay in there. "No long story, short version?"

Samir gritted his teeth to keep a less than kind response from leaving his lips. "Your boss isn't human."

Jenny blinked and her brow furrowed as she processed that simple statement. "Guess that explains a few things. Details later then. No squirming out of it."

Samir nodded, grateful that she had accepted the truth with such ease and decorum. He turned his back on her as she opened the glass doors enough to poke her head through. He didn't listen to what she was saying, but he was confident that she would be able to calm the nerves of those outside, though his own were on edge as he approached the door to the inner office unsure of what he would find in there.

A glance over his shoulder showed that Jenny had everything under control. He slipped into the room and his first thought was that he wished that he had a pair of sunglasses with him. He put a hand in front of his face and almost swore he could see his bones as if he had stepped into a giant x-ray machine. He wasn't sure how it wasn't burning him.

"Can we, uh, turn the lights down in here?" He asked, not thinking he would get any response, but the light dimmed.

Samir blinked away the spots that danced in front of his eyes to see for the first time, the being that had called himself Keeler in a human form. It was still Keeler though, that hadn't changed, and he struggled to wrap his mind around that fact. He'd seen plenty of these kinds of beings in his time, but this was the first time seeing one that he had known as human.

"Kees?" He hated that quiver in his voice as he asked and tried to quell the fear inside of him that told him this was dangerous, that these beings were unpredictable. It was what had been steeped into him through years of training. He reminded himself that he knew this being, this was Keeler. Trapped in a body or not, he knew him.

His inquiry was met with a brief pulse of light, not enough to blind him but he didn't think it was a coincidence. Most, not all, of the beings he encountered struggled with verbal communication, he'd been prepared for that and took the pulse as a positive response.

"Are you okay?" Another simple pulse, but this time a tendril of light reached out towards him and stopped short of touching him. He stared at it, knowing what Keeler wanted. He had no idea what would happen if he allowed the tendril to contact his skin. He could see the smoke still rising from the places where lightning had struck, knowing it could have killed him.

"Okay." He ignored the voice at the back of his mind that screamed at him for his foolishness. It sounded far too much like his father. This was a risk, he knew that, but he didn't know any other way to communicate. He needed to try. He closed his eyes, stepped farther into the room, and braced himself for anything.

He couldn't really feel the tendril of light brushing against his face, other than that familiar warmth and tingle. It was like every time that Keeler had reached out to him, but a thousand times stronger. He closed his eyes, enjoying the sensation. It felt like he was floating, an island on a lake of sweet, warm light. It lasted for a long second before the emotions came crashing in on him.

He'd never felt anything so intensely in his life, not even his own emotions could compare. He had no basis to equate them to, nothing that would even begin to help him understand everything that he felt. Some of these emotions were entirely alien to him. There were others that he understood, ones that he knew Keeler felt, but not the extent to which he felt them. Not until now as they carried him away to somewhere else.

An aching loneliness dug at him and carved its way into his soul until there was nothing left but a canyon of darkness that he could not see across. It made him want to weep, but as he recognized it the emotion passed and another one came crashing down on him. It was like he was standing inside the sun itself and it filled the dark corners of the canyon that loneliness had built. It burned him in a way that made him crave more. More and more emotions rushed through him until he thought he would lose himself to the onslaught.

Then they stopped. Samir staggered a few feet forward. He tried to catch himself on the desk but missed and landed on his knees. Slowly, he realized that it was only him in his head and the emotions were his own. He could remember how it felt, how intense and overwhelming it was. He looked back up at Keeler and wondered if these emotions had been as intense when he was trapped in his human prison. He couldn't imagine what it must have been like, to feel things that intensely and have no way to express it.

It was not a thought that did him any good now. He had more important things to deal with, like the ten-foot-tall pillar of light that he was staring at. Samir shoved himself back to his feet. "That was a bit much. Easier next time, okay?"

His response was another pulse of light and, once again, the tendril reached out to caress his face. Samir braced himself for another barrage of emotional discord, but this time it was calm and peaceful. Still and light, he could stay here forever, but he didn't have forever. He had no idea how this kind of communication worked, but he needed to try something.

"Keeler?" Samir called out into the stillness. No one spoke back to him, but he got a sense of affirmation and smiled. He should have figured that they communicated through emotions after all the time he had spent with Anela. Her emotions drove her, they were everything, but he had never associated that with Keeler. Obviously, he'd been wrong there. "Are you okay?"

It was too complicated of a question. While this time an emotional response did not overwhelm him, it was far too nuanced to decipher. He had to keep it simpler until he got a handle on understanding this form of communication. "Do you know what happened?"

Confusion, frustration, and despair were the predominant emotions in the response. He could understand how something like this would throw him for a loop. It was clear that this had been a surprise for Keeler as it had been for him. A thought occurred to him. "Can you sense Anela?"

Fear and worry. It confirmed for Samir his suppositions. This was not limited to Keeler but affected Anela as well. He had no idea what that meant for her but for him, it meant that he had a lot of work to do. "Can you release me for a second? I need to make a phone call."

Stillness and warmth dissipated leaving Samir with cold, harsh reality. He wanted nothing more than to crawl back into the stillness, warmth, and light, but that wasn't something he was allowed to have. Even like this, he had to force himself to accept reality even if he didn't like it. He pulled his phone out of his pocket and called Liana.

"This is not a good time, Samir. Is it important?" She wasted no time on pleasantries. That wasn't her style and he was glad of that today.

"No, this is not a good time." Samir kept his tone even but a small part of him wanted to laugh since now there was no keeping him out of the field on this one. He was already sitting at ground zero. "I'm staring at one of two reasons why your alarms are having a field day."

"Wait, what?"

"I'm sure the sensors picked up a couple nuclear level energy bursts?" Samir smiled at Keeler, not even sure if he had the capability to see it. "And I know why if not how it happened, but that is not as important as containment right now. I am sure this was no accident and I have a suspicion that the same person who abducted Anela is responsible for releasing her."

"That only accounts for one of the bursts," Liana mumbled. Samir could almost see her pouring over the reports, trying her best to make sense of the information there in relation to what he was talking about. He'd been in her position before.

"I know, but the other one is a non-issue. Don't worry about it. I've got it handled." Samir wasn't sure she would believe him, but he didn't know how to convince her other than to tell her the whole truth. He wasn't willing to do that and she didn't need it.

"What do you mean handled?" Caution colored every word and he understood well how she felt. He needed her to trust him on this.

"Yes, I'm near Park and 15th, so whatever you have in that area just ignore it. It's the other one that you have to worry about." Samir found all amusement disappearing as he thought about what he was about to do. He wasn't in a position to give orders, but that didn't mean he couldn't insinuate what needed to be done. "That one will be Anela and I have no idea what state she might be in. If this is the work of Connor Yates, then I would go in prepared for anything. Get her contained any way possible. You know the damage she can do; you've read the dossier."

"It's that serious?" Liana sounded sympathetic for the first time since he'd called. She understood what it took for him to say something like that. "You know this is my call, not yours."

It was no more than a token statement. Whether he was on leave or not, he was still the director and she would listen. "Just do it."

Samir hung up before she could say anything else. He had no time for this. Now that his mind was on Anela, all he could do was worry. He didn't want to leave it in Liana's hands. There was no telling what extremes she might go to if things went wrong. He couldn't hold it against her though, he'd given the order. He simply needed to get to Anela first.

"Is anyone alive in there?" Jenny's voice called out from the door.

Samir almost cursed. He'd been so caught up in what was happening that he'd forgotten about her. "Yes. It's all okay."

She peeped her head through the crack and her eyes went wide as she took in the tableau before her. The ten-foot-tall light creature, the ruined office and Samir frowning with his phone in his hand. "Okay. Well, this isn't what I expected. I'm assuming the pillar of light is Mr. Lim?"

"Uh, yes." Samir had no idea how she could take all of this in stride as if it were a normal part of business. He had to give Keeler credit for picking a stable and practical assistant.

"Right, so I will schedule someone to come in and renovate the office. That is if you plan on returning to human form and coming back to work? I'm not sure how these things work." Jenny frowned as she walked into the office for a better look around.

"He, um. Well, he can't answer you, but, yeah, do that." Samir stammered. If it weren't for the situation, he would have loved getting to know her better. She was a hell of a woman and, in different circumstances, he'd even consider recruiting her into the Nergal. Anyone who could handle this with barely a pause was the kind of person he wanted at his side. "I'll ask you to not say anything to anyone about this."

"I would think that's a given." Jenny frowned as she surveyed the office, glanced at Keeler, and sighed. "I've got everything smoothed out and back to normal out there. If you need me, I'll be rescheduling appointments. Again."

"Right…" Samir watched her saunter out of the office. He chuckled and smiled up at Keeler. "I think I like her. She's a pretty amazing woman."

Even without a single touch, Samir could feel hints of jealousy radiating from Keeler, which only made him laugh a little harder. "Don't worry, I have more important things on my mind than chasing after anyone else. We need to find Anela, do you know where she is?"

Once again, that bright tendril reached out to touch his skin. Affirmation colored with a deep concern that made Samir wonder what was going on where she was. "If I pulled out a map can you point me to her? I don't think Liana would be forthcoming with the location if I called and asked."

He hadn't expected an overwhelming wave of joy that required no touch for him to feel. A burst of light struck an invisible point in the room. A swirling vortex appeared where the light had struck. Keeler moved towards it, but Samir stayed where he was unsure of what was on the other side of that swirl of light.

Waves of comfort and assurance drifted over him. Not knowing what else to do, he took a deep breath, closed his eyes, and stepped through.

CHAPTER THIRTY

Samir felt stretched out like a rubber band to the point that he thought he would snap. He would have screamed if he had lungs, but he couldn't find his lungs. Or his body. As he realized this, everything snapped back and he found himself stumbling forward onto hard concrete. He caught his breath, but no longer found the need to scream. Everything was fine in the bright afternoon sunshine that filtered in from the filthy windows.

He looked behind him to see the portal closing. Keeler reached out to brush away the hair that had fallen in his eyes, but his hair didn't move. It was such a familiar gesture from a new form, even though it had been unsuccessful. It made him smile as feelings of concern and caring flowed over him. "I'm okay. Where are we?"

Samir knew that he wouldn't be able to get an answer to that question from Keeler, but his phone had GPS. He pulled it out, but it wouldn't turn on. Whatever form of travel they had used had fried it. He looked around for any sign of location, but there was nothing. Their travel had taken them from the opulent office tower to an empty warehouse.

If that were a conscious decision, he had to admire Keeler's choice. This was a good place for them to appear. There was no way he could have gone walking down the street with a pillar of light and not be noticed.

"Stay here," Samir said. He walked towards the door and peeked outside. He had no way of knowing for sure, but he didn't think they had left the city. He turned back to Keeler. "Do you know where she is?"

Once again, he got the emotions that indicated he did know where she was—either he was getting more sensitive or Keeler was getting better at projecting without the need for touch. "Can you point in her direction?"

A second tendril emerged to point straight across the street, which triggered emotions of worry and concern again. Samir frowned. Anela was in trouble, but that was not a surprise. He checked up and down the street. No traffic or pedestrians moved, but that didn't mean that they might not be seen. He had no idea what to expect when they entered the other building; he needed a team, but he wasn't going to get one of those.

"What am I doing?" Samir hadn't meant to say it aloud. This was more reckless than wandering into the office without backup. For all he knew, Connor had found a way to control Anela, to use her the way the monks that had summoned her—and incidentally Keeler as well— had wanted to do. If he had figured that out, there might be no stopping him.

Keeler appeared to have no such concerns as he pushed through Samir across the street and into the other building. Samir hadn't expected him to move through solid objects. He should have known better. Many that he encountered chose to be in a corporeal form while here, but in a non-corporeal form, things like walls didn't matter as much.

Samir dashed across the street after him. He paused at the door, trying the handle. It wasn't locked, but he wasn't going to barge straight into potential danger. He cracked it open and peered through to the relative darkness inside. It took a moment for his eyes to adjust from the bright sunshine outside to notice that it was an old reception area. He couldn't see anyone from here, so he slipped inside and closed the door behind him.

He stayed low as he moved towards a door that he assumed led into the main warehouse. He listened closely for any sound, but he couldn't hear anything. Samir pushed himself up enough to look through the reinforced window of the inside door. He couldn't see anyone from here. The short hallway between him and the main warehouse area limited his view, but he recognized the light that Keeler created. He was in there, and that meant Anela would be too.

He wanted a weapon, any kind of weapon, but there was nothing in this room that he could use as such. He would be going in blind. He had experienced the kind of power that Connor was capable of. This time it would be expected, and he would be able to counter it more effectively. He was rested and feeling strong. That meant his energy levels would allow for a good chance for him to take Connor out in one shot. If he was lucky.

This was insanity, he knew that. Going in there alone and unarmed was likely a death sentence. If Connor controlled Anela, no amount of power was going to keep him alive and he wasn't going to count on Keeler to protect him. On the other hand, if he waited for Liana, he would be shunted aside and there would be nothing he could do but wait and watch. He couldn't do that to either of them. He needed to try.

Opening the door a crack, he could hear something now. Someone was speaking, but the words were indistinct. Samir crawled into the hallway and eased the door closed behind him. He stayed low and hugged the wall as he inched his way forward. A bright flash lit up his vision. He waited for the spots to disappear from his sight before he could get close enough to assess the situation.

Connor stood in the middle of the room, his back towards the hallway. A darkness that was more than a cloud but less than solid seemed to be standing between him and the light that he knew to be Keeler. Samir could only assume that this dark form was Anela. It made sense to him that, with them being usesima, they would be opposite in appearance.

Keeler surged forward towards Connor, but the darkness blocked him. Another blinding flash filled the room and he swore he heard thunder rumble. It was obvious that somehow Connor had managed to find a way to control her. He knew that the Nergal had once researched ways to do so but had failed in their attempts. Obviously, it wasn't as impossible as he had been told. Somehow, this man had figured out a way to make it happen.

This was a dangerous situation for him to walk into. He wished that he could call Liana and let her know what was going on. Her team would be walking into something that they might not be prepared to deal with. If he could stop Connor, then maybe Keeler could get Anela under control. It was worth the risk.

Samir prepared himself as best he could. He would likely only get one good shot at trying to stop the man. He'd rarely had a need to use spells or rituals on other humans, and never with the intention to do more than disarm them. If he could, this once, he would go for the kill.

With Connor's focus on the struggle between the two entities in front of him, Samir attempted to get closer to him. He moved silently and quickly, pulling from all the power he had and letting it build to dangerous levels inside him. He knew the consequences of trying to harness that much power as a human. It could burn someone from the inside out. How Connor did it, he might never know.

Despite Samir's silence and speed, Connor whipped around and a portion of the darkness moved to block Samir's blast. He didn't have time to stop the attack he had planned, and he let loose with a blast that was enough to kill an average man.

The darkness absorbed it. All of it.

Drained and exhausted, Samir collapsed to the ground. He had put everything into that single blow—and failed. He hoped when Liana got a crew together and showed up that things would go better for her.

He waited for Anela to strike him down and hoped that she wasn't aware enough of what she was doing to feel guilt over it later. He closed his eyes, but nothing happened. Profusive cursing drew his attention towards Connor. Samir squinted to look through the brilliant cloud of light that stood between them. Anela's darker form swirled above Connor as if she were confused as to what to do. Samir didn't know if she was starting to get control of herself or something else was happening, but he was grateful for the reprieve.

Keeler struck out at Connor again only to have the darkness block it. Whatever control Connor had over her, it was still enough to keep him safe from Keeler's attempts.

Samir closed his eyes again, he needed sugar and rest, neither of which he would find here. Warmth, sweet and bordering on pleasure, flowed through him. A surge of affection came with it, and he knew where it came from.

Rejuvenating and wonderful, his only regret was that he couldn't stay and bask in the moment. This was his second chance to stop Connor. Samir pushed himself to his feet.

"Well, well, well." Connor fixed him with a glare. With a snap of his fingers, the darkness that was Anela settled around him. "I see that you ain't the type to go down without a fight. I'm not either, but if you call off your little pet, maybe we can talk like two reasonable people."

"He's not my pet." Samir flexed his fingers. He needed to stall long enough to figure out a new plan of attack or for back up to arrive. He wondered how much it drained Connor to control Anela, or if there was any energy needed now that the initial ritual was complete. He didn't think it could take much; he looked too strong and healthy.

Connor smiled at him. "He? Ah, that other one that came rushing into the room in Dallas. Interesting that those who serve the devil choose to use the light like a lie. It is the darkness that has consumed this world and darkness that will purify it again. Why stand in my way? Admit it, this world is a cesspit. It has been corrupted beyond redemption. Stand aside and you will be counted among the good and pure of this world."

"I can't do that. I can't let you use her that way," Samir warned him. "Backup is on the way. Give up now and we might show you some mercy but if you don't release her, I will make sure you suffer for what you've done. We're a private organization and there's no limits on what we can and will do. No government oversight, no Geneva Conventions."

"Have it your way. Be counted among the filth that pollutes the Earth and you will be dealt with the same as the rest." Once again, Connor snapped his fingers. The darkness swirled but didn't move from where it was.

It took a moment for it to dawn on Samir what was happening. It gave him hope that there was enough of his friend still in control. There was hope that he could stop Connor and save Anela. "She won't attack me, will she?"

"It'll do as I say it will. I will cleanse this Earth of the wicked and unworthy. I will make this planet the paradise it always should have been." Spittle flew as he declared what Samir could only assume was his manifesto. Religious zealots were the worst and he had encountered many over the years from all different walks of life. None had Connor's talents for the arcane, for which he found himself retroactively grateful.

"No, she won't." He was aware that Connor was more than capable of dealing a fatal blow, but he had Keeler on his side. He grinned even though it was the last thing he wanted to do. He wanted to throw Connor off his game, and he needed to play the part of confident and cocky to do it. "That means your control isn't as complete as you think. Surrender."

"Not a chance of that happening. I have worked too long and too hard to make this happen. Zi Asbu is mine to control. Even if it refuses to consume you, I am still in charge." Another snap of his fingers and Anela charged at Keeler, the clash releasing a rumble of thunder that shook the walls of the old building. Samir flinched as a bolt of lightning shot across the cavernous room.

Connor used that moment of distraction to pull out a revolver and pointed it at Samir. It was one of the things that he hadn't expected to encounter. His mind hadn't been on the mundane, but the supernatural and he cursed his stupidity. There were no armed associates this time and it only made sense for Connor to have something more ordinary for backup when his energy ran low. Samir wished he had managed to figure out that bullet dodging trick because at this distance there was no way he would miss. "Tell me again how you won't let me do this?"

Samir put his hands up and took a half step back. It wasn't the first time he'd had a gun pointed at him, but he'd never been in this situation alone before. His mind ran through scenarios and options, but he wasn't sure how he was going to extricate himself from this safely. He didn't even have the benefit of a bulletproof vest this time.

A door slammed open and daylight flooded in from more than the dust-covered windows that were near the ceiling.

It was enough to distract Connor and Samir took the opportunity that was given. He charged forward and grabbed for the gun to wrestle it away from the madman, but Connor wasn't as distracted as he thought, and he wasn't going down without a fight. The gunshot echoed louder than the thunder.

Samir swore he could hear someone call his name, but he had no idea who it was as another shot rang out followed by another. He didn't feel the pain, but his legs gave way and, for the second time since he arrived in this place, he crashed to the ground. He could see several figures silhouetted in the light spilling through the door. He was sure he recognized one of them.

"Samir!" He recognized Liana's voice over the gunfire that echoed in the background. He couldn't see what was happening, but he had an idea of what was going on. He'd been involved in enough response teams to have an idea, but he couldn't bring himself to care as the agony began to creep up and steal his senses until there was nothing but the pain.

"Samir! Shit. What the fuck are you doing here?" Liana's face came into view, fuzzy and unfocused. His eyes focused on the single strand of bright red hair that escaped her helmet. "Hey, hey. Look at me. Right here."

Samir tried to do as he was told as the ground under his head shifted and softened. No, not the ground, his head was being moved. He closed his eyes. Easier that way; he was tired and the pain wouldn't leave him be. He wanted it to go away.

"Samir, no. Open your eyes. Come on. Stay with me, man." Liana's voice broke and he tried to open his eyes, but it was too hard. No, he would keep them closed. It was fine. He was fine and the pain was going away now. He needed to rest a little. That was all.

"Samir!"

He tried to respond, but he coughed. It was hard to breathe. No, he would sleep.

CHAPTER THIRTY-ONE

Anela stared at her cellphone and debated texting Samir. He had promised her that he would go see Keeler today. She was doing her best to stay out of it, but she wanted desperately to knock their heads together until they both had a little more common sense about things. She pushed the phone away. He'd either do it or he wouldn't and there was nothing she could do to change that.

"I'm going to go get a coffee," she said to Susan who sat in the cubicle next to her. She hit the 'Away' button on her system. She didn't really need a coffee, but she needed a few seconds to get her mind clear before she could focus on work.

"Already?" Susan rolled her eyes. "I swear you're going to give yourself a heart attack with all that caffeine."

Anela faked a little laugh and shrugged. "You've got to enjoy the time you're given, and I enjoy having coffee by the bucket."

She was saved from Susan's answer when the phone rang on her extension. Quietly, Anela walked over to the break room, relieved to find it empty. She filled her coffee cup and stretched against the counter.

"Come to me."

She whipped around, swearing it was Connor speaking to her, but she was alone in the room. She shook her head, leaned back against the counter, and closed her eyes. She took a few deep, therapeutic breaths as she tried to push the memories of that madman away. She may not like the Nergal, but she trusted them to do their job in this case. Connor should never be able to bother her again.

"I said come here, now. Do not make me ask again." His voice was stronger this time, more demanding, and it wasn't coming from anywhere in the room. It was in her head. He was calling her and, the worst of it, she felt herself moving towards the door even though she wanted nothing to do with him.

Fighting against it, she struggled to reach out and grab something to hold her here. She forced her feet to stop before she made it out of the break room. Frantically, she patted at her pockets for her phone to call Samir, but she had left it on her desk out of the reach of her temptation to text him.

"Now, now, darling. You don't have a choice in this matter. I called you and you will come to me because I have commanded it. I have bonded the blood of your vessel to mine, you can hear my voice and you will listen." Connor sounded more amused than angry with her even as she fought against the overwhelming urge to do as she was told.

Her body had no fight left in it, and she found herself walking out of the office, unable to respond to the questions or comments from her coworkers. When fighting against it proved fruitless, she tried to detour towards her desk to grab her phone, but she failed to make the turn. Before she knew it, she had hailed a taxi and gave the driver an address to a place that she didn't know.

She tried to speak up, to tell the driver a new address but her voice was silenced before she could even do more than twitch a lip. She could hear him chuckling in amusement and she gritted her teeth. If she didn't try to fight it, he let her be, her body her own. One of the spells he had done had worked as intended—at least to this point. She could only hope that, if he did release her, he may have overestimated his ability to control her. It was the only thought that comforted her.

She walked into the old, abandoned warehouse to find Conner grinning like the madman he was. He couldn't hide his true stripes now that success was so close in his mind. A fevered look in his eye told her more than she needed to know. He hadn't stepped off the deep end, he'd dived in with joy.

"Well now, I'm glad you were able to listen to me." Connor walked around her, inspecting her as if she were a precious ancient artifact. "I hadn't quite completed everything when your boyfriend showed up and nearly ruined it all. However, I have an hour until the stars are in proper alignment to release you. Won't it be nice to stretch your metaphorical legs a little?"

"You won't succeed. The moment I'm released I will crush you and rejoice in every tortured scream of your damned soul as I do so," Anela spat back at him. She may not be able to leave here, but she wasn't going to be meek and mild. She would fight him with everything she had even if it killed her, but she would be damned if she would let him use her.

"I do love that spirit of yours. Like a wild horse, you're pretty much begging for me to tame you." Connor stopped his circling and faced her. He reached out and tapped her on the tip of her nose. "We're halfway there already because you can't even make the attempt to hurt me without considerable effort."

Anela did try to hurt him when she realized he was about to touch her, but he wasn't lying. It was like walking through cement. By the time she could gather enough power to direct at him, he'd already removed his finger. Her heart sank at the realization that he might actually succeed in this crazy endeavor. She hoped she was wrong.

"Well, now, let's get on with this. Don't want to miss my window of opportunity." Connor pulled a folded sheet of paper from the front pocket of his jeans. She could tell it had been written by hand and she wondered if he'd created his own spell to control her or if he had copied it from somewhere else. Not that it would matter if it worked.

He began to recite it and she could feel something happening. Had she been at work, she would have thought it was nothing more than an upset stomach, but the feeling grew and expanded. She could feel it building and she knew that this body wouldn't be able to hold it in for much longer. Her skin cracked as the darkness pushed out of her and soon there was nothing left of the prison that had held her.

Sight was an afterthought; her world was a pulsing of energy and emotion. Everything she had seen clearly before faded away. It was as though she were viewing the world through clouded glass—but everything else was so bright, so strong. She stretched herself, sensing things thousands of miles away and it was amazing.

So rich and yet so limiting at the same time. No taste, no touch, no smell, but an ever-changing kaleidoscope of colors influenced by emotions. She couldn't see Connor, not as she was used to, but she could still sense him. His unique energy and presence were still there.

She was free. Limitless and powerful. And angry. She turned her attention on the energy she recognized as Connor's and descended on him. She wanted to destroy him, to make him suffer more than any man had ever suffered before. She surrounded him, but he stayed calm in the darkness. She tried to hurt him and there was nothing. She screamed, a low moaning sound. It was all she could do.

"I know, darling. I told you I wouldn't fail. I confess to being a little disappointed that you still seem determined to destroy me, but I can think of a better use for that anger of yours." Connor couldn't have sounded more pleased with himself than he did now. "Let's go cleanse this filthy place."

She didn't want to do as he said, but like her body before, she couldn't refuse the command. She started to follow him towards the door when a bright light—one she knew well—charged through the wall towards her. She would have rejoiced if not for the unspoken command to destroy it. If she had a heart, it would have been heavy with sorrow, but there was no heart in this form as she charged towards the light that was Keeler to stop him.

Who she was, everything that six thousand years of human life had created, became lost deep within the overpowering darkness. The need to consume was pushed to the forefront. Anela fought against the control like a wild animal, but it was fruitless.

On command she charged at Keeler again. All her anger and her frustration were directed by Connor's will towards the only target that presented itself. He matched her blow for blow. That was easy.

Each time they clashed, she could feel him trying to get to her, to help her find control. He was trying to reach her, trying to get through the anger and the darkness to reach the person that she had become. He was trying desperately to remind her of what she was not a creature made of only darkness.

His emotional entreaties had little effect on her. Though she tried to reach out to him, to communicate in some way, even that had been denied to her. She couldn't reach beyond that consuming darkness. Whether it was the control Connor had or her own hopelessness in reaction to her dark nature that blocked him, he couldn't reach her. He couldn't free her, but he also didn't give up on her either, for which she was grateful. It gave her a reason to keep fighting, to try and meet him halfway in his battle for her freedom.

It wasn't the gunshots that caught her attention; she could not hear the shots as they echoed through the room. Nor was it the arrival of all those small vessels of controlled anger and fear that came pouring into the room. They weren't enough to concern her as focused as the others were on each other. It was a single chilling sensation that caused both of them to pause in their battle, a moment preceded by a distress that reverberated within the room. It cut through everything like a knife and then the brightest light flickered out.

It broke through the darkness, the anger, and the hopelessness. It reached Anela in a way that nothing else could have. This was her connection to the world. This was the one thing she could not consume because her orders were to destroy the wicked and unworthy—those whose souls had tipped towards darkness—but he was the opposite of all of that.

Until now. Now, there was only darkness in this place.

And it hurt.

Keeler's own pain echoed hers sharply, it spilled out of them both and filled the tiny vessels that surrounded them. Pain changed to anger and instinct cried for her to strike out and destroy that which had taken away, what had stolen her light. Keeler's anger seemed even greater than her own.

They turned all their attention to the source of an emotion that should not be. All around them was pain and confusion. Except for this one small point of dark triumph. Whatever spell controlled her was weakened, but it was still there. She reached to Keeler for help, this was her chance to destroy that man who had torn her life apart for his own selfish reasons.

For the first time since they had been released from their prisons, their emotions and intentions synchronized. There was one thought, one goal, one emotion between them both—and that was angry retribution. Darkness mixed with the light, neither consuming the other until they were one.

Connor's mental screams to attack, to defend him from the other entities in the room, had no effect on her now. Merged in intention and form, the image of Connor slowly burning from the inside out was shared. It seemed too good for the life he had taken. He deserved to suffer, deserved to be destroyed in the slowest and most painful way they could manage until there was nothing left but ash and dust.

CHAPTER THIRTY-TWO

Even with all that had happened, Liana trusted Samir's opinion—if he said that the situation on Park was under control, she believed him. It also meant that when those energy signals converged on this location, she had suspected he would be inside. It was that thought alone that prompted her to make the call to enter despite the fact that she wasn't sure they were prepared to deal with what was inside.

She'd barely made it through the door when those gunshots demanded her attention. Trusting her people to handle things, she ran towards the source of the sound, fearing what she would find there, and at the same time, grateful that she had chosen to come down to talk to him in person. She'd had a few questions for him that weren't the kind of thing she wanted to say over the phone. It was the only reason she was here now.

Charging inside, into the chaos, she wanted to curse him when she saw him lying on the ground, confirming her suspicions. Now, her worry was that she might be too late as she called out his name and received no answer. Her feet skidded in the pooling blood and she dropped to her knees beside him.

She lifted his head onto her lap, even as she surveyed the damage. He glanced up at her and then his gaze drifted away. It didn't look good, but she begged him to stay focused, to keep his attention on her. If he could hang on long enough, they might be able to save him. There was always a chance.

She held onto Samir knowing she should let go of him and go do her job, but she couldn't tear herself away. Sparing a glance over her shoulder, Liana saw her team uselessly trying to subdue both the intrusions. It was the man standing behind them, not caring about the creatures overhead or the soldiers that surrounded him that she recognized.

That man was the only person who could be responsible for something like this. She didn't hesitate to give the order. "Ignore the intrusions, take out the human."

Samir's eyes had closed and she gave him a gentle shake, once again begging him to look at her, to keep holding on. His eyes fluttered and she held her breath, but he didn't open them. "Samir!"

He tried to say something, but instead of words, there was only blood, and his chest stilled in its struggle to rise. She checked for a pulse but there was none. He was dead. The realization that he was gone hit her like a ton of bricks, all other thoughts gone under the weight of that terrible truth.

He was gone and there was nothing she could do.

She sat there, frozen, his head still cradled in her lap and her uniform covered in blood—Samir's blood. Death was always a possibility in their job, and she had lost people before, but he had been her mentor. She had never considered losing him and found it near impossible to accept that this was reality. Her instinct was to blame him for being reckless, for being here when he shouldn't have, for being…him. Except, none of that mattered anymore.

A sound like metal scraping against itself tore her attention away from Samir. It was a sound she'd only heard in recordings. One she never thought she would hear in her lifetime. Both creatures had paused in their battle. They had no eyes, no way of telling where they were looking, but she had a feeling that their attention was entirely focused on her and Samir. Again, the sound came louder, a moan of pain and anger that seemed to echo forever through the warehouse.

Others had stopped what they were doing as well. Some of the less experienced had covered their ears to protect them.

"Orders?" One of her soldiers asked. She heard the question clearly, but she had no answers for them.

As she watched, dark and light began to swirl around each other, twisting together and joining into something new. Something that was more than the sum of its parts. It was the first time she realized that she wasn't dealing with two entirely separate beings, but usesima. She wondered if Samir had known. She wouldn't have put it past him, but that was dangerous knowledge to have kept to himself.

Relief flooded through her as its apparent attention moved away from her. She couldn't be sure, but it seemed as though it were turning on Connor Yates. Some of her team were still following orders, not that it did any good. He was unscathed. She'd heard about this from the last encounter. It had been in Samir's report. Liana shouted, "Hold fire."

Gunfire slowed and then ceased. She debated giving the order to retreat as she realized that something was about to happen, but she was too mesmerized by what she was seeing. Those creatures, deep black and brilliant white, swirled and blended together. Hints of rainbow brilliance shimmered from where they connected.

Connor's eyes went wide and he began to scream. It was a raw sound, one that grew quickly hoarse as he collapsed to his knees. It wasn't a sound she had ever heard another human make. Smoke rose from his mouth and his skin bubbled and blackened as though an invisible fire was consuming him.

Liana covered her nose as the noxious smell of burning flesh filled the room. Her only wish was that she could cover her ears at the same time. That scream continued as Connor fell the rest of the way to the ground, curling into the fetal position. A small bright blue flame ignited his hair and she gagged as the smell grew worse, averting her eyes away from what was happening.

Someone, she wasn't sure who it was, puked. Others, the less experienced members of her team, backed away. It reminded her that she was still in charge and this situation was out of their control. There were dangers when dealing with any usesima once they merged and they definitely were not prepared to handle this. She needed to get her team out of here—better late than never. "Get out of here, now!"

Liana wasn't willing to leave Samir behind even though she knew she should be with her team. Only one person paused long enough to notice that she was still on the floor with a dead man's head in her lap. She waved him on. She didn't think she was in any danger at this moment and she was willing to take the chance to stay. "Go!"

The door slammed behind them as they vacated the warehouse, leaving her in silence with a corpse, a smoldering pile of ash, and a usesima that might try to kill her. For a second, she felt like maybe Samir had rubbed off on her. This was entirely against protocol. She shouldn't be here. It was a feeling that intensified as the being moved in her direction. It unwound, the dark and light separating to become two forms and those morphed back into human shapes. Shapes she recognized. Anela, she had expected, but the other one was the creature that Samir had brought to the university.

She should have known, and there was little doubt in her mind that Samir must have suspected the connection between them. Maybe that's why he had been with that other intrusion at the time of release. Always trying to do things the gentler, kinder way. She had admired his determination, but she still thought that his ideas for how things could be were foolish.

Knowing who these creatures were did little to quell her nerves though she put on a brave face as they approached. Neither spoke to her, nor looked at her. Their gaze was fixed firmly on Samir. She may as well have not even existed.

A small part of her mind screamed at her to retreat, regroup, and reassess. Liana refused to listen to that voice and stayed kneeling in a pool of blood and cradling Samir's head in her lap.

As they got closer, her instincts overrode her desire to stay and she backed away until she hit the wall. She held steady there, her curiosity demanded it. As the man knelt beside Samir, his long dark hair fell to partially block him from her view.

"What are you going to do to him?" She hadn't meant to say anything, and certainly not a question that sounded more like a challenge.

He glared at her but didn't answer. It was Anela, still standing slightly behind him, who addressed her. "Trying to help."

She didn't trust him, or Anela for that matter, but she was more than aware of how much they seemed to care for Samir. That and the incredible power they could wield was enough to remind her to watch her tone and emotions.

CHAPTER THIRTY-THREE

All this power, everything he was capable of, and Keeler still hadn't been able to protect Samir. His death, that sense of a light that connected them both suddenly disappearing from this world, had been enough to break through Connor's hold on Anela. Destroying the man responsible wasn't any consolation, as much as he had enjoyed that part.

Sensing that Samir was gone wasn't enough. He needed to see, he wanted to hope. Finding that familiar human form again was easier than he had thought it might be. He almost regretted it as his eyes added the gory details to the story his other senses had told him. Confirmation that Samir was gone. Completely and totally gone.

Keeler looked at Anela, there was no need for words between them. It was a strange sensation after being a solitary being for so long to feel this kind of connection with anyone else. He had no hope of his own now, so he held onto hers instead. Her waves of encouragement and worry made him try to see if they could both be wrong.

He placed his hands over the wounds in Samir's chest and forced them to heal, coerced his heart to beat and the lungs to move oxygen. Keeler wanted it to not be too late. Healing the body was easier than ever before. He was stronger now that he was no longer trapped and bound within a vessel. He didn't feel as drained by the effort as he forced the body back to life, but Samir didn't return. It remained an empty shell.

He wasn't ready to accept this. Not knowing what else to do, he poured more of himself into Samir's body, trying to find any hint of what he wanted to be there. There was nothing. He didn't know what else he could do to bring Samir back. Even now, with all his power, he couldn't raise the dead.

He reached out and brushed the hair from Samir's face, wondering how to mourn the loss. He knew of no words that could describe the extent of the anguish that filled him. It was another death to carry with him as the centuries wore on.

A cool touch took his attention from his thoughts. He looked at Anela who placed her hand over his. Where they met, the human form dissipated and a rainbow of light appeared. He could feel her pain as deeply as his own, but she didn't mourn. She offered him hope instead.

He could sense what she wanted to do—to go beyond and retrieve him. He had no idea if it was even possible, but they would have to leave the constraints of a human form to do it. He let the façade slip away.

Together they focused their entire attention on searching for a singular energy. Like everything in this world, nothing was ever gone. It changed from one form to another. They knew they were looking for that special signature in the waves of energy that screamed to them 'I am Samir'. It felt as though they travelled through every inch of every universe within seconds.

Without even a hint of where he might be.

They almost thought the effort lost when they sensed the barest hint of something familiar outside the limits of all that was known. Clear, crisp, and sweet. It was him.

They reached out, pushing through the boundaries of all that existed to a place that screamed to them, *"you do not belong here."* They pushed on anyway until they encircled the energy that was Samir and attempted to drag him back to his body where he belonged.

He didn't move. He was stuck in this place. It held onto him—unwilling to let him leave.

Anela let her own darkness split from Keeler's light to fight against it. She would not give in to that which wanted to hold what she held precious. She needed to bring him back with them, and all of existence wasn't going to stop her. How long it took them, they had no idea. There was no time in this place, no sensation of any kind.

Despite the want of this place to hoard the energy, she won her fight and pulled him back. Keeler joined her as they once again pushed through a barrier that now demanded for them to stay. It was an effort that sent them soaring back, faster than they could have done on their own. A sense of being slammed into their own forms brought them back to where they had started.

Keeler and Anela took form immediately and stared at Samir expectantly. He had returned with them and had crashed into his corporeal form. His unique essence didn't seem to want to stay. Even as they stared, he was starting to slip away again. His body was alive, but even that wouldn't last forever if they couldn't make him stay.

Anela shook Samir's body like she was trying to rouse him from a deep sleep. "Come on, Sami. Come back to us. You can't leave now. You promised me you had a long life left."

Keeler placed a hand on her shoulder. He wasn't ready for words yet, but he was willing to try one last thing. It was a desperate measure. What they had already done had been risky. What he was considering was something that seemed impossible, but he had to try. They'd come this far. He wasn't about to give up now.

"We might lose him completely." It was the only argument Anela had. They would lose him either way, but if Keeler failed it would mean there would be no other chances to try. Everything that was Samir would be gone, irretrievable.

"I have to try." It was only a whisper, barely louder than a breath.

Anela nodded and stepped away, joining Liana by the wall. He ignored them both as he closed his eyes, needing to focus, to calm the worries. This had to work. If it didn't work, he wasn't even sure what he would do at that point.

Keeler took a deep breath and leaned forward, pressing his lips to Samir's. It wasn't a kiss, not in the traditional sense. It was close to an ethereal type of CPR. He needed as much contact as possible so that he could let everything that he was—the light, essence, and energy—flow from him into Samir. He filled him as completely as he could. He enveloped Samir's energy, grabbing it tightly as he filled the vessel with his own essence in an attempt to anchor him in place.

His power waned, but he pushed on. He hadn't even thought it possible, but he had never poured this much of himself into anything before. Even if there was nothing left of him, he was willing to do this to save Samir. He would rather not exist than carry the responsibility of another death—this death—with him.

Suddenly, he could pour out no more of himself. It wasn't that he had nothing left, but the vessel before him was full. It could take no more.

Keeler tried to sit up, but he didn't have strength. He let gravity carry his physical form to the ground, not caring about the now tacky blood that still covered the ground. He placed his head on Samir's chest, watching his face for any signs that he might be in there, alive.

Had he the strength, he would have begged for a sign, but he wasn't even able to do that. All he could do was wait for Samir to wake, or for his strength to return so he could try again.

CHAPTER THIRTY-FOUR

Anela was more than willing to step away. This was not something that would benefit from her presence. Her powers may have allowed her to bring Samir back from beyond, but it took the light to hold it here. She looked over to see Liana standing against the wall watching them intently. She went to join her, tasting her fear and uncertainty as she approached.

"We're trying our best to bring him back." She kept her voice low and smiled gently to show Liana she meant no harm. She had never liked the woman, but that didn't mean she had to be mean to her. She cared about Samir in her own way and Anela respected that. They didn't have to see eye to eye for her to be kind.

"Can you?" Liana asked, her eyes not leaving Samir and Keeler.

"I don't know, but we can try. Well, he can try." Anela leaned against the wall beside Liana to watch them. She hoped it would work, she didn't want to think about what it would mean if it didn't. It hurt her to consider that, even as nothing more than energy in another realm, Samir might not exist at all. "His body lives, but his soul or essence or energy, whatever you want to call it, doesn't want to go back. It is fading. Keeler is trying something. It is dangerous, but there are no other options."

"Is that its name?" Liana mumbled, her eyes still on what was happening.

Anela ignored the pronoun. It wasn't the time to make a point. She could feel the last of the adrenaline leaving Liana. "Yes, perhaps it would be best to take a seat? This might be a while."

With a nod, Liana slid down the wall to sit. Anela sat beside her, calm and collected as she felt the energy build up. It was coming soon. She bit her lip, waiting and watching, praying to nothing as there was nothing above herself that she believed in. Still, there might be a being somewhere that was listening, that could reach out and help.

It seemed to go forever. Keeler's energy waned to the point that Anela was starting to worry about him, though she still doubted he would want her help or that she would be able to. When she thought he would be able to take little more, Keeler collapsed. Liana was quick to her feet, but Anela held her where she was.

She shook her head and pressed a finger against her lips. She could sense his exhaustion. He had poured a lot of energy into this attempt, but it wouldn't take him too long to recover. More importantly, she could sense Samir deep within the cocoon created by Keeler's own essence to tie him into his body. It was weak, but it was there.

She didn't want Liana to get closer in case something went wrong. She was afraid, with the amount of energy involved, that things would be dangerous if anything went wrong. It would have been safer for Liana to not even be here, but Anela knew that she would never be able to make her leave. And if it all went well, then there would be no need for it. She would be able to witness something that should have been impossible.

Most of her attention was focused on Keeler and Samir. Each second that ticked by in which she was still able to sense Samir made her hopeful that this might work. Even Keeler's energy seemed to be coming back. He sat up. Even now, fear and despair still outweighed the hope that what he'd done would work.

Her heart broke a little for him. When they had joined, the depths of his attachment had become clear to her. Not that he would ever admit to it. She loved Samir; he was her family and her friend. Though love was a newer emotion when compared to the length of her life here, there was no denying the strength of its impact. Her heart, her will to continue, were almost destroyed when she'd realized that Samir was gone. For Keeler, this emotion that he wasn't even willing to fully acknowledge, was brand new. This hurt so much more for him.

As the time ticked by, her hope turned to worry and impatience. Samir needed to wake up. He needed to be okay. She could sense that desperation bearing forth like a wild animal in Keeler and Anela wished there was something she could do to comfort him. He ignored any emotional treaties from her, his only care and attention was Samir.

She perked up at the spike of joy, the hint of hope that came to her from Keeler as Samir's eyelids fluttered and opened. Keeler pulled Samir a little closer, blocking him from her view, and she tried not to be too annoyed with him.

"Is he…" Liana whispered, not finishing the question.

Anela smiled and nodded. She stayed where she was, wanting to give them a chance and was glad that Liana seemed to be following her lead. She was sure that once he was awake, Keeler was bound to forget that there was anyone else here, and she hoped the distance would prevent Liana from seeing too much.

Keeler leaned down and kissed Samir's forehead. It was a much more modest response from him than she'd expected. With a nod to Liana to tell her it was okay now, she got up and walked over to see Samir for herself. She had expected Liana to join her, but she hung back, her discomfort clear to Anela.

"Sami." Anela put as much joy and cheer into her voice as she could, but she wasn't sure she liked the pallor of his skin, nor the hint of fresh blood on his lips. "Let me help you."

She took him from Keeler and helped him up into a sitting position. He was weak and there was a distinct sense of something wrong, but he also seemed strangely alive and vibrant. It was an odd contrast. Samir looked around as though everything were new and surprising.

His eyes fixed on Keeler, still kneeling close. "Kees?" It was little more than a hoarse whisper, barely audible. That one small word was enough to make Samir cough. Blood spraying from his lips. She hoped it was the residual effects of the wounds and not something more serious. Samir looked down at himself and fingered the holes in his blood-soaked shirt. He looked back up at Keeler. "Wha—"

More coughing, more fresh blood coated his lips. He wiped at it with the back of his hand, for all the good that did.

"Take it easy, darling. You've been through an ordeal," Anela cooed at him as if he were a child. She didn't want to worry him. She wanted him to stay calm, though she feared what this might mean.

Samir took a shallow breath and spoke again, keeping his voice soft and slow. "What happened?"

Anela looked at Keeler who was, thankfully, good at keeping a neutral expression. His concern was as strong as hers, perhaps more so. His guilt told her that he was probably blaming himself for this. She decided it would be best if she answered that question. "We can talk about it later. We should get you out of here and to some medical care."

Samir shook his head even as Keeler grabbed his other arm to help him to his feet. Though he had managed to move his hands and arms, she'd failed to notice that the moves had lacked any finesse. Now that they had him standing, it was easy to see that he was struggling with his fine motor control and laboring to produce the right movements.

"Liana?" He said it loud enough that it sent him spasming with another fit of coughing and more blood.

"Hey, take it easy," Liana said, her smile subdued and a sheen to her gaze that could only mean she was close to crying. Considering how much she prided herself on being tough, Anela was surprised at the depth of her concern and relief. It was clear from her emotions that she knew something was wrong as well. They all did except for maybe Samir, whose emotions were fuzzy and indistinct to her. "I—"

Liana stiffened, turned, and moved away from them as she pressed a couple of fingers to her ear. Anela had almost forgotten that there was a whole team of Nergal waiting impatiently outside. Her entire focus had been on what was happening inside the building. She expanded her senses outwards, picking up the fear, uncertainty, confusion, and even some revulsion from those gathered in the street waiting to find out what had happened.

She kept her voice low and her response short. She turned back to face them, frowning as she looked at Samir. "I've dismissed my forces since there is no need for backup now. However, I want to get him back to the university for a full checkup. We need to make sure he's okay and we have the necessary facilities to do so there. Although I am not sure a commercial flight will be a good idea in his condition."

Anela wasn't about to argue. As distasteful an idea that she found it to be, she couldn't disagree with Liana. "No, a commercial flight won't do. Not to mention, you look like hell."

Liana nodded in acknowledgement; her brow furrowed in thought. "And driving will take too long."

"Can you bring them here?" Anela asked as she shifted under Samir's weight, trying to get more comfortable. What little strength he had was quickly disappearing.

Liana chewed on her lip. "No, that won't work. Too much of the equipment doesn't transport easily."

"Portal?" Anela quirked an eyebrow at Keeler.

He shook his head. "It would be quick, but I'm worried it'll hurt him. That kind of travel is hard on physical forms. It was stupid that I had even brought him here like that in the first place." His discomfort increased as he looked at Liana. "I have access to a plane."

Anela understood his reluctance to say anything. He didn't want the rest of the Nergal to know more about him than they already did. She knew it was only his concern for Samir that prompted him to give up what remained of his anonymity. Anela sent him her silent gratitude.

"A private plane?" Liana gave Keeler a hard look over and nodded. "That would be ideal."

"I'll need to make a call. Do you have a phone?"

Liana unlocked her cell and handed it over with no hesitation. It was a short conversation, with a small break to hand the phone to Liana so that she could give Jenny the address and her clothing size at Keeler's insistence.

"Okay, let—" Anela didn't finish that sentence as the slow burn of pain she had sensed in Samir exploded into a bright heat. It was so intense that she nearly dropped him before she could block it out. They needed to hurry.

CHAPTER THIRTY-FIVE

Keeler collapsed into a seat and closed his eyes. "He's resting. For now."

Battling Samir's pain as well as his own fears and guilt over what had happened were taking their toll. He had been doing his best to keep Samir asleep and comfortable, floating somewhere far away in a cloud of quiet, blissful pleasure. But there were times when the pain came strong enough to nearly overwhelm his attempts.

He could have pushed harder against it and drowned everything out, but that would have taken a depth of connection that even now would be too much for him. Too tempting. No matter what, he had to keep Samir's words in mind and maintain some sort of distance between them.

A tickle at the back of his mind told him another wave was coming. With so much of himself in Samir, the connection was unavoidable. His brief respite was already over. "I need to get back in there."

"Good luck," Anela said as he walked to the small private room at the back of the jet. It wasn't much, but it had been useful on his longer journeys. More comfortable than the seats, no matter how much they reclined. He'd always considered it a bit of a luxury, but he was glad to have splurged on it now.

Samir didn't move when he entered the room, his consciousness was as intermittent as the pain. Though it was concerning that as the periods of pain increased, Samir's times of conscious lucidity decreased. He stood by the doorway, not wanting to disturb him yet. He needed the rest that came naturally, and not what Keeler had been forcing on him.

He had searched for a physical source of the problem, anything that he might have missed. Healing was a tricky art, and as easy as it was with his power regained, he had still hoped that he could find something he had missed. The body appeared to be in perfect health. Keeler worried that the pain might stem from what he had done when he secured Samir's essence to the body.

He hadn't said anything, but he feared he had done more harm than good with his efforts. In those few lucid moments between the pain, Samir seemed perfectly normal, as if there was nothing wrong and he wasn't spending more than half his time in agonizing torture. Keeler wished he could do more than keep the worst of it at bay, but at least he could do something.

It was coming soon, the next wave. Keeler crawled into the bed and curled up beside Samir, wishing that this was something different than what it was. He could dream, even if it was clearer than ever that he had been right the first time he'd met Samir—he should have left. Not that he regretted most of it, only the pain and suffering he'd caused. Involvement with humans was, inevitably, never good for the human, even for those accustomed to being around non-corporeals.

"Kees?" Samir sounded weak, but with another episode of pain so near, it surprised Keeler that he was awake and aware at all.

"Yeah?" Keeler propped himself up so that Samir could see him better, resting his other hand on Samir's chest. Contact was needed for this to work, especially with the protections he had as a Nergal. More points of contact made it easier. Thinking about it, the intimacy of what was required was a distraction he could ill afford. He had to keep his mind on the reality of things. He needed to be prepared when the pain came so that Samir would not suffer more than he already had.

"Why is this happening?" He barely got the words out as the first wave hit and he gritted his teeth. Keeler did what he could to counteract it. This was a mild bout, the first wave of something bigger, he was sure. Samir relaxed a little but held on stubbornly to consciousness.

"You should rest." Keeler wasn't sure Samir was in any condition to know the details of the situation, but it also wasn't fair to keep it from him. He deserved to know the truth, but not when another wave—a bad one from the feel of things—was coming. "We can talk about it later."

"Please, tell me." Samir forced the words out, still battling the effects of Keeler's touch that were meant to keep him in a state of blissful peace.

"Will you rest if I do?" Keeler asked. He stopped trying to fight against Samir's own will to stay awake and focused only on mitigating the worst of the pain.

"Yes," Samir agreed as the current bout of pain subsided. These short ones were becoming more infrequent, and the stronger debilitating ones came more often now. It also meant that the moment of peace would be even shorter before the pain was back.

"You died," Keeler admitted. "Connor shot you and I didn't get to you in time to save you. We—I—tried something risky to bring you back because I wasn't willing to be—"

He cut himself off. There was no reason for Samir to have to carry that burden. It was his own. He needed to not make things worse. He'd done enough already in that regard.

"I died?" Samir asked, disbelief coloring his words.

"For a little bit." Keeler saw no reason to also tell Samir that he had no idea what was wrong with him now. "It's going to be okay."

"You're a terrible liar." Samir tried to laugh but started coughing again. Keeler grabbed the towel that he kept for this reason and wiped away the bit of blood. He searched again for the source of the bleeding, but it didn't seem to be coming from anywhere. There was nothing for him to heal. It was frustrating.

"Rest," Keeler commanded, and he could feel Samir fighting it. Another wave, stronger than the last, tingled at the edge of his senses. He wanted to have Samir long past the point consciousness where the agony would be little more than an abstract and distant concept before it arrived.

"Kees?" Samir tried to reach for him, his hand landing awkwardly against Keeler's shoulder. He still had a hard time controlling his limbs—something that was getting worse as the pain increased. It disturbed Keeler to see him so helpless like this. Samir's brow creased as he concentrated, his hand dragging upwards until he managed to reach Keeler's face. He cupped his cheek, his expression deepening to one of heartfelt sorrow. "I'm sorry."

"You have nothing to be sorry for," Keeler tutted. It was silly of him to apologize for anything with the state he was in.

It wasn't his fault. None of it was. Keeler was willing to shoulder all the responsibility for what had happened. Samir would never have been in the warehouse if he hadn't taken him there. And it was most likely his fault that Samir was suffering like this now. "You need to rest and get better, okay?"

"No, I do. I am," Samir said between gritted his teeth. The new wave was here before Keeler could stop him from feeling it. He started the process of pushing it away. Samir shook his head. "No, please, let me talk. I need to say this."

Keeler didn't want him to suffer, but he wanted to respect his wishes too. He focused on the light sense of pleasure, on dulling the nerves that screamed as though they were on fire. If this was what Samir wanted and needed right now, then he would do his best to make it possible. It wasn't any easy process, but he could feel Samir relax beneath him as the pain was subdued. "Okay. What could you possibly have to apologize for?"

Samir gasped. "I should never have chosen the job."

It was such an unexpected statement and Keeler had no idea what to say in response. Honesty, this kind of honesty, was new to him. He'd spent much of his long life shutting everything out. Until now. He only wished that this could have come sooner. Staring down into that warm, sweet face, he knew what he wanted to say, but they were not words that had ever passed his lips before. He doubted that they ever would. He settled for a small smile. "It's okay."

"No, it's not." Barely a whisper, Samir's words were edged sharply with regret.

He wanted to soothe away the sadness there even as he wished to ignore the words that only served as a reminder of what he couldn't have. He couldn't even blame the change of heart on the situation, emotions told a more complete tale of where the words came from. His only recourse was to beg for Samir to get some sleep. "Please rest."

"No…" Samir said, dragging it out and refusing to give in to the gentle mental soporific that Keeler created. Again, he relented, unwilling to force anything on Samir that he didn't want. Despite the weakness in his grip, he attempted to pull Keeler closer and he didn't resist. He didn't want to. If this was all he could have, another stolen moment, then he would take it.

With slow, deliberate consideration, Keeler carefully sampled every emotion, but refused to name them. There was a certainty to these feelings he had never sensed before. It was almost intoxicating as they washed over him; each one unique and inviting, drawing him further in. He let his lips brush softly against Samir's, wanting to prolong this and forget about everything even though the pain was still there, crowding in on them like an unwanted visitor.

This time, he let himself give in to his own emotions and held nothing back. There was no point in that. He wanted it all. The full experience and, he wanted to share everything that he was with Samir. Allowing the kiss to deepen, he searched for a closeness he'd never allowed himself to have and found it.

Samir returned his efforts with all the passion he had, more than could be expected considering the state he was in, and Keeler melted into it, letting it temporarily quell his worries and fears. He gave more of himself than he thought possible, letting that ethereal pleasure build until even the pain could no longer be sensed, fading away like fog on a bright summer's morning.

Keeler wanted nothing more than to linger in this place where he could believe in having what had always been denied. His hunger had no power here. What he craved had moved far beyond such basic instincts. He didn't want to let go of this, the moment or the man, but Samir needed to rest. He drew away, letting reality slip back in. It reminded him that this was neither the time nor place.

"You need to rest," Keeler whispered against Samir's lips before kissing him gently on the forehead. "Please."

Samir didn't resist his efforts this time and Keeler sent him to a place where the pain would have a harder time reaching him. He was exhausted. He couldn't deny that, but he was willing to give everything he had to make this better. To make it right. Samir deserved that from him, even if there was nothing else he could give.

With a three-hour flight ahead of them, there was only one thing he could do now. Keeler curled up closer to Samir and rested his head on his chest. He listened to the rhythmic heartbeat, willing it to soothe him into his own much-needed slumber. His guilt for the pain he had caused followed him into his dreams.

CHAPTER THIRTY-SIX

Anela tried her best to ignore the surge of emotions coming from the bedroom. It was not what she had expected but she wasn't unhappy about it. She had been pushing for Samir to stop putting the job first for years. It seemed, like with many humans, it took dying for him to understand how short a life was. She waited until everything had subsided into the subtler sensations of sleep before saying anything. "He's resting again."

Liana nodded at the statement without looking at her. She sat several seats away, lost in her thoughts. Anela casually followed the emotions but left her alone to think. Even she knew a decision needed to be reached before they landed—especially the consideration of what to do with her and Keeler. Anela knew the difficulty of many of these decisions. Samir had often come to her to talk things out.

She hesitated to intervene even though her fate was one of the ones that needed to be decided. She'd never been a fan of Liana, mostly because of the antipathy that the woman had for non-corporeals. Considering her introduction to this world, Anela could almost forgive her for it—almost. Still, she knew Liana would never come to her for advice without being prompted.

"You seem troubled?" Anela asked pointedly. She phrased it as a question even though she knew it to be a fact. There was no point in making Liana more uncomfortable than she already was. An hour into the flight and the silence on top of the emotional atmosphere was driving her near insane. She was no longer accustomed to silence and she needed to know what Liana was thinking, not only the emotions attached to it.

"What makes you say that?" Liana snapped at her. Anela was sure part of the response stemmed from the fact that she wasn't used to being questioned, especially not by non-humans. She shook her head and held up a finger to stop Anela from responding. "No, don't answer that question. Tell me what makes you think you should even be talking to me about it."

"You have been silent for this trip. Your concern for Samir is evident even to those who cannot pick up emotions." Anela moved closer to Liana so that she could keep her voice low and, therefore, more confidential. "We may not like each other much, but that does not mean that I can't sympathize with you. Or talk to you about it. Samir is my family. I care deeply for him."

Liana turned her gaze out the window. "He's my mentor. Hell, he's saved my life more times than I can count. We may not always agree on policy and procedure, but I've always looked up to him. And... I don't know what to do going forward from here. These are not the kind of decisions I'm good at making."

"Samir once told me that you were one of the most promising field agents he'd ever worked with. It's one of the reasons that he pushed for your promotions, but he also said that you weren't ready to be in charge. There is a need for a flexibility that you had yet to learn," Anela recounted, knowing that he'd never said those words to Liana. He'd always kept his opinions of those he worked with to himself. Encouragement and feedback were handed out where necessary, as was discipline and lectures, but Samir's focus had always been on what was best for his staff from an administrative standpoint.

She had accused him more than once of being too analytical with the people around him and he would laugh, saying he'd learned from the best. Some days she wasn't sure if he was referring to her or his father. Then again, her father had to learn from someone too. He hadn't always been as he was now.

"He's right," Liana admitted. Anela appreciated her honesty about her own shortcomings. Not many people seemed capable of that.

"Or maybe he was wrong. You are thinking hard on things and not falling back on what policy dictates for you to do in this situation. I know it well, perhaps better than you do." Anela had become good at talking to humans over the years. Many of her coworkers treated her as their own personal counsellor, more than once telling her about how insightful she was. Liana was one of the few who knew where that insight came from.

"I don't know." Liana sighed. "This puts me in a difficult position. Samir needs help, but the situation borders on so many no-go areas of policy that I don't even know how to proceed. I mean, no offence, but both you and Keeler should be officially detained now that you are no longer trapped in your human bodies."

Anela nodded. She had expected to hear as much, but she knew there was more to it than that. "There is a 'but'?"

"But I'm grateful to you both for saving Samir. Even if it didn't work out as expected. Whatever you and that thing did to him, I don't know how to explain it to the medical staff, but hopefully one of you two can," Liana said. Anela winced at the words 'that thing.' Liana must have noticed as a slight tinge of guilt colored her emotions. "Sorry."

"It's alright. Just a small difference of opinion. I like to think of myself as a person, and you like to think of me as some unwanted alien intrusion. Nothing we can't look past temporarily." Anela shrugged and let go of her annoyance. She had more significant things to worry about than her own feelings about old issues. She had long ago given up changing the minds of any Nergal, though Samir was more optimistic than her. He was also a heck of a lot younger. "More importantly, what are you going to do?"

Liana slumped back in her chair and stared up at the ceiling. "Hell if I know."

"Do you mind if I give you some advice then?" Anela asked, trying not to read anything into the initial reaction of revulsion and anger she saw there. An initial reaction of any being was simply how they had been trained or raised to feel about things. She had learned long ago that it was the emotion that followed the initial instinctual kick that mattered. That is what told her how the person wanted to be if change had not sunk that far into their core yet. And of course, how they choose to act afterwards made all the difference.

Liana didn't look at her as she continued her inspection of the ceiling. "What?"

"Do what you believe to be the right thing. Don't go by policy or procedure. In the end, those are just pieces of paper. You need to be able to live with the decisions you make, so do what you think is right even if it means going against what you've been told to do." It was advice that she had given Samir on many occasions and it had never steered him wrong.

Liana looked at her sharply. Anela had no doubt that it was not the kind of advice she had been expecting. "I will keep that in mind. Thank you."

"You're welcome." Anela smiled and poured herself a glass of water. A human habit, but it passed the moment and allowed her to pretend the silence in here wasn't near as awkward as it was. She watched the passing landscape, leaving Liana to sort out what she was going to do. Anela had given her two cents, and seemed to have settled some of the conflict that had been bothering Liana. It was an un-ignorable spike in discomfort that prepared her for an inquiry that may have otherwise caught her off guard.

"Hey, can I ask you something?" Liana posed the question almost hesitantly, as if she weren't sure she wanted to know the answer.

Anela tried not to smirk at the curious indecision. She raised an eyebrow, wondering what had brought on the sudden surge of interest. "Of course you may."

"You and Samir? Have you two ever...." Liana left the question unasked.

Anela laughed this time, not at her discomfort, but at the fact that she was the first one who'd ever had the courage to ask. She knew there were others that wondered at the exact nature of their close relationship, but few were comfortable asking the boss if he had hooked-up with the creature he was charged with watching.

Anela struggled to mute her laughter as Liana's discomfort grew almost palatable and shook her head. "Oh, oh no. Never. I've known him since he was a little child. He is my family and that is all there ever has been. I love him as my family, and I believe he feels only the same for me. He's not driven by a need for relationships, though I have tried to encourage such things. He's always been more focused on the job than anything else. Not to say he hasn't dated in the past, but it's never worked out well for him."

Liana relaxed with a small chuckle. "Ah. I know how that goes. The last time I had a date I had to leave early on a call. How do you explain having to go out on a call in the middle of the night when your day job is working as a research assistant at a university lab?"

"And no one within the Nergal has caught your eye?" Anela leaned forward and grinned. Sometimes she couldn't help her flirtatious attitude. While appearance was the least of the things that attracted her to her partners, she did appreciate a pleasing aesthetic and made note of such things. "I am sure someone as beautiful as yourself has garnered some attention from within the ranks as well."

Liana shrugged. "When you're being groomed to be in charge, it feels awkward to date someone who you might have to order into danger in the future. It doesn't seem wise. In the meantime, there are one-night stands and serial dating if they're worth more than that. I'm okay with it. I've never been the settle down type, but I always felt like Samir would be more than happy to find someone to settle down and build a home with."

"Oh, he is very much that type." Anela's grin faded slightly at the thought that he might never get that chance now. "He hasn't found the right person I guess."

Liana glanced back over her shoulder towards the room and Anela had a good idea what she was wondering. It was obvious to anyone with eyes how much Keeler cared about Samir, but without the ability to sense emotion it was not immediately evident that the opposite was also true. It was a pity that it took dying for Samir to accept that.

"We should be landing soon enough." Anela got up and went back to her own seat. There was nothing but the quiet emotional overtones of sleep coming from the bedroom. She was glad. It would be awkward if there had been anything more than that when they landed.

CHAPTER THIRTY-SEVEN

Anela shifted awkwardly in her seat. She hated hospitals of any kind, but this was worse. To be within the Institute, surrounded by people who hated her for her mere existence as she watched the only real friend and family she'd ever had fade away, was a new definition of hell. She was useless. She couldn't help Samir; reducing pain was Keeler's specialty.

She could produce the sensation of pleasure, but it didn't come from a place of joy and light. For her it was based in the darker euphoria that could be found in pain and fear. None of her partners had complained about the sensations she could create, but for this kind of thing her abilities were useless.

Not that Keeler had much to do right now either. Drugs took care of the pain and all they could do was wait. They weren't allowed to leave the Institute. Not that either of them wanted to leave Samir's side, but they weren't officially detained either. Not yet. Their status was in limbo as no decisions had been made as to what to do with them. So, they sat in silence and waited for the doctors here to figure out what was wrong.

Liana had been in and out to visit when she could. Most of her time was tied up in dealing with Nergal business. Each brief visitation was colored by the stress of dealing with everything that was happening on top of day-to-day operations. None of the doctors would talk to either of them and all their progress updates came during these visits.

"I'm so sick of this waiting." Anela paced back and forth in the small room. It had been close to a week with no improvement in Samir's condition. There had to be something more that could be done other than keeping him sedated. All the tests the Institute had done were inconclusive at best. No one knew anything more than they had the day they arrived.

"Pacing won't help." Keeler didn't look away from Samir as he spoke. There was no emotional emphasis behind his words, only habit of routine. This was a conversation that had happened to various degrees already and his focus was on keeping track of the cycling between pain and normality. Try as she might, there was no distracting him from this and, unless forced to, he'd hardly left his seat at Samir's bedside, holding onto his hand the entire time. With the amount of drugs that had been pumped into Samir's system, it was the only way Keeler could sense anything.

"Nor does sitting there acting like a grieving widow," Anela snapped at him. Part of it stemmed from her own worries about Samir's condition. They both could feel that he was fading away, disappearing as the anchors that Keeler had created slowly unraveled. It was something that couldn't be measured by any machine or test and there was nothing either of them could do to fix what was wrong. It was pure torture.

There was also the fact that she was not used to being cooped up like this anymore. Being here reminded her too much of things she preferred forgotten. No matter what, she wasn't going to let them keep her here for another few thousand years. She enjoyed her time as a human far too much to let it go now. She would fight for it if she had to.

"What else am I supposed to do?" Keeler tore his eyes away from Samir long enough to glower at Anela. Pain and worry painted a picture on his face that showed only a small portion of the vast depth of emotions he hid from everyone, though he could not hide them for her. The agonizing guilt, his determination to carry the responsibility for it all. No matter how many times she argued with him about it, he stayed as immovable as a mountain in those beliefs.

"I don't know!" She threw herself into one of the chairs and crossed her arms in frustration. "I wish they'd let us do something, anything to help. I feel so useless sitting here and waiting for him to either get better or…"

"You know why," Keeler reminded her. He turned his attention back to Samir, his emotions and energy consumed in monitoring his condition. Their hands were tied in this place. They could do nothing without the permission of the Nergal or the Institute, and neither organization wanted their help. All either of them could do was wait for the doctors to find a way to fix what was wrong. She only hoped they would figure it out soon enough.

"It's not a good enough excuse," Anela mumbled as she slumped farther down in her chair. There had to be something they could do. Any idea was worth consideration. Anela was willing to grasp at straws. What they needed was one of their own kind, one who had more knowledge than they did of these things.

She perked up at that thought. One of their own kind. Without being bound into a human form by a long-lost ritual, there was a possibility it could work. Even her sudden movement and change in mood wasn't enough to get Keeler to look up. "It's our intervention that caused this to happen. If their doctors could fix this, they would have done it already. I don't want to sit here and wait for him to fade away. I won't."

"I don't want to talk about this." Keeler sighed, still fixed on watching Samir. Anela knew that she could use a far more persuasive form of argument, but she had chosen to use words. They'd both become attached to being human. It had become an easy form, a familiar form.

Anela leaned forward in her chair. "Then don't talk and listen to me. We aren't stuck in human form anymore. It was the only thing that ever kept them from sending me back. That and their fear of what would happen if they released me from my prison, but that's not an issue."

"What is your point?" Keeler snapped impatiently. She didn't hold it against him, the strain of the wait was weighing on him. He was tired, far too tired.

"We may not know how to fix this, but there might be someone from our dimension who could help us." Anela bit her lip as Keeler considered her suggestion carefully. There were merits to it. She hoped that he could see that, but she wasn't sure how it would work. Or if it could work. She was a little surprised he hadn't thought of this before her; it was something Keeler once said that he oft longed for during his life.

"Do you really think that might work?" A sudden glimmer of hope lit somewhere in the pit of despair that he had been wallowing in and she was glad to see him show interest in something. It was an unknown risk for the Institute to agree to it. Of course, nothing else was working and there was a chance they could be desperate to try anything. Or, if not the Institute itself, perhaps Liana would agree to it. "Do you think they'd even let us try?"

Anela shoved herself out of her chair and started to pace again. "At this point, I think they might listen. You can feel their confusion and despair as well as I can. They have no clue what's happening and no ideas on how to stop us from losing him. If they're unwilling to admit to the obvious, then he is lost to us anyway. We can't keep sitting here. I can't watch the only family I have die like this."

"Then talk to Liana. She might listen to you." Keeler turned his attention back to Samir as another cycle of pain coursed through him. Even she could feel it this time. There was no doubt that though he was unconscious, Samir could feel it too. His heart raced a little faster and a sheen of sweat showed on his brow. "Go before it's too late for us to try anything at all."

Anela didn't need to be told twice. With or without his consent, she would have tried to talk to Liana about her idea anyway, but she preferred to do it with his agreement. She left the room in search of Liana. Anela wasn't sure if she would listen, but it was worth a try. Keeler had a point. If they waited much longer there would be no use in even trying. She could feel Samir slipping away from them a little more with each passing day.

She found Liana in Samir's office, sitting at his desk, and staring at a photo that he kept there. She could feel so many emotions, but mostly there was sadness and hopelessness. She wondered if it all had to do with Samir or if it was something else. She knocked on the open door and Liana looked up at her with surprise. "Anela? What brings you here?"

She stepped into the office and closed the door behind her. "I came to talk to you about Samir."

Liana averted her gaze, not that it mattered. For Anela, the pain and sorrow that radiated from her was a flashing neon sign. It was too bright and too overpowering to be missed. She walked in and took a seat at the desk. She reached for the picture that Liana had been looking at. It was of her and a much younger Samir. She smiled at the memories it evoked. "I remember this day. It was the first time I had seen the ocean. We had ice cream and walked for miles along the shore long before he became the director. He thought I would love the vastness of it. He was right."

Liana's mouth curved into a professional smile that didn't reach her eyes. "Doctors haven't given me any new updates since you last asked. Is there anything else I can help you with?"

Anela put the picture back on the desk. "He's dying."

"His vitals are stable," Liana countered, as if that were the only measure of health. They both knew it wasn't his body that needed saving and there was nothing they could do for something that they didn't even have the proper terms to describe. Although measurements of brainwaves were now showing a slight, but noticeable reduction in activity, it didn't paint a pretty picture.

Anela leaned forward on the desk. "You know what I mean. Your machines can't measure what's important here. Time is running out. I don't want to sit here and do nothing but watch it happen."

Liana pressed her lips together. "Our doctors are doing the best they can. This is unknown territory for all of us."

"It is, but as good as they are, we both know that it isn't enough. We need to try something radically different. Something that we wouldn't consider under normal circumstances." Anela lowered her voice. "And I have an idea, but it's risky."

"Risky how?" Liana leaned back from her and Anela could still sense the innate distaste that she had for those that weren't human. It was less than what it had been before, but it still existed. She didn't think it would ever go away completely. It was too ingrained in who she was.

"We want to take Samir to our dimension where we came from, in hopes that someone there can help us fix what went wrong." Anela presented her idea as casually as she could, but inside, her stomach was doing flips. She had no idea how Liana might react to the suggestion; she could only hope that she'd take more than a second to consider it.

"You want to take him… elsewhere?" Liana repeated back to her with deliberate slowness.

Anela continued, emboldened by the lack of immediate rejection. "With your permission and assistance, we would like you to send us back to where we belong and we would like to take Samir with us."

"We…" Liana paused and cleared her throat. "I don't know if Samir has ever talked to you about this, maybe not. We've done experiments to see if we can open a portal to elsewhere, and we can, but not for corporeal things."

Anela frowned as she considered this information, then asked the only question that mattered now. "Has the experiment ever been done with a non-corporeal willingly facilitating the transfer instead of machines trying to replicate what we can do?"

"It's never been done before." Liana pursed her lips. Anela gave her time to process the idea knowing this was something that would have never been considered by any of the humans. She perked up and stared intently at Anela. "How do you propose it to be done, and how would you bring him back?"

"Let's tackle one problem at a time," Anela said. "Although, if you have a better suggestion, I'd love to hear it."

Liana shook her head. "I don't have any other suggestions and, I want to say yes. I want to make this happen, but I can't move ahead without permission from the council. If I take this to them, I need to have all the answers."

"I wish I had them. I don't know how this will work or even if it will work. I don't know how we'll get him back." Anela tried not to feel discouraged as she admitted to her lack of knowledge. "I only know that we need to do something."

Liana sighed and pushed back from the desk. "I'll take it to the council and see what they say. It might take time for them to research the possibility and get back to us. I can't make any promises, but I will try my best to make sure they do consider it."

"Don't let them take too long in deciding," Anela warned her, standing as well. "Time is precious."

"I know," Liana said curtly. Anela let the response go. She was tired and stressed with her attention torn between tracking down the sources that Connor had garnered his information from and hunting down his remaining followers on top of the day to day operations. It was something that would stress anyone out and Anela knew that.

She nodded her head in thanks and left Liana alone. She had no idea what would become of her suggestion, but she felt far less useless now that she had done what she could. Without the help of the Institute, they wouldn't be able to return to where they came from. No one had ever taken a human with them, not that they knew of anyway. It would be an experiment. One born of desperation, but a fascinating possibility all the same.

CHAPTER THIRTY-EIGHT

It had taken less than a day for the council to deliberate on their decision. It was an unequivocal 'No.' They gave no explanation and Liana hadn't expected one. The answer had come quickly enough that she knew no one had even given it more than a second of consideration, and she had no idea how to tell Anela that the council refused to consider such an extreme. For the last few days, she had managed to avoid her by switching offices until she could figure out what to say. By her math, she had another day or two before she had to say something.

"Good morning. Ms. Na'im," an unexpected rich baritone voice said from the door of the old office she'd chosen to hide in today. "You're hard to find."

She had no idea how anyone had found her here. Curbing her temper, she looked up and froze at the sight of the man standing there. Had she been a believer in ghosts, premonitions, or time-travel she would have thought the unsmiling man in front of her was Samir in another thirty years. It took a few seconds before her brain caught up to her eyes.

This wasn't a ghost from the future, but Samir's father. She'd heard of him. He was a legend within the Nergal. As she studied him, she noticed the small differences beyond the lack of a smile and his age. His skin was darker, but his eyes weren't soft and kind. This was a much harder man than Samir. A man who fit the stories she'd heard.

"Are you going to say something or sit there looking like an idiot?" Despite his words, there was no anger in his voice. It was the same even tone in which he had said 'good morning'. He ventured no farther into the room as he waited on her to verbally acknowledge his presence.

Liana bit back her initial response to that comment. It was something she had a lot of practice doing in her lifetime. If this man was who she suspected him to be, she would be better off treading lightly. "My apologies. You surprised me. I didn't think anyone knew where to find me. Can I help you, sir?"

"Ms. Na'im, I am Hamid Amin." He dipped his head in a brief nod of greeting before entering the room, making sure the door was secured behind him. He took the only other seat in the mostly barren office.

"Your reputation precedes you Mr. Amin." Liana wondered why he was showing up only now. It was pushing onto the second week since Samir arrived at the facility. Even with a nine-hour flight from London, she would have expected him sooner. "Would you like me to take you to see Samir?"

"No," Hamid said. "I am here in both an official and unofficial capacity."

Liana wasn't sure what to make of this visit or this man. She would have thought he'd be more eager to see his son. "I was under the impression you had retired."

"I am, but if you would please check your emails you will see correspondence from Councilman Stephane LaCroix that will explain my presence here." Hamid waved his hand in impatience at her hesitation. "Now would be a good time."

Liana did as she was told, her annoyance growing with each word he spoke. She had no idea how someone like Samir could be related to him. There was an email from Councilman LaCroix, as he had stated, and she read it with a growing disbelief. Despite the firm and direct order to not proceed with Anela's idea, this email from one of the senior members of the council was telling her to move ahead in secret with the plan and Hamid's assistance.

She pretended to read for a bit longer than necessary as she considered what this might mean. Retired or not, the man before her could make her career difficult if she didn't follow through with what was being suggested. "What brought about this sudden change of mind? I was under the impression that the decision had been unanimous."

"In public, yes. Different arrangements have been made privately," Hamid answered cryptically.

She didn't expect him to expand on that, but she still was hesitant to go forward without knowing more. "I thought, and I am quoting the council here, that this plan was 'too dangerous to even consider.'"

"As I said, the public stance and the private arrangements do differ. The council is well aware of what will be happening. We can proceed with or without your assistance here." There was no doubt that Hamid's veiled threat wasn't a ploy. He had pull, and Liana was sure this would be the most she would ever get out of him. This was a man that rarely had to explain himself. He was a legend, a hero. The great Hamid.

"I see." Liana kept her face neutral as she adjusted to the new information. Temporarily, she was to follow all instructions given to her by Hamid in respect to this situation. As much as she wanted to follow the rules, Samir had trained her and, for once, she found herself listening to his advice regarding blind obedience.

She weighed her options. She couldn't question Hamid further about this change without risking her career. As much as she wanted to find a way to save Samir, something didn't seem right about this decision and she didn't like the position that this put her in. She had no arguments, no idea of how to phrase her questions. This was territory she had never been in before. It was Samir who questioned everything, who made his own path and fought the council tooth and nail when he believed in something. "Well then, when would you like to go forward with things?"

Hamid stood up as if this was all the discussion the matter needed. "From what I understand, sooner would be better. I suppose I should go see him, where is he?"

"Yes…" Liana tried not to bristle at the way he had said it, as if Hamid had little interest in seeing Samir beyond the expectation that he should do so. She stood up even as she cursed herself for not being able to stop doing what she had always done—follow orders. She continued. "He's in the medical wing. I can show you the way if you like."

"That would be appreciated." Hamid stood stiffly and allowed Liana to move past him so that he could follow her. "This facility was only in the planning stages when I retired. I'm not as familiar with the layout as I should be."

Her uneasiness grew with each step as she led him in silence towards the medical wing. Instinct continued to scream at her that something wasn't right with this situation. She kept it to herself for as long as she could, but with the last set of doors before they reached the wing and the final hallway that would take them to Samir, she had to ask one thing. "Can you tell me why the council was so quick to deny approval for this, but specific parties were so quick to approve it in secret?"

Hamid gave her a tight-lipped smile and she felt her stomach sink a little. She was already regretting asking the question. "The reasons for denying it are those you already know: too risky, too dangerous and most likely to end up as most experiments to send corporeal things to the other dimension—messily. As for why it was approved, that is above your pay-grade."

"Oh." Liana had heard the rumors about the experiments, most people who had been around as long as she had been knew of them. Messy was the nice way of describing the results of them. It's why she had taken the risk to tell Anela that it might not work when it was suggested. This time would be different though. They'd never done this with the help of a non-corporeal.

"If you perform well in this task, I am sure I could put in a good word for your promotion to the position of Director." It was a bribe, she knew that, but it was a tempting offer even if she wasn't sure she wanted the promotion. It wasn't nearly as important as having Samir back—preferably with him in charge as well. On the other hand, a good word with the council could go a long way from someone like Hamid even if she didn't want the position.

"Thank you, sir." Liana had no idea what else to say or do in this situation. For now, she would do the only thing that she could. Opening the door into the secured section of the medical wing, she did her best to squelch the uneasiness that simmered at the back of her mind. It would do no good to have either Keeler or Anela pick up on it as she gave them the apparent good news. She only hoped that she wasn't going to regret this.

"He's in here," she said as she opened the final door.

Hamid entered ahead of her. He came to a jarring halt before fully entering the room. His back stiffened. She had forgotten to tell him about Anela and Keeler.

CHAPTER THIRTY-NINE

Anela sat up straighter in her chair at the person who entered the room. Keeler didn't look up; he almost never bothered to look away from Samir for any reason. Even the doctors had grown used to working around him now. The man who walked in was one of the last people she had expected to be here. "Hamid?"

"Anela. How are you?" he asked with a false warmth in countenance. She wasn't sure why he bothered. There was no one here that would care if he had greeted her more coldly. Of everyone, she was one of the few who would understand the coldness to his demeanor, but she did appreciate the effort.

"I've been better." Anela smiled out of habit and glanced at Liana who stood off to the side, her unease filling the room. Hamid had that effect on people. He was a legend within the Laibiruzi Institute and the Nergal. If he said "jump" there were many who would do so without question. It made no difference that he had retired over fifteen years ago. "It is good to see you again."

"And you." Hamid nodded, his gaze drifting to Keeler who still hadn't bothered to acknowledge the presence of anyone else in the room. A hint of annoyance broke through the emotional wall that he kept in place and Anela raised an eyebrow. Hamid stiffened and the emotion dissipated. He stood stiffly; a smile that didn't reach his eyes fixed on his face. "Of course, I heard of your suggestion that the council rejected."

Anela knew she shouldn't be disappointed by that news, but she was. Hamid's presence here made more sense to her now. He was here to push through his own agenda and nothing more. It was too much to hope he'd soften enough to visit his own son. "I see. And?"

"I've read the reports from the doctors. It is clear to see that there is little they can do." Hamid's eyes tracked back to the still silent Keeler before he continued, another brief flare of emotion surfacing only to be repressed. "You will be allowed to privately attempt what has been suggested."

"We're sending you both back with Samir," Liana clarified, her unease growing as she spoke.

Anela wasn't sure if she should be worried or overjoyed at this news. She wondered what else was going on behind the scenes. She pushed her concerns over Liana's nervousness aside. She smiled, this time a far more genuine one. "That's wonderful."

Hamid turned and finally addressed the silent Keeler. Distaste was the emotion that surfaced this time, and was quickly suppressed. "You must be the other one that I heard about. I take it you tried to save his life, and this was the result?"

Keeler stared at the man without blinking, sitting straighter in his seat. Anela tried to flash him a warning, but she didn't think he was in the mood to listen to her. Keeler said, "I did the best I could to make sure he survived. I regret that I didn't have the abilities to do better than that."

"From what I heard, you brought him back from the literal dead. Not something that has ever been done before. I am amazed that you managed to do even that." Hamid dipped his head briefly. "So, I owe you some measure of thanks for the attempt at keeping my son alive."

As much as his words showed gratitude, Anela could feel little emotion behind them. Keeler finally glanced at her, searching for guidance, but she had none to give. Hamid was not an easy man to understand or deal with—not even for her and she probably knew him better than anyone. Anela responded, her voice casual and cool, matching Hamid's tone of voice. "As always, you know Samir's safety and wellbeing is something I've always taken seriously. I am sure I have you to thank for making this attempt possible. It is the only solution that I can see as viable."

"I agree," Hamid said with a nod as Keeler turned his attention back to Samir. "We'll make this happen before the end of the day."

Without a word more, Hamid pivoted to leave. Liana rushed to grab the door for him. As soon as the door clicked shut Anela began to giggle. It quickly turned into a full belly laugh.

"What was that about?" Keeler asked as soon as her vocal amusement waned, his eyes on Samir again.

Anela shook her head, a goofy grin plastered across her face. "I was thinking that I should have called Hamid first, but it never even occurred to me to do that. He would have had the suggestion approved within the hour. Back in the day if you wanted something done, he was the man to get it done. Some things never really change, and it was amusing to see Liana act like a nervous new recruit around him."

"He seemed…" Keeler frowned before finishing the sentence with a word that they both knew wasn't the right one, "…odd?"

"That is one word for it." Anela shrugged, her grin fading. "Another word would be intentionally emotionally distant. As in the distance between here and Pluto is too close for his emotions. Long story."

"Hmm. They're not very much alike beyond the surface, are they?"

Anela snorted. That was a hard question to answer knowing both men as well as she did. In many ways, they were a lot more similar than most people thought. "As I said, it's a long story."

"Right." Keeler didn't press the issue. She was grateful for that, but no matter how well things seemed to be going, she needed to do one more thing.

"I'm going to stretch my legs." Anela didn't waste time waiting for a response. She had more important things on her mind. One of which was talking to Hamid. She hadn't spoken to him in a long time, but there was clearly—to her— something wrong. He was normally so much better at repressing his emotions than he had been today.

Between the sheer size of the complex and her power repressed here, she had a hard time tracking him down. He was reading when she found him in the dorms. She knew he could have ignored her and left her standing out in the hallway, but he allowed her in.

"Give," was all she said.

"Give?" Hamid put his tablet aside. "You will need to be more specific."

"Hamid…" Anela sighed and shook her head. "I am the one who taught you the repression techniques when Kate left to help you deal with the pain. I know when there is more going on and I know you well enough to understand that those hints of emotion mean much more than any other of my kind might know. Talk to me. You know I can keep a confidence. I have kept yours for a long time."

"Not this time, Anela." Hamid stiffened as he said it.

"What machinations are you up to?" she asked, not expecting an answer. She wasn't disappointed. Hamid greeted her question with a sigh, letting his annoyance seep out. "Fine, keep your secret, but if things go wrong, do not find anyone else to take the blame. I know you pushed for this against the wishes of the council. I don't even want to know what favors were called in or who you blackmailed to make it happen. I only wish to know why."

"You can leave now."

She wanted to be angry with him, even if she had gotten her way in this matter, it still bothered her that there was something going on here that she didn't understand. There was more to this story, to what was driving Hamid to push for this risky solution.

It was something she was going to have to think about before she said anything else. For now, she had to focus on how to get Samir to a home she couldn't remember. He needed her more than Hamid did right now.

"Fine. Perhaps we can talk when I return."

As the door closed behind her, she heard him mutter in a tone that wasn't meant to be overheard, "I hope so."

CHAPTER FORTY

It was late into the evening before anyone came to the room to retrieve them. Keeler didn't mind the wait. He wasn't sure what would happen to them when they reached home. *Home.* It was a strange thought to him. His knowledge of the place was nothing more than foggy half-remembrances. He'd almost begun to think of this place, this planet, as where he belonged. It was clear that was exactly how Anela felt though. This was home.

She'd been subdued as they waited, unusually quiet—especially for her. He'd noted her mood when she returned but hadn't bothered to ask why. He was too lost in his own head. Samir was fading far too quickly. That wonderful, sweet essence that had first caught his attention was barely even there anymore. Failure was a thought he didn't want to entertain. It had to work.

Liana slipped in; her whirlwind of unsettled emotion was the only reason Keeler knew who it was. He stiffened when he heard Hamid's voice. He hadn't sensed the man at all. His presence was an utter blank, no more feelings than a wall. "Are you ready?"

It was, from what he could tell, a rhetorical question. Ready or not, this was happening. He stood, still holding Samir's hand. This was little else he could do, not even sure if his presence was known.

"We're ready," Anela answered for them both.

"As you are aware, this area is warded from your abilities. We have a room specifically designed for these sorts of things," Liana announced, sounding more confident than she had the last they were in. "We've done some research and have decided that, since you both are new to travel, we will assist the process with a few of our available senior field agents."

"I'm sure that won't be—"

"The assistance is appreciated." Anela cut Keeler off, her tone of warning hard to ignore. He had no idea what it was about, but this place was her territory. She knew the Nergal and these people better than he ever could.

Liana continued as two white-suited medics came in to begin the procedure. "We'll have to move quickly once the doctors take him off the IV. From what we understand, it won't take long for the pain to overtake him and we are not sure what the effects of that will be. We have a stretcher ready unless…"

Her expectation was not lost on Keeler and he would have smiled if it were in his nature to do so. "I will carry him. It'll be faster and I can monitor his condition along the way."

He almost jumped when an unexpected hand landed on his shoulder and gave it a squeeze. It was one of the last things he had expected Liana to do. Her gratitude washed over him before the words could leave her lips. "Thank you."

"Shall we?" Hamid asked in his already too familiar calm and emotionless manner.

Keeler tried not to let it frustrate him too much. It didn't matter if he thought that Hamid should show more depth of emotion where the wellbeing of his own son was concerned. This wasn't his place to say anything. He stood, easily scooping Samir up in his arms. He enjoyed the feeling, trying not to think about if this would be the last time. He'd had time to think. Perhaps too much.

No matter what the outcome, his mind was decided.

He waited for the medics to unhook the monitors and IVs. He could feel Samir's body burning through the drugs, pain already pushing in on him. Keeler did his best to soothe it away, but this was beyond anything he had felt before. It was nearly relentless. He paid no attention to anything else as he followed the others through the complex.

Hamid was the last person to enter and he locked the door behind him. In total there were nearly twelve people crowded into the small room. Keeler spared a moment to taste the emotional resonance within the room, from Liana's worry, fear and hope to the general disgust and curiosity directed at him and Anela. One thing was clear, apart from the blank spot of Hamid, everyone here cared and worried about Samir.

It was touching, but he could spare no more thought for it as the pain blazed forth, almost drowning out his own senses. Keeler struggled to push it down, wishing he had more privacy for the contact needed for his attempts to be more effective. A hand touched his shoulder and he could feel his focus strengthen. It was enough to push this wave back temporarily. "Thank you."

"We'll get him fixed soon," Anela said. "Save your strength for the trip. This isn't going to be easy, and it's never been done with a corporeal."

"It'll be easier if you both take non-corporeal forms," Liana informed them, pointing to a series of concentric circles on the floor. "Put him in the middle and stay as close to touching him as you can."

Anela looked at Keeler who gave a stiff nod to tell her he was ready for this. He placed Samir down gently and almost regretted having to let go. He lingered only as long as he dared with so many watching. As one, they both shed their human forms. A pillar of light and a swirl of darkness hovered around the unconscious human.

"Good luck," Liana whispered, the intent of her words more noticeable than the words themselves. Freed of the human constraints, he was undeniably more powerful. It was strange the compromises he made by being in a human body even when he did it by choice.

Instinctively, he reached out for Anela, wrapping around her, merging to become more powerful.

He could sense the humans around them, their own energy focusing on a place that resonated as 'elsewhere' with them. A place that they had sent many others of his kind. He could feel the tone of the words reverberate around the room, creating a pattern he could feel vibrate through even his own person. It was an interesting and unexpected sensation.

Samir's pain flowed through him, overwhelmed him. Much like the portal, there was a sensation here of stepping between two places, but instead of a crack in the sidewalk, he was stretching expanses that were near impossible to perceive. With the help of Anela, he pulled Samir through with him, the pain receding behind in the room where he had once been.

This reminded him of when he retrieved Samir from the other place, but slower. This distance didn't feel anywhere near as far away, for which he was thankful. Lights shot by—

sharp points of emotion in the darkness. Vast and seemingly endless tracts of emptiness rushed by. A thought pushed in on him, something vague and bothering. A sense of complete wrongness, but he wasn't sure why.

In the expanse, something screamed. Even without a body, he shuddered. It was getting harder to pull Samir with him, harder to hold onto something that was halfway between solid and nothing. It was new and different.

Again, there was a scream in the darkness, demanding and hungry—not for a connection as he and Anela had often craved. No, this was something malicious.

Pain slammed back into Samir before Keeler could do anything about it. He had no idea how Samir could even feel it; as far as Keeler could tell, he no longer existed. He could feel him there, but he couldn't reach him, couldn't stop the pain from overtaking everything.

Then there was only silence.

To be continued in...

Rising Darkness

Solving the problem of how to keep Samir alive isn't a simple matter. Most in non-corporeal realm are hesitant to even help them—and not even sure that they can.

Things are made more complicated by the fact that what Keeler did to save Samir has brought him to the attention of a dangerous being. One that is bent on revenge against the non-corporeal realm that Keeler and Anela once called home, and it will stop at nothing to achieve its goals.

No matter what decision Samir makes—to live or allow himself to die—the universe is at risk simply because of what has been done to him.

As Samir willingly walks to his fate, other plans are being made without his knowledge. Will the struggle to save his life be in vain? And if he survives, what will it mean for his relationship with Keeler?

Read on for a sneak peak of the upcoming sequel...

CHAPTER ONE

Silence. Darkness. Limitless and peaceful. Only distant bright points of energy filled this featureless expanse. Each of them a confluence of power and emotion that indicated sentience. Beings that were similar—almost identical—to him. It was impossible to know how many others there were, but it was more than Keeler had ever sensed in his long human existence. This place, as unfamiliar as it was welcoming, reminded him of a time he had nearly forgotten from before he had become trapped and powerless. He longed to reach out, to touch and to know them, but he needed his energy focused on keeping Samir comfortable, alive, and here.

For an infinity that lasted a fraction of a microsecond, he could have sworn that they'd lost Samir. It was a sensation far too much like when they'd brought him back from the dead—as if something were barring Samir's entry to this place. The level of pain he'd sensed during that moment, and throughout this brief journey, had been higher than he thought any human capable of withstanding. Keeler couldn't help but wonder if this had been a mistake. If those that called this place home didn't have a solution, he wasn't sure Samir would survive the trip back to the corporeal realm.

Another fraction of a microsecond, this one passing far too quickly as the empty peacefulness broke into a chaos of jagged colors and shapes. Walls coalesced around them, forming a bubble—a prison without doors or windows. White, sterile and reminiscent of a hospital room. Or rather it appeared that way to the limited vision Keeler had in this form, but it felt different. Something about this replica wasn't right.

Outside the walls, he could sense others approaching rapidly. Confusion, concern, and familiarity were the emotions that marked them. He couldn't blame them for the first two, but he was put off by the familiarity. He didn't know who or what had sparked that emotion.

Color flowed, dripped down the walls, changing the scenes from a sterile hospital-like room into a rough approximation of Samir's apartment then quickly switched into Anela's kitchen then a beach, and back to the hospital room. Though their surroundings continued the kaleidoscopic shifting, Keeler found himself grateful for his lack of vision. Even as it was, the changes were dizzying.

Despite the apparent solidity of the room that had formed around them, there was no gravity. They continued to float in the middle of it as Keeler encompassed Samir, unsure of what was happening and wanting nothing more than to keep him safe. Anela flitted back and forth throughout the room, her anxiety and worry nearly overwhelming Keeler's focus. He didn't even have the energy to spare to make her stop.

Beings closed in around them, the shifting landscape stabilized and then melted back into the empty, unending nothing—except for the dozen or so pulsing lights that surrounded them. Fear, anger, and another emotion so subtle Keeler almost missed it. They were waiting for someone else to arrive. Someone in a position to do something other than contain the source of their distress.

Keeler did his best to project an aura of calm assurance in spite of his split attention. Anela took her cue from him and did the same. He could only hope it would be enough to make sure those around them know they meant no harm as they waited for someone—anyone—to acknowledge them directly. Anela tried to engage, but her attempts were firmly ignored. She ended up crowding closer to Keeler and Samir as it became evident that nothing would happen until someone else arrived. He had no idea of what to expect and hoped that everything would work out well.

Reverence filled those surrounding them, directed towards three others that approached from different tangents. Fast, slow—it was hard to get a true sense of things with no markers to indicate distance, and time seemed to have no hold in this place. Everything took forever and happened in a split second. It was disconcerting and yet, Keeler found himself adjusting easily to the strangeness. As if this were normal, and the single-minded forward march of time that he had grown used to as a human had been entirely wrong.

He made no move to greet the new arrivals despite the urgency of the situation. The last thing he wanted to do was anger those whose help they sought. Samir was slipping deeper into unconsciousness, further out of reach, and there was nothing he could do about it. His only option was to wait for these beings to acknowledge them in some way.

Anela shared in his worry about Samir, but not his patience. Despite sharp warnings from those around them, she intruded on what appeared to be a private conversation. Even here, among effectual strangers, in a land they could barely remember, she made her demands known. Shock and mild outrage came from those who surrounded them, but the new arrivals steadfastly ignored her attempted intrusion.

Keeler took his attention from Samir to warn her from trying a second time. He didn't disagree with her sentiments only with how she went about making her point. They couldn't wait much longer for these beings to decide what they wanted to do. Another cycle of pain crashed down on Samir and he was unable to even dull it. Sharp abstract forms violated the emptiness and the ghostly hint of familiar shapes stood between them and the others.

A mental shriek tore through the illusion as it reached a jarring crescendo, sending the colors and images scattering into oblivion. Anger, directed at the human in their midst, overrode all other emotions—though Samir was unable to feel their wrath. He did not belong here. Pain seemed to be a foreign concept in this place, as alien as the use of speech to them.

Keeler, unsure of what would happen now, circled tighter around Samir as Anela crowded closer. The three who seemed to be in charge turned their attention towards Samir, the moment the pain had washed over them. He could feel none of the animosity from them that the others projected, but an emotion he couldn't identify. Something subtle, but equally as unwanted. It was as if they were nothing more than bugs under the microscope of an indifferent scientist.

Once again, white walls formed around them. It was the same strange bubble prison from earlier, slowly it shifted into the rough approximation of a hospital room—perhaps even one pulled directly from their own memories. Unlike before, this time the barrier felt more solid, not a passing creation, but something real—a place separate from the emptiness. He could sense the others vaguely in the same way that he could recognize someone through frosted glass as a human—indistinct but identifiable.

Gravity—a concept that Keeler had nearly forgot existed—slowly began to take hold of the space. He wasn't about to leave Samir lying on the floor, but he had no idea how to move him towards the bed. As the thought occurred to him, the room shifted, and the bed was below to stop his descent. Unsure of what else to do, he continued to hover over Samir.

Outside of this strange bubble, he could sense the others calling to him and Anela, but he was reluctant to leave. He'd barely left Samir's side since the day he had died, and he didn't want to do so now. He brushed a tendril across Samir's face and wished he could feel it in the traditional sense. Instead, he picked up on the hints of his cool and sweet essence that was still there, trapped in place by the light and life he had poured into this vessel. It was the closest he could come to touch—more intimate but far less satisfying than physical comfort. It was odd how he missed that part of being human when he had spent so long hating everything to do with being human.

Anela's impatience to find out what was happening urged him to leave—though he was unsure how to do so. With a mental shrug, he attempted to flit through the wall and found himself back in that endless nothing. He could sense Samir behind him but couldn't see the place that these being had created. There was only single point of shifting light that gave a sense of otherness. Anela reached out to him and he let her. It was the most comfort he would find in this place and at this moment.

All attention was on them, some of those that had gathered previously had drifted away, but the three late arrivals and several others remained. Keeler faced them as he would a firing squad, with quiet resolve and grim determination. Somehow, he had to explain to these people why they were here, and he wasn't sure how to do so without the use of words.

With some effort, Keeler did the best he could with Anela picking up the threads of the story whenever his own abilities trailed off. She was far better with expressing her emotions—he wondered if it was because he had repressed his own for so long. It was intricate a tale and difficult to tell with only emotions when neither he nor Anela had much practice at this type of communication.

As the conversation wore on, it became easier. Almost second nature, as if this was a language he had once know well. It was, in a way, like returning home. Keeler would have laughed if it were possible, this was his home—their home. It was strange for him to think of anywhere as being such after spending so much of his human life wanting nothing more than to not exist.

They weren't interrupted until they faltered and went silent. Then, the questions were asked, and clarifications demanded. Keeler kept is his patience, though he wanted to rush them to a decision. When no more explanations were requested, Keeler repeated the same thing he had asked for since the beginning—for their help to save Samir. Silence greeted his plea. Anela pushed the issue, not worried about offending those whose help they sought, and trying to stress the importance of this corporeal creature to herself and Keeler.

Another of those hints of an emotion more complex than he could understand, came and disappeared before Keeler could analyze what it meant. There was a reluctance there, a hesitation to help, and he didn't know why, but he was determined to find out. He tempered his impatience, but it wasn't easy to hide the depth of his emotions as he tried not to read into anything.

This was a unique situation; one that these beings had probably never encountered before. It was understandable that they would be hesitant to suggest a solution that may not work—at least, that is what he wanted to believe. He was mostly thankful that Anela managed to keep herself under control this time.

Eventually, one of the beings that had stayed for the entirety of the discussion suggested the assistance of someone who might be willing to help. An entity who had spent time in the corporeal realms and, more specifically, on Earth. Another flash of that strange and unrelatable emotion reverberated through them as the trio came to a quick consensus.

Keeler made a mental note of how they summoned someone at a distance, it was new to him—though that could be said of many things in this place. Much like the arrival of these three beings, it seemed to take forever and no time at all. The being arrived; marked by jovial undertones and an intense curiosity directed towards the newcomers in their midst.

It took only a fraction of a second for them to be updated on the situation. His desire to help was immediately apparent. There was no hesitation, only that continued curiosity and an eagerness to meet the strange human that had come to a place where physical things did not typically exist. It was a relief to find someone here that was neither indifferent nor afraid of this human intrusion into their home.

The being drifted towards the point of energy that marked the entrance to the bubble that contained Samir. They waited there, pulsing with excitement for Keeler and Anela to join them. There was no point in waiting, they made the journey back inside.

A rotund human form greeted them as they entered. It was as unexpected as it was welcome. Though Keeler couldn't see the smile, he could sense it. Conclusive evidence that this being had been to Earth before. His deep voice echoed in the near-empty room. "You can take form in here, but out there such things are not easy to do and probably shouldn't be done. It's not a place meant for that which is corporeal—like your far too solid friend here."

Keeler wasted no time in taking human form. There was room for only one thought as he rushed to Samir's side and took his hand. Brushing his fingers over his pale face, Keeler assessed the situation. He was there, barely. There was so little of that sweet essence—the energy that was Samir. Keeler took a deep breath of air not knowing or caring if it was real or an illusion and gave a silent thanks that time, as it was here, had not passed long enough for Samir's condition to further degrade.

"Can you help him?" Keeler turned to face the man, taking him in for the first time. He was dressed as if he had walked straight of an old west movie—complete with an oversized handlebar mustache.

"We'll see, but there's no big rush right now." He stretched and twisted as he spoke. It was as if he were trying to readjust to a long-forgotten physical form. "So, do either of you have names from the human world? Something I can call you in this temporary pocket of corporeal creation?"

"I'm Anela." She glared at Keeler before he could say a thing, and it was probably for the best. It wouldn't do to antagonize the one being who was willing to help them. He stayed impatiently silent as she did the introductions. "Anela Masterson and that is Keeler Lim. Nice to meet you, mister…?"

"You both may call me Dr. Jack. That's what I went by the last I was a human. They knew so little about illness and disease in those days. Sometimes, I'm surprised that bunch could make it out of the primordial ooze from which they came." Dr. Jack stepped over to stand beside Keeler and leaned over Samir to study him closer. "I'm assuming things have changed?"

"Significantly," Keeler drawled the word. He had no interest in casual conversation typically and less so now. He squeezed Samir's hand a little tighter and wished for a chair. At the thought, one appeared, and he accepted its presence, resuming the far too familiar position beside Samir's bed.

"Glad to hear that." Dr. Jack chuckled. "Ah, I've missed corporeal form. It has some wonderful benefits. I do need to go back sometime. I miss food and drink."

"Can you help him?" Keeler snapped; his patience worn thin. If Dr. Jack wanted to go back to a human life, then he could do that later. Right now, the focus should be on Samir, about fixing the damage that Keeler had done.

"Oh ho, what do you think I've been doing kiddo?" Dr. Jack's tone didn't change as he winked at Keeler. "He's not doing so well. Never seen anything like this before. Then again, never thought a corporeal would be capable of making it past the barriers either."

"But can you help him?" Anela repeated before Keeler could say anything that would be considered offensive. His emotions on the topic were more than enough to give him away and he let go of his biting retort.

Dr. Jack frowned. "Of course, I've never known anyone brought back from total death before either. I've personally brought people back from near death, but I understand you dragged his essence from the beyond and shoved it into this corporeal form. Then you bound him to it using your own essence. Is that right?"

"Yes," Keeler admitted and bowed his head, not wanting to look at anyone. It was hard to admit that he had been so selfish as to force Samir back into a body that his energy had willingly vacated. He shouldn't have done it, he knew that, but he hadn't been able to let him go. Though he pressed the guilt and responsibility as far down as he could, he knew that the others could sense it.

"I think there might be something we can do to stabilize him." Dr. Jack flopped back, a chair appearing from nowhere to catch him. Keeler tried not to get his hopes up it wasn't a promise of a cure. Dr. Jack pursed his lips as he studied Samir. "However, it won't be a permanent solution."

"Is there a permanent solution?" Anela asked as Keeler stared at Dr. Jack, waiting for a better explanation than what he had given them so far. A temporary fix still gave him hope, but it was useless if it was only another stopgap measure.

"Well, that's the thing, isn't it?" Dr. Jack answered cryptically and lapsed into silence. His emotions were muted, near unreadable. Keeler waited for an answer that made more sense, but no verbal one was given. Instead, Dr. Jack allowed fear and uncertainty to slip through with a hesitation that came from somewhere far more complex than he could understand.

"What's going on?" Anela's words fell like stones in a pond, creating overlapping ripples of concern throughout the room. There was no doubt that Dr. Jack wanted to help Samir, but something was holding him back from doing so.

"It's not my place to tell you about these things." Dr. Jack spoke slowly, choosing his words with care. "What you did was extremely dangerous. It was something that, had you known what you were doing, you would never have done it. Everything exists in a delicate balance and, sometimes, beings fall through from one place to another occasionally by accident, usually by intention. The difference between these movements and what was done here is the difference between moving a pebble and pushing a mountain." Dr. Jack sighed heavily. "It's a tricky situation you kids are in, what with the potential consequences and all."

"The damage is done." Keeler forced the words through gritted teeth. He knew that it wasn't Dr. Jack he was angry at, but he had no other outlet for his rage. "What you aren't telling us is what these consequences are and if you're going to save him or not."

"You'll need to talk to the elders about the consequences. There are extenuating circumstances on whether or not you can be told. This isn't a standard situation we find ourselves in here." Dr. Jack shrugged as if it was all unimportant to him, but the undercurrents of fear and worry in his emotions told a different story. "As you said, the damage is done, and we can only deal with each problem as it appears."

Keeler lowered his head until his forehead rested against Samir's hand. He should have known better. The phrase that ran relentlessly through his mind. It didn't help his guilt to know that, given the same choice, he would have done it again.

"Don't worry there young one," Dr. Jack huffed as he pushed out of his seat so he could look down at Samir. "We'll get him a bit more stable which ought to take care of the pain. After that, well, you are going to have to talk to the elders."

"Keeler, if you could stay as you are, we will need to return that borrowed energy back to you." Dr. Jack placed a hand on Samir's chest. "This won't take long."

His hand and part of his arm disappeared into a deep green glow. Tendrils reached out, surrounded Samir until it looked like was in a shimmering cocoon of light. Keeler monitored closely. He wanted to trust Dr. Jack to do the right thing, but trust wasn't something he was practiced at and there was plenty of room for worry here. Samir's breathing slowed and Keeler held tight to his hand. He could feel the binding he had done on instinct alone alter ever-so slightly. His own energy released or absorbed as Samir's strengthening essence took its place.

The green light pulsed several times and then faded away. Dr. Jack stepped back to stand by Anela. Though his voice was soft, Keeler heard him clearly in the silence of the room. "This should be interesting."

Time ticked by, uncounted and uncountable, as they all waited to see if it had worked. Pressure on his hand caught Keeler's attention. He perked up, hoping that this was a sign that Samir was waking. His movement was greeted with a sharp gasp from Samir—sounding more like a man who had nearly drowned. Pain, sharper than any before cut through the room like a blade as Samir's body arched upwards and then slammed back onto the bed. His hand gripped so tightly on Keeler's that his knuckles turned a shocking white. A bolt of bright white lightning crackled through the room, jumping from Samir to Keeler.

Everything stilled—including Samir. He was there, Keeler could feel him more strongly before. It gave him hope that this might have worked, but he was somewhere far away, deep inside a dark slumber. It was a far more restful place and it allowed Keeler to relax back in his chair, eyes closed.

His world relaxed, tension slipping from his shoulders now that he had hope that Samir might survive. All Keeler needed now was for him to wake so that they could finish the conversation that had been started on the plane. Providing that he could find the courage to apologize for the part he had played in Samir's death.

"When will he wake?" Keeler said, his voice unexpectedly hoarse.

"I don't know. This isn't something I've done before." Dr. Jack's emotions carried with them a comforting apology.

"So, what do we do now?" Anela asked.

"We wait and we hope." Dr. Jack said quietly.

ABOUT THE AUTHOR

Crystal L. Kirkham is a multi-genre speculative fiction author and podcaster. She has published several full-length novels and has been a part of multiple best-selling anthologies.

Originally from the west coast of British Columbia, she now chooses to call a tiny hamlet in central Alberta her home. She is an avid outdoors person, unrepentant coffee addict, part-time foodie, and companion to several delightfully hilarious canines.

She will neither confirm nor deny the rumours regarding the heart in a jar on her desk or the bottle of readers' tears right next to it. However, she will confirm that she once broke the metal handle to a 4-tonne car jack with her bare hands.

You can find out more about her and her work on her website crystallkirkham.com or find her hanging about on Twitter at the handle @canuckclick.

MORE FROM DARK BREW PRESS

Urban Gothic by Stephen Coghlan

Burned out and drugged up, Alec LeGuerrier spends his days faking it, barely ekeing out an existence while living in a haze of confusion and medicated mellowness. That is, until he stops a gang of nightmarish oddities from killing a strange young woman with indigo eyes.

Dragged into the lands of the dreaming, he must come to terms with his brutal past and his grim imagined future in a land his body knows is real, but his mind refuses to acknowledge.

The Cranes of Blackwell by J.D. Kellner

Bergden and Alyssa Crane are dutiful citizens of the Regime. Bergden, a Regime blackjack and Alyssa, a faithful wife, do what they can to provide for their son, James even when it means sacrificing their very freedom. But when Bergden is accused of treason, the Cranes must flee for their lives to escape the terrible reach of the Regime. During the escape, Bergden and Alyssa become separated.

Now, Bergden and Alyssa will do whatever they must, and against all odds, to unite their family. With the tyrannical Chancellor Kroft hunting them night and day, both must discover their inner strengths to conquer their fears and find each other's arms.

Little do they realize that a greater threat lurks in the shadows.

The Cranes of Blackwell by J.D. Kellner

Bergden and Alyssa Crane are dutiful citizens of the Regime. Bergden, a Regime blackjack and Alyssa, a faithful wife, do what they can to provide for their son, James even when it means sacrificing their very freedom. But when Bergden is accused of treason, the Cranes must flee for their lives to escape the terrible reach of the Regime. During the escape, Bergden and Alyssa become separated.

Now, Bergden and Alyssa will do whatever they must, and against all odds, to unite their family. With the tyrannical Chancellor Kroft hunting them night and day, both must discover their inner strengths to conquer their fears and find each other's arms.

Little do they realize that a greater threat lurks in the shadows.

OTHER BOOKS
FROM CRYSTAL L. KIRKHAM

Gateway

New Perish is a technological wonder in a land gone dark. War, famine and disease have decimated much of the world. Only a few beacons of society remain and technology is all they have left to rely on for survival. GLE is the corporation that keeps the people of New Perish alive by using Trackers to find those who use or develop unapproved technology. They are chosen from orphans that are healthy enough to be able to survive the modding and forced to serve until the tech used to create them, kills them.

Lara is the youngest Tracker ever created. Maybe that's why she's managed to live longer than anyone before her. Modded at only 12 years old as an experiment, she managed to override the coding that kept her loyal to GLE and escape into the desolate wastelands outside of the New Perish bubble.

Now, at 17 years old, she needs to return to find her old friend "The Butcher" who is capable of repairing an arm damaged in an altercation. She's ready to run as soon as she's fixed, but he wants her help to find out who is behind a new liquitech drug called "Gateway". She's got nothing left to lose since the tech is starting to do what everyone expected it to do—kill her—but the shocking truth that she uncovers might also save her life.

Alert

One way in, one way out, and nowhere to go.

Shannon is a researcher at an observatory located near Canadian Forces Station Alert, a remote listening post and the northernmost permanently inhabited place in the world. When a visiting reporter falls ill with a mysterious illness, the station gets put on lockdown as the rest of the world deals with the spread of the same strange illness attributed to a new, tropical parasite.

As those around her fall, she must figure out a way to survive in the deep darkness of an arctic winter.